"Angela Ruth Strong has gifted us with a ⌣
romance! Brimming with perfect doses of heart and heat, Hero ⌣ₑᵤ₊ᵤ
made me laugh, swoon, and sigh in happy-reader contentment. A
must-read for inspirational rom-com fans!"

BETHANY TURNER, award-winning author of
The Do-Over

"*Hero Debut* had me alternating between swooning and laughing as
screenwriter Gemma Bennett tries to make a grumpy cop her very
own hero. Once again, Ms. Strong combines comedic moments with
gospel truth, delivering another page-turner as she did with *Husband
Auditions*. I can't wait to see what she comes up with next."

TONI SHILOH, Christy Award–winning author

"Angela Ruth Strong writes characters who immediately become your
friends. *Hero Debut* is a witty romp that plunges beneath the surface
of a typical rom-com and will leave the reader not only laughing but
also reflecting."

BETSY ST. AMANT, author of *The Key to Love* and
Tacos for Two

"What a delight to read! Any author who can write a romantic comedy that is as witty as it is romantic and still carries an impressive dose
of depth is an instant hero in my book. If you loved *Husband Auditions*, get ready to fall head over heels for *Hero Debut*."

BECCA KINZER, author of *Dear Henry, Love Edith*

"With fearless and fun writing right from the start, Strong has penned
yet another arrestingly delightful romance—so much heart, spark,
and sizzle, it'll require full lights and sirens. Absolutely smitten."

NICOLE DEESE, Christy Award–winning author of
All That Really Matters

"*Hero Debut* is another witty and real offering from the talented pen of Angela Ruth Strong. You'll laugh, love, and enjoy all the feels in this classic book about the ultimate of opposites who end up attracting. Happy reading!"

CAROLYN MILLER, best-selling author of the Original Six series and the Muskoka Romance series

"In *Hero Debut*, Angela Ruth Strong continues to play to her strengths: a fun premise, charming characters trying to make their way to each other amid complicated issues, and a hilarious and satisfying ending that will leave the reader smiling."

HEATHER WOODHAVEN, author of *The Secret Life of Book Club*

"Angela Ruth Strong is at it again with another hilarious story sure to delight readers of Bethany Turner and Melissa Ferguson. *Hero Debut* is the bookish escape you've been looking for!"

SARAH MONZON, author of the Sewing in SoCal series

HERO DEBUT

HERO DEBUT

A Novel

ANGELA RUTH STRONG

KREGEL
PUBLICATIONS

Published in association with the Books & Such Literary Management, 52 Mission Circle, Suite 122, PMB 170, Santa Rosa, CA 95409-5370, www.booksandsuch.com.

Scriptures taken from the Holy Bible, New International Version®, NIV®. Copyright © 1973, 1978, 1984, 2011 by Biblica, Inc.™ Used by permission of Zondervan. All rights reserved worldwide. www.zondervan.com. The "NIV" and "New International Version" are trademarks registered in the United States Patent and Trademark Office by Biblica, Inc.™

Library of Congress Cataloging-in-Publication Data
Names: Strong, Angela Ruth, author.
Title: Hero debut / Angela Ruth Strong.
Description: Grand Rapids, MI : Kregel Publications, [2023]
Identifiers: LCCN 2023002361 (print) I LCCN 2023002362 (ebook) I ISBN 9780825447938 (print) I ISBN 9780825470608 (epub) I ISBN 9780825468636 (Kindle)
Subjects: LCGFT: Romance fiction. I Novels.
Classification: LCC PS3619.T7756 H47 2023 (print) I LCC PS3619.T7756 (ebook) I DDC 813/.6--dc23/eng/20230320
LC record available at https://lccn.loc.gov/2023002361
LC ebook record available at https://lccn.loc.gov/2023002362

ISBN 978-0-8254-4793-8, print
ISBN 978-0-8254-7060-8, epub
ISBN 978-0-8254-6863-6, Kindle

Printed in the United States of America
23 24 25 26 27 28 29 30 31 / 5 4 3 2 1

Dedicated to my personal hero,
Cathleen Dialogue, who is a beautiful example
of keeping her faith, loving her family, traveling the world,
riding motorcycles, and fighting breast cancer

CHAPTER ONE

GEMMA

*When you slip on a banana peel, people laugh at
you; but when you tell people you slipped on a
banana peel, it's your laugh. So you become the
hero rather than the victim of the joke.*
—NORA EPHRON

Karson Zellner is my hero. Not only because he's the police officer who busted into my town house to rescue me from my roommates when he'd thought they were my captors, but also because I'm literally using him as inspiration for the hero in my next script.

He's not aware I'm here, though, because I registered for Citizen's Safety Academy at the door. All to prevent him from finding someone else to teach the class in an effort to avoid me.

As he scans the conference room in search of supervillains, I duck behind my journal. Not because I fit the supervillain profile, but because I'm Lois Lane on assignment.

I peek over the top of my journal.

He's gone back to talking with another policeman by the entrance, so I'm in the clear. There's time to take in all the details that will make my story come to life.

I scribble notes. Karson is about medium height, medium weight, and medium-brown hair, so he's more similar to Marvel's superhero Hawkeye than Superman, but that's not a bad thing. Like Hawkeye, he buzzes with an inner strength and intelligence. He's constantly on alert, ready for shootouts, motorcycle chases, and taking down corrupt government agencies.

My heart plays a drumroll in anticipation of the moment our eyes will meet. There's nothing average about his eyes. I'd call them cornflower blue, like the weird crayon in kindergarten that looks darker than it actually shades. In the same way, Karson's light eyes appear darker when brooding underneath his constantly creased forehead and widow's peak.

He's in uniform, of course. I've never seen him without it. Would I even recognize him in civilian clothes? It's as if he was meant to wear a shiny badge, a black button-down, and the thick belt holding all kinds of gadgets.

He stands at the doorway to the modern conference room in the back corner. The officer next to him laughs and shakes hands with the civilians entering the room.

Karson keeps his arms crossed. He's always so serious that it makes me feel flighty and frivolous in comparison.

"Are you hiding behind your diary, Gemma?" asks Charlie from the seat on my left. He's got Ashton Kutcher's good looks but not the smug smile. He's too literal to be smug.

Charlie is only here because he's thinking about directing a documentary on police reform. He doesn't hide from anything and doesn't understand why he's always upsetting people by bringing up politics and religion. I mean, he started a Bible study at one of the most liberal film schools in America. I'm grateful because it brought the three of us together, but occasionally it can get embarrassing.

After we graduated from college, I headed for SoCal with high hopes. I wouldn't say Hollywood ate me alive, but it did try to serve me as an appetizer. One director literally told me I was just another pretty face. So I'm back in Oregon, teaching high school English by day and writing by night. I admit this sounds like failure in many ways, but there are benefits to coming home. For example, the safety of renting a room from Charlie versus sharing an apartment with random roommates found in the classifieds section of the *LA Times*. I mean, if the police have only been called to our neighborhood because of me, then it's pretty safe.

Kai, our other roommate, sits on my right. "If anyone is hiding, it should be me," he says. He has the deep voice of Keanu Reeves, but his head is rounder than Keanu's. Maybe I should be comparing him to Henry Golding.

I smile at Kai as I recall the moment he answered the door to a cop while I was bound to a chair with duct tape. "You're just saying that because Karson pulled a gun on you."

"Exactly." Kai huffs dramatically enough that he could get a job acting in front of the camera rather than operating it. "Forget the journal and give me a bulletproof vest."

I turn back toward my hero and find Charlie staring directly at my policeman. As I mentioned before, Charlie's not versed in the art of subtlety. I slap his arm. "Stop staring."

Charlie has literally turned his ergonomic seat sideways behind the long tables to face Karson. Charlie twists his body to frown over his shoulder at me. "Why?" His hazel eyes flash with confusion. "I thought you were here to watch him."

"Not like that." Kai answers for me. "You should *never* watch anyone like that."

"Oh," Charlie says, as if this is new information and he's recalling all the past times he's stared at strangers.

I tilt my head to soften the blow. "We want to observe Karson in his natural habitat, and it will be hard for him to act natural if he sees us all staring."

Charlie holds his hands wide, still confused by the try-not-to-stare thing. "He's the instructor. Everyone is going to be watching him once he starts."

I'm not sure I can reason with Charlie, but maybe he'll understand a direct request. "Will you wait until then?"

"Okay." He spins to face forward, folds his hands on the table, and looks around as if he needs to find another purpose. He has too much energy to be good at waiting, so this is probably the best we'll get.

I glance back at Kai with a smirk. I suspect he's making jokes about Charlie in his head, but instead of laughing at Charlie, he's narrowing his eyes at Karson.

What in the world? That's even worse than how Charlie gawked.

"I don't know what you see in him," Kai grumbles. "He looks so angry all the time."

"He's on duty." I defend my crush. "Law enforcement officers have a lot of responsibilities on their shoulders."

"Yeah," Charlie agrees, though I'm not sure if he's agreeing with me or Kai. At least he's turned to face us now so he can't stare at the police officers. "I don't think I'd put him in front of a camera. His anger would shine a negative spotlight on the Portland Police Bureau and that light has already been pretty bright. However, Karson's partner might be perfect."

Charlie spins his chair around again, and my gaze lands on the cheerful guy in uniform with biceps the size of Mt. Hood. The man shakes hands and offers high fives, his laughter carrying across the room. He's his own spotlight.

Karson says something to his buddy, and the man claps his hands. "Let's hit it!"

Karson leads the way to the front of the room. His gaze washes over the class, so I should have been bracing for impact, but the moment he spots me, I'm toppled by a sneaker wave. I lose my breath as I'm tossed in the depths of his ocean-blue eyes.

His head swivels, holding our eye contact, while he continues forward. What's he thinking? He doesn't smile, but I knew not to expect joy.

My chest tickles, and I'm suddenly an eight-year-old at Six Flags with my family. Mom had agreed to go on the free-fall ride with me because nobody else would. Strapped in seats, we faced outward, our legs dangling a couple of hundred feet in the air. At the very top, in the seconds before they dropped us, Mom yelled, "I can't believe I'm letting you do this!" I yelled back in terror, "*I* can't believe you're letting me do this!" Then we plunged toward possible death. After the screaming stopped, we got back in line to ride again. There was nothing else as thrilling.

Could Karson be feeling the same thing? Is he thinking, *I can't believe I'm letting you do this?* Is he afraid he's about to fall for me? Charlie grips my arm. "He saw you."

"You think?" Kai quips.

A few of the participants glance our way.

I pat Charlie's hand to hush him.

Karson's cool gaze travels from me to Charlie, then back across me to Kai. He's reached the front of the class, but he keeps walking toward the whiteboard, turning his back on us for a moment. He lifts an arm to run a hand over his short hair.

I curl my toes in my canvas slip-on sneakers.

He pivots to face the room but barely brushes me with his gaze before addressing everyone else. "Welcome. I'm Lieutenant Karson Zellner."

Ooh, he's a lieutenant now.

Charlie leans toward my ear as if he's about to whisper. If only he knew how to whisper. "I wonder if he's become lieutenant because so many cops have been taking early retirement or quitting."

Karson crosses his arms and waits for us to quiet. This time when his gaze meets mine, an eyebrow arches in challenge.

I put the *grin* in chagrinned. He's just so cute when he's one-hundred-percent business. Which I'm beginning to think is always.

Rather than look away again, he narrows his eyes, so I know his tiny headshake is for me.

I feel special.

His eyes roll to the ceiling before he extends an arm toward his colleague. "Officer Drew Harris will be helping me lead this training. Our goal is to educate in order to create a greater understanding of public safety's role."

I sigh with sweet anticipation. I have my summer off from teaching to really focus on writing, and I can't think of a more inspiring way to spend it than right here. Thanks to my new muse, I may even become the next Nora Ephron.

"That's right," Drew chimes in. "During the first four weeks, you'll be here at the police department. Then, for the last four weeks, you'll be training with firefighters."

Oh, I didn't realize that. I hope Karson has to oversee the firefighting weeks as well.

Karson glances at me as if he'd heard my thoughts and disapproves. "Here at the PPB, you're going to get some experience with self-defense, work with our K-9 unit, and even race our cars through the practice course."

Charlie straightens at the mention of a racecourse. "Seriously?"

"Seriously." Drew nods. "Though you'll have to get through tonight's hands-on training first. And by hands-on, I mean we'll be taking your fingerprints and running background checks."

The class chuckles in response, but I'm too lost in my daydreams of Karson to join in. His eyes bulge my way in warning, and I realize I'm staring. I'm as bad as Charlie.

Karson clears his throat and angles his body so the two of us are not facing each other. "We're simply making sure our trainees are law-abiding citizens. We don't want any trouble here."

I'm pretty sure he's thinking about me again. I can't wait to prove him wrong.

Drew shrugs. "No need to worry if you have minor infractions like speeding tickets or being reported for disturbing the peace when you threw a party in college."

Charlie raises his hand but doesn't wait to speak. "What about if your neighbor called the cops because she saw your roommate duct-taped to a chair through your window, and she didn't realize said roommate asked to be duct-taped so she could practice escaping for a script she's working on?"

Or what about if you have murderous thoughts toward your roommate for bringing up your history with the police in front of your whole class?

Kai turns his head sideways and covers his face as if he's trying to hide. Maybe he'll take care of Charlie for me. Except we both know the dummy truly believes he's helping.

Drew blinks. No doubt he's never had to answer such a question before.

Karson's brooding expression doesn't change, and his arms remain crossed. "In such situations"—meaning my situation—"I've recommended the actress stick to acting and leave police work to professionals."

My mouth gapes. How could he think such a thing? "I'm not an actress. I'm a writer."

Drew's dark eyes widen in delight. He motions my way. "That was you?"

Both of Karson's eyebrows arch this time. "Did you or did you not act in the superhero TV show that was filmed downtown?"

So he'd recognized me from the TV show I worked on last summer. I'd only taken that job with hopes it would open the door for selling my screenplay to the director.

Chairs squeak and clothing rustles as everyone else in the room twists to see if they recognize me too.

But what I want to know is, after I appeared, did Karson keep watching the show or turn off the television?

The role wasn't my finest work. I'd tried suggesting some changes to the writers so they could make it more believable, but then they poisoned my character. Which was actually much nicer than what other writers have done to me.

Ahh . . . poison. The most dignified of murder weapons.

"Yes, it was me," I respond to both policemen. "But—"

"I thought you looked familiar," a slouchy guy in the front row interrupts.

The frumpy woman next to him harrumphs. "You said she looked like a Barbie doll."

I don't need that kind of judgment in my life. Even if I'm judging her for wearing such crazy bright sneakers. I lean forward against the edge of the table to present my case. "I do a little acting when the opportunity presents itself, but I'm here to learn about police work so I can write more realistic stories."

"Really?" Karson's chin raises.

Does he guess that's only part of the reason I'm here, and he's the other part?

"Is there anything realistic in Hollywood?"

Whew. He's not questioning me. He's questioning the whole film industry.

Charlie jabs a thumb to his chest, taking the opportunity for himself. "Actually, I film documentaries, so reality is my focus. I'd love to put together something about the issues you deal with on a day-to-day basis."

"Whoa, boy." Drew gives a loud clap of his hands. "Are you all in the movie biz? What about you, dude?" He snaps his fingers at Kai.

The term "dude" fits. Not only is Kai actually a Hawaiian-born surfer, but he looks like one too, with his shaggy hair and puka-shell necklace. He shrugs his broad shoulders. "I just take pictures."

I elbow him. He should be proud of his art. "Actually, Kai's a cinematographer. He does beautiful work."

More rustling and murmurs.

"All right then." Karson calls our attention back. "Anyone else here make movies?"

I scan the room to see if a producer will out themself among the twenty or so participants, providing me the chance to pitch my latest script treatment. I may not live in Southern California anymore, but Portland has a few studios and a big indie vibe. Our airport even has a theater where they play shorts for free. But nobody else in the room admits to being in showbiz.

Karson clears his throat. "Now that we know we've got some filmmakers in the class, let me get a few things straight."

I grin at him, excited for whatever he's about to say. Yes, my roomies are filmmakers too, but I feel like he's talking to me personally.

"In real life, police do not shoot bazookas from helicopters like *Rambo.* That would have sent the chopper crashing down. In real life, we do not swing off rooftops on fire hoses while the top of the building explodes like Bruce Willis in *Die Hard.* His character should have definitely died hard."

Charlie smacks a palm on the table. "I've been saying that for years."

"Why are you ruining action flicks for us, man?" demands a biker in the back.

"But"—Karson holds up a finger—"most importantly, in real life, we do not take our shirts off to rescue anyone."

Is he mixing up screenplay writers with cover designers for romance novels?

He crosses his arms. "If someone were drowning in a lake, I would dive in with all my clothes on to save them."

Okay, he might have me there.

"I don't know, Zellner." Drew's body shakes as he cackles. "If I looked like Terry Crews, I would take off my shirt."

The hilarious thing is that Drew does look a bit like Terry Crews.

"Not funny." Karson holds up his hand to halt Drew's laughter. "Nobody stops to remove their shirt before a rescue."

Our class keeps laughing along with his partner. If these guys played "good cop, bad cop," Drew would be the good cop.

Karson nods at my little group. "If you're going to write about police, don't romanticize our job. We give out tickets, we arrest people, and we use our firearms when needed. We're the ones who show up after a crime has been committed. Nobody wants to see us. Though we risk our lives to protect the public, they often attack us for doing our jobs."

Charlie jabs at my journal. "Write this down for me. This is good stuff."

I slide my journal along the table so Charlie can take his own notes. This is one of those rare occasions where life is more fascinating than anything I could write. I'm enthralled. No wonder Karson is angry all the time.

The florescent lights flick off overhead except for one panel in a corner that casts the room in a dim silver glow.

"Lieutenant Zellner is getting a little dark," Drew jokes. He points a remote control at the projector on the ceiling. "So, since we're talking about police movies, I'm just going to show you film of what police work looks like in real life. This footage is from body cameras."

"Yes!" Charlie jots in my journal.

I'll rip the pages out for him later.

Movement flashes on the whiteboard. An image of the front tire of a bike on a dirt trail fills the makeshift screen. "This first recording is from Zellner's camera," Drew narrates.

Karson groans. "Not the bike clip. Harris, we talked about this."

Drew's laughter drowns him out. I join in, not sure yet what we're laughing about, just excited to find out what Karson is trying to keep hidden.

CHAPTER TWO

KARSON

*What makes Superman a hero is not that he has
power, but that he has the wisdom and the
maturity to use the power wisely.*
—Christopher Reeve

Gemma Bennett is my kryptonite. Well, not her specifically, but women like her. Yeah, she's stunning with her long hair and even longer legs, but keeping up her appearance like that is not about true beauty. It's, in a word, fake. Who has a tan already in Oregon? And either her hair isn't naturally that blond or her eyelashes aren't naturally that dark. I'll just stop there, before I get to her more feminine attributes, which also can't possibly be as perfect as they appear.

I know to stay away from women like her, even if they claim to only want info on Citizen's Safety Academy. For example, I'd successfully ignored Gemma's Facebook stalking. Also, I'd escaped into a bathroom the time I'd been temporarily assigned duty at the airport and she showed up to drop a friend off for a flight. Plus, I'd turned the channel when she starred in my favorite show. (Well, after I saw how it was going to end, of course.) I'd also wondered if she would register for this class, but her name wasn't on the roster yesterday, so I'd mistakenly assumed I was safe.

Yet here we are. I'd thought her note-taking on my every move in her little pink diary had been bad, but now she's watching a recording of me flipping over the handlebars of my bike when I hit a rock. And she's laughing.

I glare at Officer Harris. The whites of his eyes flash my direction in the darkness, so I know he sees me, but apparently my intimidation tactics don't work on him anymore.

The video ends. The mirth continues.

Harris even has to wipe tears away. "That's the best."

It's really not. "I would have preferred you use this recording as blackmail material, Harris."

"So you could arrest me?"

"Absolutely."

Gemma watches us with her chin resting on one palm like an enamored teenager. Though her infatuation can't be with me. She could probably have any man she wanted. In fact, she's got a couple of lookers on either side of her right now. Why isn't she interested in them?

Oh. I nod. My uniform. She likes the power it represents, but she wouldn't like the hours, risk, and public perception that come with it.

I'm a little surprised the bike-wreck video didn't remove the hearts from her eyes. Especially with that moaning sound I couldn't stop from making when I'd had the wind knocked out of me. Though maybe she sees the video as fodder, since she considers herself a writer.

Am I going to end up in one of her movies? The policeman who can't ride a bike? She needs something actually impressive to inspire her.

"How about we show the class a clip I can enjoy too?" I suggest to my former partner. "You have any car chases uploaded from dash cams?"

Harris points the remote and clicks onto another recording. "You know it."

A hush falls over our audience, which is then replaced by the sound of sirens. Aw, yeah. I relax a little at the sight of a MINI Cooper zipping around like a clown car. Bozo the Driver makes the mistake of turning down a dead end. When he notices he's in a cul-de-sac, he whips around and tries to cut through a lawn but ends up hitting a tree. The footage shows patrol cars surrounding him, and the dark scene gets a little brighter from all the blue and red lights flashing. The suspect is barely out of his car when our men surround him. All in a good day's work.

I cross my arms in satisfaction.

Officer Harris laughs and loads up a few more videos. He fields the questions as well.

I stand back and try to avoid eye contact with a certain playwright. In my peripheral vision, her face repeatedly turns my direction. I really hope nobody else notices. Namely Harris. He doesn't need more to joke about.

Eventually Harris finishes up with Show and Tell, allowing me to flip the light switch. We all blink in the brightness. "If there are no more questions, we're ready for our tour of the precinct."

The dark-haired guy on Gemma's left is the first to line up in front of me. Though we are pretty much standing face-to-face, he raises his hand. "Can we film the tour?"

"No." It's not that I don't trust him—the guy is too direct to be able to lie about anything—but there are people out there I don't trust. A lot of people I don't trust. So I'd rather they not have video footage on the layout of my precinct.

Harris takes his place at the end of the line forming. He'll bring up the rear to make sure no stragglers have the opportunity to cause problems. He expands on my simple answer. "While you can't film, there will be a couple of areas where you can take photos. I'll let you know."

"Great." The guy who'd asked the question waves for Gemma to join him. He even steps back to let her cut in front.

She squeezes between the two of us and smiles at me with clear blue eyes that I wish I could believe were as innocent as they looked.

But I catch the scent of coconut, as if she's wearing sunblock because she just came from the beach. The beach on a workday?

Maybe her tan is natural after all. Not that it makes her vanity any more respectable.

I look past her to my former partner and current co-instructor. The sooner I can move, the better. "We ready?" Harris shouldn't have any trouble with the end of the line today, because trouble is leading the pack.

The officer pauses in the multiple conversations he's holding with the participants around him to wave me forward. "All set, boss."

I do an about-face and take a deep breath of coconut-free air to cleanse my senses. This isn't the first time I've had women in class want my attention. The good news is that it will only last the first four weeks, until the firefighters take over. After Gemma meets those rescue heroes, she'll forget all about me.

I lead the way out of the briefing room and stop in the lobby by a gray bin that resembles a mail-collection box. "This is our drug disposal location. As it's dangerous to flush or throw away medication, we offer a safe place for people to get rid of old prescriptions. No questions asked. It also helps prevent drug abuse."

"Ooh . . ." Gemma acts as if this is the most interesting thing she's ever heard, but maybe she just wanted an excuse to purse her dewy lips in my direction. Or maybe she's got a prescription drug addiction she needs to kick. That would be one way to explain her disconnect with reality. Either way, I'm out.

I walk backward and hold a glass door open at the front of the building. There's a second glass door that exits into the parking lot, but I herd our class into the vestibule between. Once Harris brings up the rear and closes the door, the sun shining in makes it feel as though we're in a sauna. The students look to me for an explanation as to why we're roasting here.

I motion to the doors leading back into the building. "These are locked at night." I motion to the doors leading to the parking lot. "These are not. So if anyone is being chased, they can run in here and hit the intercom button that connects to our 911 dispatchers. Officers on duty have the ability to remotely lock the front door to keep the victim safe until they can get out here to help."

Gemma points to the door on the parking lot side. "Is that glass bulletproof?"

I pause in surprise. Either she's more perceptive than I realized or, on top of being a druggie, she's also planning a way to break into the police department. "Yes."

She grabs her pink diary from her roommate and busies herself with writing notes again. She jots some more when I lead them to the practice lot that resembles the back lot of a movie studio but is used for tactical training. And even more when I show the map room, where the locations of crimes are pinpointed so we can try to predict the next strike.

I finish the tour by leading our group into the holding room, where we'll take fingerprints for background checks. I'm not too wary of anybody in this class. There's a bearded gentleman in Harley gear, which means he could be involved in one of the outlaw biker gangs coming into our area, but it's more likely he belongs to the ninety-nine percent of motorcycle clubs that follow the law. You just never know though. It's probably the sweet, middle-aged stay-at-home mom in bright retro high-tops who I'll find out has served time for embezzlement.

Harris leans against the doorway, obviously not too concerned either. "Citizens are allowed to take photos in here if they wish."

He isn't even finished making the announcement before the Hawaiian guy has his phone out. He snaps a few selfies with Gemma and the other member of their entourage, then the three of them take turns posing on the line painted for sobriety tests in positions that make them look as if they can't walk straight.

And she claims she's not an actress.

"I hate to break up the party." Not really. I'm a professional party pooper. "But we need to get started if we're going to make it through everyone's fingerprints. If anyone wants to volunteer to get their prints taken for the background check in front of everyone, I'll show you how we do that right now."

Gemma jolts forward.

I should've known. Though, with the way her torso tipped before she took steps to catch her balance, I'm guessing one of her male friends had something to do with her being so quick to volunteer.

"The lieutenant will practically have to hold your hand to take your fingerprints," her talkative buddy says, confirming both my suspicions that he can't tell a lie and that he pushed her to volunteer.

Harris gives a little hoot from the door, which I ignore. I'll deal with him later. Right now I'm too busy trying to figure out this *Three's Company* dynamic.

If Gemma's roommates are encouraging her to get closer to me, then maybe they're not interested in her as more than a friend. I find this surprising, which means I'm admitting to myself it would be hard to spend a lot of time around the beauty and not be attracted to her. Though I'd rather deal with looters and rioting than go down that relationship route again.

Gemma squeezes between a couple of other attendees to plant herself in front of me and the scanning device, where I'm going to roll her fingers one at a time so they will appear on the computer monitor. "I'll volunteer," she offers sweetly.

I don't realize I'm inhaling deeply until I smell coconut again. I decide to hate that scent since it's going to make me think of her whenever I smell it now. She's summer vacation personified. I'll have to make my time with her quick so I don't get burned.

I type her name and info into the computer, concentrating on the cursor and letters. But I feel her presence warming my arm like rays of sunshine.

"This has been really fun." Her voice is all soft and dreamy.

I have to look at her then to see if she's serious. Because I never think of my job as fun. And I especially don't get soft and dreamy about it. Law enforcement is pretty awful most of the time. Just ask my ex.

Her eyes sparkle, and I realize she's not thinking about the realities of police work. She's thinking of Sylvester Stallone and Bruce Willis with their shirts off.

I place this thought in the forefront of my mind as I hold out my hand for hers.

She raises her long slender fingers. They are bronze, of course. She wears one thumb ring that looks like a bunch of little rings stacked together. Her nails are short and rounded, clean and painted peach.

Her jewelry and nails aren't pretentious. They're also more appealing than I'd expected. I take a moment to mentally chastise myself, then I take her smooth palm in mine. Since when do I have expectations about hands?

I robotically press all her fingers down onto the glass at once. The slopes and swirls of the designs from her finger pads appear on the monitor in front of us. Thankfully, the computer doesn't show any blurs or smudges, and it beeps its acceptance so we can move on.

"I'll start with the index finger on your right hand."

She curls the rest of her fingers in and waits for me to grip her wrist and guide her. "I'm so glad you don't have to use ink anymore."

I can't help giving a snort before rolling her finger to create a print from one side of her fingernail to the other.

"What?" she asks, and with the way I'm tipped forward over her hand, her breath tickles the back of my neck. It's warm, but somehow it makes me want to shiver.

The light underneath the glass pad flashes green, and I don't wait for her to switch fingers for me. I curl and straighten them myself. Her fingers glide easily between mine, and I remind myself they are probably still moisturized from all the sunblock she slathered on earlier.

"If you don't like getting your fingers dirty, you'd hate this job," I finally answer. I chance a look to see how she'll respond.

She doesn't actually flutter her lashes, but they lift slowly enough to have the same feminine effect by the time our gazes lock. "I might surprise you."

My guts twist in a warning that I know as instinctive. I'm being lured into danger. The word "siren" comes to mind, and I wish I meant the kind attached to my patrol car.

"I don't know." I extend her bare ring finger and roll it along the glass. "Your skin is too soft for manual labor."

I didn't mean that to come out as a compliment, but by the way the pulse in her wrist throbs harder under my touch, she must have taken it that way. I'm thankful everyone else in the room is too busy joking around with Officer Harris to notice Gemma and me noticing each other. I've never appreciated that guy's jokes more.

Time to get my head back in the game. I have twenty-four more people to fingerprint.

I finish and submit the prints. I could step away from her, but I need to stay near the computer. "All right, guys. I've put a rush on Gemma's background check. In a moment, we'll know if she's robbed any banks or has a history of grand theft auto."

Gemma's head drops back in laughter, and I enjoy the tinkling sound almost as much as the way her silky hair slides over her shoulders. The rest of the group seems to enjoy her merriment as well, because they smile in our direction. It's actually kind of nice that I'm getting the laughs instead of Harris for a change.

"Is grand theft auto bad?" the Harley rider quips.

Another round of chuckles circles the room.

Gemma grins again, and I can't help considering the laid-back attitude that makes her seem authentic and unpretentious. Maybe I'd like it if she surprised me the way she'd suggested.

The computer chimes that her results are ready. Harris explains more about the system as I click to open her file. Her name flashes red, and the sight might as well have been a punch to the gut. My insides spasm. This was not the kind of surprise I'd been expecting. This is kryptonite hidden in a lead box.

Gemma Bennett has a warrant out for her arrest.

CHAPTER THREE

GEMMA

*If you can't be a hero, you can at least be
funny while being a chicken.*

—INA MAY GASKIN

I'm still tingling from the lieutenant's touch, and I'm thrilled Charlie shoved me to the front of the class, forcing me to volunteer for the fingerprinting. Maybe Karson feels our connection too, finally. He seems to be thawing a little with his curious glances and the gentle but authoritative way he rolled my fingers across the glass. Not to mention, he called my skin soft.

He could have backed away when he finished the fingerprints, but he's still right beside me, smelling like cinnamon and inciting flash-backs to Big Red gum commercials. He jerks straighter, giving me the impression he can somehow read my thoughts. I may have done some acting in the past, but I tend to be embarrassingly transparent in real life.

Only he's not looking at me. He's looking at the computer monitor.

I follow his gaze. There's a bunch of information on the computer screen I can't decipher. He's run my prints, so it must be about me.

Perhaps he discovered my parking tickets from college. I kept for-getting to pay them and ended up getting a boot on my tire. Is that going to keep me from taking this class? Or worse, from going out on a date with him? I get that he has to be careful about who he associ-ates with, but it's not as if I'm a criminal or anything.

"There's a warrant out for your arrest." His tone is low, and I strain to make out the words.

Yikes. I guess he's not looking at my info after all. I glance around to see who he's talking to. Probably the scary-looking biker. Except the biker is on the other side of the room with Officer Harris. In fact, there's nobody else within hearing range.

I frown at Karson in confusion.

His narrowed eyes are accusing me. As though I tricked him somehow. As though I'm the one with a warrant out for my arrest.

"What?" I squeak. Surely I heard him wrong. "I paid my parking tickets."

"Wait right here." He crosses the room toward the other law enforcement officer, leaving me alone with my overactive imagination.

I gape after him. Had I accidentally committed a crime I don't remember? Maybe I did it while sleepwalking. Maybe I was hypnotized or had temporary amnesia. I hope I wasn't an assassin in my forgotten life, like Jason Bourne.

I test the memory of my childhood and relief floods me when images pop into my head. I picture my mom, dad, sister, and a betta fish that only lived one week but still holds a place in my heart. I told all my troubles to Mr. Bubbles. Though I don't think I've ever been in this much trouble before.

Karson and Drew bend their heads together. Drew looks my way as if he's in as much shock as I am.

"Gemma," Charlie chides. "You told me we aren't supposed to stare at people like that."

I hold a hand to my thundering heart. Staring has become the least of my worries. "He said I have a warrant out for my arrest."

Kai chuckles as if he thinks I'm telling a joke.

"That's preposterous." Charlie shakes his head. "Unless . . ."

My head snaps his direction. "Unless what?" Does he know about my parking tickets?

"Wait." Kai rubs his chin. "You're serious?"

Both men scoot closer and form a huddle.

I motion for Charlie to continue. "Unless what?"

His long forehead wrinkles, drawing dark eyebrows together. "Remember when we were making that student film in college?"

The scene hits me like Jason Bourne remembering how he joined Treadstone. No, I wasn't an assassin, but I did hold a gun in the staged robbery of a Dairy Queen. Passersby apparently like calling the police on me. "Oh no." I cover my mouth.

"What college film?" Kai's dark eyes ping back and forth between Charlie and me.

I'm still trying to connect the dots. Yeah, the ice-cream shop had been surrounded by squad cars, but once I'd gone out with my hands up and Charlie explained, no charges had been filed. That I knew of.

Charlie wipes his forearm across his forehead before responding to Kai. "Remember the 48 Hour Film Project where you were having an Achilles surgery and couldn't join us?"

"Yeah." Kai grimaces at the memory he does have before focusing on the experience he missed. "That was the only film competition you didn't win, due to poor editing by my replacement." Before either of us can explain further, his head straightens and his narrowed eyes lock on mine. "That's the time the cops thought you were robbing a DQ."

I hold my arms wide, both shrugging and enjoying my freedom before handcuffs restrain me. "I didn't do anything."

Kai nods. "Exactly. Now you know how I felt when Officer Angry Eyes accused me of kidnapping."

Kai has never had a warrant out for his arrest. Plus, Karson's eyes aren't necessarily angry. More like justice-seeking. "Not helping."

Charlie slices a hand across his throat in the "cut" motion before turning from Kai to me. "I'll vouch for you. Again."

"Again." Kai echoes with a snicker, still not taking my situation seriously. "You know this kind of thing would never happen to anyone else, right?"

Charlie's face scrunches in contemplation. "Maybe you're more suited to writing romantic comedies than suspense, Gemma."

I'd never considered writing romantic comedy before, but I really hope this is something we can all laugh about later. Unfortunately, as Karson heads back our way, his justice-seeking eyes flash police-light blue.

Charlie steps in front of me. "She didn't actually rob a Dairy Queen. It wasn't even a real gun."

My roommate blocked Karson's face from my sight, which is probably a good thing. I can't imagine his statement caused a positive expression.

"What gun?"

I peek around Charlie.

Does Karson seriously not know about the gun?

The set of his jaw tells me he's even more serious than usual. If he doesn't know about my almost-arrest for armed robbery, then what could my warrant possibly be for?

"No gun," I rush to explain. "I was acting in a robbery scene and someone called the police."

"It wouldn't be the first time," Kai quips.

Charlie holds up a finger. "Actually that *was* the first time. The duct-tape scenario was the second time."

Karson rubs his temples. I may be giving him a headache, but that's not illegal.

"Isn't that why there's a warrant out for my arrest?" I hope. What else could I have done? Unless my amnesia is so bad that I've forgotten I have it.

"No." Karson huffs and crosses his arms.

I straighten to hide behind Charlie once again. My feet and hands tingle. I assume this is the start to a panic attack and take mental notes for writing about such emotion in the future. At least I'll have lots of time to write in jail. Would I describe this sensation as pinpricks or as the feeling one gets when a limb starts waking up after falling asleep? The wake-up description is accurate but kind of verbose. I'll go with pinpricks.

Drew whistles for the group's attention, as if the class isn't already hanging on his every word. "We're going to head back to the briefing room now. I'll be taking everyone else's fingerprints with ink, the old-fashioned way."

I close my eyes and cringe. Because I have the feeling "everyone" doesn't include me. I'll be staying here to smile pretty for my mugshot.

I open my eyes to find Charlie has removed himself from being my human shield, thus giving Karson a clear view for trying to read me. Exposed, I make the rash decision to fake a grin and hope it doesn't look too Joker-ish. "I guess I'll be getting my hands dirty after all."

"You're not going." Karson confirms my fears.

Charlie is already to the door. His instinct to be first in line has overridden his protective nature. At least he calls back, "We'll wait for you, Gemma."

I pray he isn't waiting too long.

Kai follows after him, hands shoved in pockets and lips pressed together. He's probably afraid of getting on Karson's bad side again. He shrugs a shoulder when he passes me as if to say, *I tried to warn you.*

I should have listened. I don't want Karson's attention anymore. I want to go on the run and start life over in a small Canadian town where I will work at a bakery and own a labradoodle. Okay, maybe I am more suited for romantic comedy than I'd thought. Had I written about Jason Bourne, his film would have aired on Hallmark instead of being advertised during the Super Bowl.

All too quickly, the door thunks shut, and I find myself alone with Karson. Ever since I met him, I've dreamed of this moment. But never in this way.

My pulse throbs in that spot between my throat and earlobes. "What did I do?" I have to know.

His gaze roves over my face, then lifts to the ceiling.

I look up too, as if seeing what he sees will clue me in as to what he's thinking. But there are just ceiling tiles. The kind that can be pushed up for access to the air ducts. Is he giving me a hint on how to escape, like in *The A-Team* when Jessica Biel passed Bradley Cooper the key to his handcuffs through a kiss?

No, he's not. He's too real for that. While I've watched too many movies.

"I want you to know this is my least favorite part of the job," Karson says.

"What? What part?" I could not be more lost. Wouldn't Karson's least favorite part of the job involve some kind of life-threatening altercation, like a shootout or riot? How can talking to me be worse than that?

He crosses his arms and levels his eyes on me. I can't quite tell if they flicker with condemnation or apology. "Getting involved in domestic disputes."

I hit pause on the story of my life to do a mental dictionary search for the word "domestic." It could mean *household* or *national*. I come up with crimes like domestic abuse and domestic terrorism but still can't make sense of how this relates to me.

I decide to play along. "Okay . . . ?"

There's that gaze once more. The probing kind. If only I knew what he's looking for. "You owe your ex-husband back child support."

Relief sweeps through me and pours out in laughter. I have no ex-husband. I have no child. Unless, you know, amnesia.

Or . . .

My laughter sputters and dries up. I cover my face.

"You must be making quite a bit of money with your acting if you have to pay your ex. Or is he simply a deadbeat who refuses to work?"

Does Karson really think I've been married and have children? Will that affect his desire to date me more or less than if I was truly a criminal? Okay, that's not what I should be worried about at the moment.

How to explain? This is even more complicated than the fake-gun thing. Now it's my turn to roll my eyes around the room looking for answers.

I cross my arms to hug away a chill. The trembling continues because it's not based on body temp but adrenaline from past trauma. I take a deep breath and simply let it all out. "I'm an identical twin. My sister and I have similar fingerprints. It actually gave us issues when Mom and Dad had our prints taken for a child identification program. After she had her prints taken, the computer wouldn't accept mine." Karson remains quiet, so I keep babbling. "The technician said it's rare, and computers are getting better at reading the differences. But . . ." I shrug. "Here we are."

He blinks, which is as fazed as I've ever seen him. "You have an evil twin?" he deadpans.

A guffaw escapes. What would Jewel think about being called my evil twin and, more significantly, why did she not immediately come to mind when my fingerprints turned up a warrant? "Pretty much."

Karson lifts his chin. "Does she live in a volcanic lair?"

A smile tugs at the corner of my lips. He does have a sense of humor. "Not quite. It's more of a three-story modern monstrosity built into the side of a mountain."

"Mount St. Helens?"

The volcano in Washington blew before Jewel and I were born, but that's still a funny thought. I imagine her laughing like a supervillain from her lair. "Arlington Heights."

"A single mom in Arlington Heights? Did she remarry?"

Does he find my story suspicious? As he previously alluded to income, he must know Jewel makes good money in order to be the one paying child support. "No. She's a psychologist."

He looks me up and down as if wondering what happened to hold me back from becoming as successful as my dear sister. Maybe he'd rather date her. I brace for his next question. "What makes her an evil genius?"

The question isn't so bad. I relax a little.

While most other twins I meet seem to be close, we had a falling out about ten years ago. "In high school she was class president, and she rigged homecoming elections so I wouldn't be crowned queen. We're pretty much Jacob and Esau because she stole my birthright."

Pause. "I can't believe I'm having this conversation."

"You asked." I drop my arms to my sides so he can see I'm being completely open and honest. I have nothing to hide.

He considers me. "What's her name?"

"Jewel."

His gaze slides sideways toward the computer screen that started it all. "That's not your alias?"

"Hardly." I can prove my fingerprints had pulled up Jewel's background instead of my own. "If you'd accepted the social-media friend request I sent you, you would be able to see all my family connections. Here, I'll send the request again."

I pull my phone out of my purse and angle it away from him so when I open the app, he doesn't see his own profile immediately pop up. I wasn't stalking him. I was just checking in on him before coming to today's class to ensure he's still single. I pretend to scroll around on my phone for a second to make him think I'm searching for him, then I hit *Add Friend.*

His phone buzzes in his pocket. He keeps his arms crossed. "I only use social media for close friends and family."

Challenge accepted. We'll become close friends. For now . . . "Fine. I'll show you."

I tap on my sister's name to pull up her profile. Her cover picture is of my six-year-old niece and three-year-old nephew at Disneyland. They're little towheads with big brown eyes. I hope my kids will be as darling. I turn the phone to face Karson. "This is Daisy and Forrest. Aren't they the sweetest?"

Karson glances at my screen. "Adorable." When his gaze reconnects with mine, I can see his curiosity has returned.

I'll take his begrudging interest. That's improvement.

"Your sister had two children while becoming a psychologist?"

Dang. His interest is still in my sister. "Yes. Her husband stayed home with them so she could finish her residency ahead of schedule. Unfortunately, her being a workaholic ended their marriage. He still keeps the kids during the week so she can pursue her career, which is why she pays him child support."

He tilts his head toward the computer displaying my fingerprints. "You mean why she's *supposed* to pay him child support."

My lips quirk into a smile. I'm relieved not to be arrested, and I'm now enjoying this bonding experience. "Yeah."

He lifts his chin, a form of acceptance far superior to the kind on social media. His eyes may still be cool, but being in their sights is as refreshing as the mist from a waterfall.

"Okay," he says. "I'll do another background check, and once I get this cleared up, I'll let you go. But you need to tell your sister to pay her child support so I don't have to arrest *her*."

My smile slips.

CHAPTER FOUR

KARSON

*Anyone who does anything to help a child
in his life is a hero to me.*
—FRED ROGERS

As I pull into the parking lot next to the cone of an extinct volcano, I can't help thinking about Gemma and her evil twin, who should build her lair here in Mt. Tabor Park. Of course, if Gemma believes stealing the homecoming crown is evil, then she would never be able to deal with what I do on a daily basis.

My eight-year-old nephew's seat belt unsnaps and whizzes back into place, releasing him to lean over my shoulder in an illegal fashion. "Is that a real volcano?"

I find a spot and shift into Park. "It was. Now it's used as an amphitheater." The typical person would never know the venue once spewed molten lava. Now the small crater is currently filled with grass and surrounded by greenery. Today there's even a band setting up in it for an after-party.

"Cool." Phillip grabs his longboard and leaps out his door to the asphalt before I even turn off the engine.

"Wait, kiddo."

Phillip stands in wonder of the skateboarding tricks going on around us, though this is how he seems to live every day. His mouth hangs open to reveal adult teeth he hasn't yet grown into, his dark eyes shimmer with the energy of freshly brewed coffee, and his chestnut hair is spiked with sweat from constant movement.

I don't think I was ever so innocent.

"Look at them."

I climb out of the decade-old F-150, click Lock twice on my key fob, and join Phillip to scan the chaos. There should really be parking attendants and security set up, but at least the pine-scented air smells fresh like the woods right here in the middle of the city, and the giant trees offer cool shade from the blazing sun overhead.

Skaters of all ages and abilities take turns between racing and loitering. The action is accompanied by an orchestra of wheels on pavement, laughter, and a loudspeaker in the distance. I'm here as the stand-in for Phillip's dad, who is currently deployed. And because Harris is competing in the Old School Downhill Race.

My former partner rolls up. He looks more like a character from a sci-fi movie than a skater in his long-sleeved black Under Armor shirt, gloves, and an aerodynamic helmet with a reflective gold visor. I can't actually see Harris's face, but it's either him or someone wearing a padded muscle costume under all that spandex.

Phillip knocks knuckles with my old partner, but I'm going to have to give him a bad time about this ensemble. "Join the dark side, Darth?"

Harris removes the helmet à la Skywalker. He flashes his trade-mark smile. "You're the one hanging out with women who have arrest warrants."

I narrow my eyes. I was able to avoid him after Tuesday's class, but I should have known this conversation would catch up to me. "The warrant is in her twin sister's name. They have almost identical fingerprints."

He chuckles, steps on one end of his skateboard, and picks it up by the other end. He strolls with us along the hiking trail toward the reservoir where races start. "There's two of them? Maybe we can double-date."

My stomach plummets like a skateboard down a mountain. Surely it's because I have absolutely no desire to go out with Gemma, and not because Harris finds her attractive. "If you're interested, you can have her."

"Oh no." Harris shakes his head. "That woman only has her heart set on one cop, and it's not me."

Phillip's eyes shine with fascination, and I realize too late that word of Gemma is going to spread throughout the Zellner clan. I should have faced off with Drew during the workweek to prevent anyone from getting caught in this cross fire.

I picture myself yelling "nooo" and running in slow motion to guard my family from gossip. I don't make it in time.

"There's a girl who likes you, Uncle Karson?"

Harris hoots. "She doesn't just like him. She's writing a movie about him."

"Not about *me*," I correct. Especially not after the firefighters take over the class. "About heroes in general."

Phillip grins his toothy grin. "Is she pretty?"

I want to say, *That's all she is*, but after our discussion over her background check, I know it wouldn't be true. Gemma is sweet and intuitive and a real pain in the booty. I don't say this either, because little boys don't understand the dangers of dating beautiful women. "She's all right."

"All right?" Drew whoops. "She's *all right* like I'm white."

Phillip laughs along, though the V-shaped dip of his eyebrows tells me he doesn't understand this either. "You're not white."

Spoken by the boy who once licked Drew's arm to see if he tasted like chocolate. I kid you not.

"Good call, big guy." Drew does a little hop and spin with the kind of agility you don't see often in muscular men. "This woman who likes your uncle is not just all right. She's so gorgeous she could stop traffic. It's a good thing he didn't bring her along today because she'd probably cause a few skateboard crashes."

"Really?" Phillip hugs his longboard tighter.

That's right, kid. Choose your own goals over a girl.

"Really. Though he should bring her here another time since this is such a romantic location." Harris points through the giant trees at the city's skyline below.

I roll my eyes toward heaven. God knows I don't need a woman in my life, and even if I did, it wouldn't be Gemma. She's too much. Too much seems like a good thing at first unless a guy has already had too much. Then it's as Proverbs says, *One who is full loathes honey.* See? God and I are on the same page. I've had honey, and it just made things sticky. "Being romantic and being stupid are the same thing."

A couple of skater girls cross our path and glance over warily.

Harris waves off their worries. "Don't mind him. Even Casanova had bad days."

Thankfully we've crested the hill, and my nephew seems to have lost interest in my love life. He yells, "This place is amazing," and runs ahead toward the crowd gathering at the reservoir.

That statement I can agree with. The huge rectangle pool of water is surrounded by an iron fence and guarded by a stone gatehouse. It's one of the seven reservoirs built on Mt. Tabor during the early 1900s to store water for local residents. After a man was caught peeing in one of the reservoirs some years back, there was a big to-do and the city stopped using them for drinking water, but they are still kept as historic sites.

I nod after Phillip. "I've gotta try to keep up with him. When's your race?"

Harris glances at his smart watch. "It'll start in an hour. If you stay for the stunts up here, you'll still have time to get to the bottom of the hill to see me cross the finish line first."

I slap him on the back before we split directions. "Good luck, old man."

There's a thousand-dollar grand prize he wants to use for a security system on his mom's house. His dad died last year, and she lives in an older neighborhood that's going downhill, but she refuses to move. I'm glad she has Harris. And I'm glad he has her. As for me, I have Phillip.

I jog after my nephew and catch up at the street that's been blocked off for the races. On the far side of the street are stairs leading down to a lower reservoir that now sits empty but offers a great scenic overlook of the valley filled with trees and skyscrapers. While people usually come here to watch the sunset, nobody is paying any attention to the view today. Instead, the crowd has formed a circle around a group of skaters lining up in front of a limbo stick.

Phillip looks to me expectantly. "Can I play?"

I scan the ages and abilities of the kids in the circle. Most of them are teenagers who are using their time waiting in line to flip their boards or practice handstands. Phillip is nowhere near that level. But there seem to be younger kids in line too, and they're all just cheering each other on.

Do I let my cop side out to keep Phillip safe, or do I vicariously relive my childhood through him? Maybe if I were a parent, I'd instinctively know what to do, but since I haven't even had parents in my own life, I'm at a loss.

"Please, Uncle Karson. Dad would let me." He plays his trump card.

"Way to send me on a guilt trip, you hoodlum."

He giggles with glee.

"Go ahead. That's what your kneepads and wrist guards are for, right?"

Phillip runs out to join the line with the kind of enthusiasm I've only ever seen in cheerleaders and small dogs.

I cross my arms and watch proudly. He makes friends with the older girl behind him, and she seems to be demonstrating how he should squat and duck to avoid hitting the pole on his turn.

When he gets up to the front of the line, I debate about whether to film him or not. If something goes horribly wrong, I wouldn't want my sister to ever see the footage. But if he does something right, I definitely want him to be able to send it to his dad.

I pull out my phone and focus.

Phillip steps one foot to the board. With a shrug of his bony shoulders, he pushes off.

The wheels whir. The crowd cheers. Phillip steps his back foot next to his front and drops into a squat so low he might as well have been sitting on the board. His blue helmet ducks between his knees, and he sails underneath the pole with almost a foot to spare.

I punch my free fist overhead in victory. "Thatta kid!"

He circles around to the back of the line before looking my way with a shy smile. My heart has never swelled with so much pride. The circle of skaters continues round and round, and every time Phillip makes it under the bar, the pressure in my chest grows.

Finally it's down to him and the girl behind him, who may or may not regret giving him advice. Phillip rolls under the pole. She rolls under the pole.

The height lowers. Phillip rolls under the pole. She rolls under the pole.

Repeat.

The crowd presses around me and cheers louder, everyone wanting to see how the competition will end.

"You've got this, Phillip," I shout over the din.

"He's good," says the man next to me.

I feel like growling, *He's not good, he's grrreat!* as if I'm Tony the Tiger. But I simply say, "Thanks."

It's three more rounds before the girl's helmet hits the pole, knocking it down, and Phillip is announced the winner.

I whoop. Then the crowd rushes in, and I can't see him.

My trigger finger tingles, ready to take action. I've sent out AMBER Alerts before. Right as I'm about to tear apart the crowd in search of a kidnapper, my nephew emerges.

I blow out my breath and shake the tension from my arms. I just need to be happy for him, not freak him out.

Phillip holds his longboard under one arm, his head tilted to one side as if he's trying to act casual despite how hard he's smiling. As if to say, *It was nothing*, when really it feels like the biggest something of all the somethings.

I feel that. "You did it." I give him a cool high five but can't stop there. I hug his little body to me. "Wait until your dad sees the video."

The man who'd been standing next to me gives Phillip a high five as well. Then he looks at me and lifts his eyebrows. "You're not his father?"

I don't like the man's tone or the judgmental glint in his granite eyes. Phillip shouldn't be made to feel as if he's missed out because his dad is defending our country or made to feel as though I'm only here because his dad isn't. I'm here because I need him more than he needs me. I'm here for moments like this.

"He's my favorite uncle," Phillip answers.

I'm not sure if he's bragging or defending, but I'll take it. No need to mention I'm his only uncle.

"You have a *funcle*," the man jokes. Maybe he wasn't being judgmental after all, and I'd only seen what I'd expected to see. He nods toward two teenage boys getting ready to jump over the stick and land on their skateboards. Kind of a game of reverse limbo. "I'm sure my sons would love to have a funcle. I'm just the boring old dad who has to bring them to these events even though I don't know anything about skateboards."

Now it's my turn to support him. "The important thing is you're here."

There are a lot of good things that should be said about boring old dads. In real life, not everyone gets to have one. And not everyone gets to be one.

I turn Phillip around and lift him up onto my shoulders. He'll think it's so he can see the competition over the heads of the crowd in front of us, but it's actually so he won't see the emotion on my face. When he looks back on this day, I only want him to remember me as his proud funcle. By the time this reverse limbo game is over and we have to head down the hill for Harris's race, I'll have had time to swallow my grief and be able to laugh again.

I may not be able to protect Phillip from his own scrapes and bruises, but I can protect him from my pain. The kid is too young to have to understand that sometimes joy mingles with sorrow.

CHAPTER FIVE

GEMMA

*Being a hero isn't about letting others know you
did the right thing, it's about you knowing you
did the right thing.*
—GRANDPA MAX TENNYSON

I'm excited to see my niece and nephew, but that's all I'm excited for. In fact, I put off this dinner with my twin until the night of the second safety academy class. I knew I couldn't face Karson again without having told Jewel about the warrant for her arrest. At the same time, going to my class after dinner is a good excuse to leave her place early.

I call it a "place" because it doesn't look like a home. From the street, all you can see is a black box of a garage with a short walkway to the front door on the right. It's built on a hill, so this is the top floor with bedrooms for Daisy and Forrest behind the garage. You have to go down two more stories, past Jewel's suite on the middle floor, to get to the main living area that steps out onto a patio. From there, you can see the beautifully terraced landscape, but from here it's all concrete, including the planters full of firs and ferns.

I suppose it's a nice place. Definitely spendy. But I don't think I'd want it even if I could afford it. I'd buy a beach cottage in Seaside, a houseboat on the Columbia River, or maybe even a cabin in Mt. Hood National Forest. Those would be homey. Someday, I'll have my own home. For now, Jewel can still give me a bad time about sharing a town house with two roommates.

With my wicker purse hooked across my body bandolier-style, my hands are free to grab the plastic case of sidewalk chalk I brought. I pop open my door to the warm kiss of late afternoon sunshine and the smokey scent of barbecue. A magical combination.

I really hope we're having steak tonight, though my stomach might be too nauseous to enjoy it. If Jewel is grilling T-bones, I suspect she'll try to use them to get something from me. I mean, Jacob used a pot of stew to swindle Esau out of his birthright. Though I really don't have much left for her to take.

I'd originally wanted revenge for stealing my homecoming crown and tried to get her suspended from school, so she'd graduated early and took off for college. She came back with these babies, and I put up with her for them. Though if she'd been as repentant as Jacob when meeting with Esau again, she would have sent gifts and called me "my lord," or at least "your highness."

I slide my sunglasses atop my head before stepping into the modern alcove entry and ringing the doorbell.

When bare feet slap against tile flooring, my shoulders finally relax.

"It's me. Aunt Gemma," I call to the kids, so they know they're safe to let me in. If we have to wait for my sister to climb two flights of stairs, we are going to be here a while.

"Aunt Gemma," Forrest echoes. Followed by, "Awesome!" He's three.

"Did you bring books?" Daisy wants to know. I'd brought her a book when I'd attended Forrest's baby shower, so she wouldn't feel left out, and even though she'd only been two at the time, she now expects a book every time I visit. Which is, as Forrest would say, awesome.

I smile at the black door still closed between us. "I brought something better. We're going to make our own book tonight. You two will be the heroes." I can't wait to ignite their imaginations. I try the pewter door handle, but it's locked.

"Can I ride a dragon in the book?" Forrest yells.

I'll need to look up how to draw a dragon, but . . . "Sure."

"I want to wear a tiara like a princess," Daisy shouts.

I can relate. "That's a great idea." It's so cute that they don't even question the possibility of me putting them into a story. They simply believe I have the power to do it. I wish movie producers had that kind of faith. "You're going to have to let me in first."

"We can't," Forrest shouts.

"Mom said," Daisy explains.

I suppose that's a smart rule. It just seems like there could be exceptions for family. There probably would be if my parents hadn't moved to Utah to take care of Opa and Oma. "Is she coming?"

"Gemma, I'm down here." My sister's voice comes from the side of the house. It sounds a lot like mine, just with an annoyed-at-the-world tone. "Would you quit yelling for all my neighbors to hear?"

I press my lips together. I haven't even stepped inside her house, and I've already done something wrong. I wonder whether or not to yell to the kids that I'll meet them on the patio, but their foot slaps tell me the race is already on.

I open a gate hidden behind shrubbery and take the stairs diagonally down the hill to the second level, where a door leads out from Jewel's room. At that point, there's a couple of chaise lounges and a switchback that continues around levels of plants and bushes down to the firepit and barbecue under a pergola. This is my favorite part of her home, but instead of enjoying the landscape design, I'm checking out the flat cement areas. If we use the driveway too, we might have enough space for all the art I plan to draw.

Jewel glances up from where she's flipping T-bones. She may be my identical twin, but she wears glasses and cuts her hair shorter. Basically, if I were to film a makeover scene in a movie, she'd be the before version of the character. This wouldn't be a bad thing except for the way she resents me for being the after version.

She glances up and takes in the plastic tub in my hands. "Did you bring a side dish? Because I stopped at the deli on my way home and picked up plenty of food."

It's totally not fair that she didn't develop my lactose intolerance and gluten allergy, and even more unfair that my diet bothers her. She hates it when I bring food, as if she thinks I don't rate her food as good enough. So I don't ever offer anymore. Especially when I'm already dreading offending her with the arrest warrant thing.

I hold up the tub. "It's chalk."

The sliding door to the living room glides wide, and the cutest kids in the universe charge out to hug me. Their little bodies press against my leg.

"Chalk," Forrest repeats. "Awesome!"

"Can I draw a hopscotch?" Daisy reaches for the tub.

"You could." I set the tub on a side table and unhook the purse from my shoulder to lay it on a seat cushion. "But there's something else I want to draw first."

Jewel points her tongs at me. "You're spraying the cement clean afterward."

"Sure." I pull my phone out of my purse to open images of my chalk-art idea. In the first photograph, there's a drawing of balloons floating into the sky with a little girl posed laying on the ground as though she is holding onto the strings and being lifted toward chalk clouds. I turn my phone screen to show the kids. "We can draw you two right into the story. I'll take pictures, then put them together in a book."

Daisy claps and dances. She appears to be doing the potty jig, but I think she's just excited.

Forrest leans in for a closer look, not quite grasping the concept. "Where's the dragon?"

"I'll draw one." I google his request and up pops a picture of a boy posed as if he's holding a shield to fight off a fire-breathing dragon. "Does that work?"

Forrest's dark eyes grow wide underneath his wispy, white-blond hair. "That's scary."

Yeah, trying to draw such detail would be kind of scary. I'll do better with simple shapes, like a moon for him to "stand" on with a big space helmet drawn around his head, or a swing under a tree where Daisy can "sit." I swipe to a picture of a boy "flying" over a city skyline. "How about we make you both superheroes?" I offer.

"Awesome!"

Jewel's lips twist as if I've almost impressed her. "That's a cute idea."

Wow. Okay. Maybe tonight won't be as painful as I'd expected.

While Jewel sets the table, we get to work, making up the story as we go.

"Once upon a time, a brother and sister decided to take a trip to the beach." I draw a shade umbrella over beach towels. Daisy runs inside the house and returns with two pairs of sunglasses for props, which make the whole picture even cuter than I imagined when they lie down on the towels. There's seriously nothing more adorable than kids in sunglasses.

Next scene . . . "The sister went swimming, while the brother went fishing." Forrest "sits" on the dock "holding" a chalk drawing of a fishing pole, and Daisy pretends to dive underwater with the seaweed, starfish, and octopus. Perfect.

We troop up to the second-level patio for fresh cement.

I stretch my stiff lower back before squatting to draw again. "But when they returned to the shore to dry off, they realized their towels were actually capes." Thus they have to fly through the sky.

We're just getting to the part where their capes stop working and they have to use them as parachutes when Jewel joins us, hands planted on hips.

I brace for criticism.

"Do I get to be in the book?" she asks.

"Uh . . ." I guess every superhero story needs a supervillain.

"You can be the butterfly," Daisy yells, as if this makes sense with our plotline.

I'll figure some way to connect it. I draw butterfly wings and my sister lies down flat. I have to climb onto a chair to get a good angle for my camera. The end result actually looks pretty good. I show her the picture.

She laughs, and it's not a villainous laugh. "Dinner's ready."

I don't argue. Because steak. Also, I want to keep on Jewel's good side.

We sit around the wrought iron table, Daisy and Forrest wiggling even as they fold their hands and close their eyes for the blessing. I follow suit, sans wiggling, though I always have trouble listening to my sister pray too.

Usually she's praying for food full of gluten and dairy to bless my body. But I guess her prayer isn't so bad with today's steak and salad. I'll be thankful too.

"Amen." I cut into my meat and savor the first juicy bite. Jewel may not be thoughtful, but she sure can grill.

"So, are you enjoying your summer off?" she asks, as though I'm a slacker.

I do love my summers, but not in the way she implies. I haven't stopped working.

I slow my chewing to think of the best way to answer and finally swallow into a sour stomach. Might as well respond with a segue into the topic I came to discuss. "I'm taking a citizen's police academy class as research for the screenplay I'm writing."

"Play is right," she says, confirming my suspicions that she only studied psychology in order to inflict deeper mental anguish on those around her. "Have you sold anything yet?"

Many retorts script themselves in my brain, one of which involves how artists have to master their art before they can make money, and we don't get paid to "practice" the way doctors do. But I can also script how she would react, and I would rather not play a role in that scene.

I reach for the kale salad to avoid eye contact. "I wrote a play the high school senior class performed this spring."

My students enjoyed the unit I taught on *The Scarlet Pimpernel*, so we came up with a parody called *The Scarlet Fingernail*, where the heroine pretends to be a Paris Hilton type. I've tried pitching it as a screenplay, but the producer I met with had never even heard of the world's very first fictional hero with a hidden identity. *Sink me.*

"Well." Jewel shrugs off my small success. "I guess that's what they say. 'Those who can't do, teach.'"

Her quote is actually shortened from a line in the play *Man and Superman* by George Bernard Shaw. But I doubt she cares so much for its origin as she does about the criticism it implies. For that reason, it's a quote every teacher detests. And she knows it.

What Jewel doesn't know is that while she's trying to hurt me, I'm being careful with the information I have that can hurt her. I mean, if I wanted to, I could pick up the phone right now and have the police come haul her off to jail. But I would never use the warrant for her arrest as a weapon. Which just makes her attacks seem all the more unfair.

I sip my tangy lemonade, still considering possible replies like steps through a minefield. I'm here because of Karson. Soon I'll get to see him in class, and I'll be able to tell him I did what he asked me to do. Then I can forget all this and focus on learning about the K-9 unit. I wonder if Karson has a dog.

Hmm . . . While thinking about Karson owning a dog is a daydream to save for later, I could definitely refer to Karson as my instructor for this conversation. That will make her put-downs seem less personal.

"Not all teachers are created equal." I set my glass on the table and make a defense on behalf of others. "My favorites are those who teach from their own experiences. For example, in my Citizen's Safety Academy, the police officers shared video footage from their own body cameras. And dash cams. We got to see a car chase last week."

Forrest stands on his seat. "Awesome!"

Jewel points for him to sit.

Daisy rests her elbows on the table, head tilted against the fist not holding her fork. "What's a car chase? Who's fast enough to chase a car?"

I smile at the cute question. "The police cars chase the bad guy's car."

"Elbows off the table, Daisy."

Daisy pulls her hands to her lap, but Forrest is standing again. His fork nowhere to be seen, he plants his hands on the table and pushes against it to do donkey kicks.

"Forrest," Jewel scolds.

I don't even think he realizes what he's doing. He's just thrilled to be alive. He keeps rocking the table with his enthusiasm. "I want to help chase the bad guys. I can fly really fast in my cape. Will you draw a police car, Aunt Gemma?"

I steady my sloshing lemonade. "Sure." I think I can manage a couple of small cars in the skyscraper scene I drew under the chalk superhero capes.

He catapults off his seat as if he's already wearing one.

This time Jewel warns him with a look that I'm pretty sure is giving her the wrinkles I haven't gotten yet. When I have children someday, I'll have to make sure not to glare at them so harshly.

Forrest bounces in place. "I ate seven bites, Mom. I ate seven bites."

She studies his blue plastic plate. "That's enough to go play but not enough for dessert."

He's already scrambling through the bushes up the side of the hill as if he has no time for sidewalks. "I don't want dessert."

"Then you need to go brush your teeth."

He pauses, perhaps considering which will take longer, brushing his teeth or eating more steak so he doesn't have to go brush his teeth right now. Oh, to be able to live in the moment like a preschooler again.

Daisy bolts from her chair toward the sliding glass door as if she's trying to escape before her mom looks at her pink plate. "I'll brush my teeth too."

Forrest follows, leaving a trail of topsoil behind, and I wonder whether the kids know something I don't. Jewel did burn last Thanksgiving's pumpkin pie. I glance at her suspiciously. "What's for dessert?"

"Ice cream." With the way she smirks, I'm guessing she didn't buy sorbet or anything else dairy-free.

I might as well brush my teeth too. Oh well. That's not what I came for anyway. I rub at the pressure building in the nape of my neck and decide to take advantage of our quiet moment. "Jewel, in my class at the police station—"

"We're talking about police again?" She leans back in her chair and lifts an eyebrow that's both lighter and bushier than mine. "You have a thing for the cop, don't you?"

I bite my lip. I'm not sure if she has the power to read my mind because she's my twin or because she's a psychologist. "Yes, but—"

She cackles. "He isn't interested in you? That's a first."

I'm not sure how to take her statement, so I cross my arms to ward off all insinuations. "Anyway—"

"Wait. Don't gloss over this landmark moment." She leans forward with elbows on the table, and I wonder why it's okay for her to put them there and not Daisy. "Is it a love triangle? Did he choose another woman over you?"

I hate how much she seems to be enjoying this, but as her ex is remarried, she might feel like this makes me more relatable. "No," I say slowly. "I think he had something bad happen in his past that has him building walls with people."

"Don't we all?" She throws her arms up in the air. "Except you. You want everyone to like you, including this one man who isn't interested."

I shift in my seat. "I'm drawn to him because I want to help him find joy again. He's got a lot of anger he needs to let go of."

"Oh, sweetie."

I sit up taller, not that I could ever be taller than my twin. "Don't 'oh, sweetie' me, *sweetie*." Yeah. I said it. I called her sweetie in a mean tone. But I've had enough.

She laughs to see me get so riled and then holds up her hand as though I'm the one who needs to calm down. "You obviously don't know much about anger, sis. So let me give you a little psychology lesson that will help you connect to your irate officer."

If she knows so much about managing anger, then why is she the one with the extra wrinkles? I want to say this, but I don't, because I'm actually curious. I do need all the help I can get with Karson. "What?" I ask grudgingly.

She leans back and crosses her legs, making herself comfortable as if she's dealing with a patient on her couch. "Anger comes from one of three areas—pain, fear, or frustration."

Like my frustration with her? "I'm listening."

"So either your cop is hurting, he's afraid, or there's something"—she pauses, looking me up and down—"or some*one*, annoying him."

She's calling me Karson's annoying someone. Which makes her *my* annoying someone.

"Well." I push my chair away from the table, steak only half-eaten, though I consider eating her ice cream. All the lactose in the world couldn't make me any sicker than I already feel. "I did do one thing that annoyed him."

The corners of her mouth curl up. "Care to share?"

If fear is one of the causes of anger, then I should prepare for her backlash. I take a breath and rip off the Band-Aid. "When Karson took my fingerprints, he thought I had a warrant out for my arrest. But it turns out that my fingerprints pulled up your file."

Her lips purse. Her eyes narrow.

"Apparently you haven't been paying your child support."

She blinks. But her lips slide back into a stiff smile. "No. That's not true."

Jewel says it in such a way that I'm actually questioning whether Karson made a mistake. Or there's a triplet neither of us knows about.

A triplet would be wild. I'd like to think she'd be on my side in standoffs such as this.

I hold a hand out while I shrug. It's not for me to determine if the warrant is real or not. "I'm just repeating what Karson said. He told me to tell you, so you can take care of your back child support before he has to arrest you."

"Karson?" she mocks, as though he's not a real cop because he's teaching a class. Just as easily, she brushes away the threat of prison. "When I started my own practice, the state stopped automatically taking the funds from my paycheck. I pay Grant directly. He just needs to let the government know."

I don't want to argue anymore. So I remain still like a hiker who just ran into a rattlesnake. "Okay."

The sliding glass door slams shut, distracting Jewel, and giving me a chance to back away slowly. "I'll finish my art with the kids before I leave for my class." I prepare my exit strategy before offering, "And maybe you should go call Grant just to make sure you're on the same page with child support."

"Shh . . ." she hisses, head tilting toward her kids as though I'm an idiot for mentioning child support in front of them. I don't think they even know what that means, so I'm pretty sure she's just using them as an excuse to end our conversation. "There's nothing to worry about. Just run along and play. I'll clear the table and wrap up your leftovers for you to take home, Gemma."

Again, there's no way for me to win. I was trying to help, and also entertaining her kids, but she's making me seem like the immature one.

Forrest and Daisy grab my hands and drag me up the path, so I turn my back on Jewel. The three of us have a great time finishing our story, and I'm surprised to see the time on my phone when I snap my last picture. Jewel has been inside for quite a while. Maybe she really is taking my advice and giving Grant a call.

I don't want to interrupt, but I have to leave for the police precinct, and I should at least stick my head inside to say goodbye. Though she may not appreciate me now, I think she'll love the photobook of her kids I'm going to put together. Then one day I'll sell a screenplay, and she'll have to take my career seriously. Take *me* seriously.

CHAPTER SIX

KARSON

Everybody loves the underdog, and then they
take an underdog and make him a hero
and they hate him.

—Fred Durst

I'm not watching for Gemma—I'm watching *out* for Gemma. Though she can't possibly cause as much trouble as she did last week.

I glance at the clock on the wall in the back of the briefing room. We've got a couple more minutes before we're scheduled to begin, but I subscribe to the belief that if any person is not five minutes early, that person is late. I should just lock the front doors right now.

Our K-9 unit is already here and ready to give demonstrations. Unfortunately for me, Harris is on that unit, which means I'll have to handle the class by myself until we go outside.

"Where's Drew?" the biker dude asks. He's dressed in slacks and a button-down today, but he still looks the part with his Grizzly Adams beard. We learned in his background check that he's a defense attorney, which I naturally consider to be worse than a biker.

"Hi, Larry," I say because, first, that's his name, and second, he prefers to be called by his club moniker "Wolfman." "We'll see Harris when we go outside for the K-9 demonstrations. He'll be introducing you to the partner who replaced me."

Larry bobs his head in appreciation. "Dope."

Dope is either a drug taken illegally for recreation or a synonym for dunce. I get tired of dealing with both, so I'm not sure how the word ever became slang for something positive.

"It's quiet in here without Drew." This comes from the wife of the middle-aged couple who sits in the front row. Aaron and Erin.

I kind of wish all couples shared the same first name. That would make remembering who they are so much easier, though I can see how it could also cause confusion. I already had enough confusion with Gemma and Jewel.

Gemma's roommates tromp through the door, creating a ruckus loud enough to satisfy Erin.

I wait for Gemma to follow so we can get started. The doorway remains empty, and I give a sigh of relief that comes out sounding like a disappointed harrumph. Weird.

"Sorry we're late," Gemma's roommate Charlie announces to the whole class. He's not technically late, but he must share my definition of the five-minute rule. "We were waiting for Gemma to get home, but she let us know at the last minute that she's going to meet us here." He looks around. "Did we beat her?"

So she is coming. "Yes." I cross my arms, choosing not to let her current absence distract me one way or the other. "We have our animal handlers here today, meaning we can't wait for her before getting started."

Kai pulls out his phone and holds it up. "I'll video so she can watch later."

I stare at the screen, unsure if he's actually filming or not. The last thing I want is for Gemma to have video footage of me. I'm not the hero she's looking for. "No recording."

Kai lowers his phone and shrugs. "Didn't realize this was so top secret."

I level my gaze on him. "We use special hand signals for our dogs that we wouldn't want shared with anyone who might have nefarious intent."

Charlie snorts. "Don't be nefarious, Kai."

Kai lifts a hand, fingers curled in so that only his thumb and pinky stick out. He wiggles his wrist in a way I've seen surfers do. "Is this a special hand signal? Sometimes I make it without thinking, and I wouldn't want to accidentally call a dog to attack or anything."

Is he for real? Because he reminds me of a cartoon character. "No."

"See?" Kai grins at Charlie. "I'm not nefarious."

I glance at the clock. This could take all night, and we are supposed to be outside for the demonstrations in ten minutes. "Can we begin now?"

"Yeah." Charlie taps his phone screen. "I'll just take notes for Gemma."

"Fine." I huff. "Besides the no-filming rule, I have one other rule for the demonstration. If you have any food in your purse or pockets, make sure you leave that inside. Dogs' noses are very sensitive, and if you smell like mints or a granola bar, it will throw them off the scent we purposely planted for them to follow."

Everyone nods.

Erin hoists her giant handbag the size of a picnic basket onto the table. "Is my purse safe if I leave it here?"

I always err on the side of caution when it comes to safety in order to prevent crimes of opportunity. Lock car doors. Leave porch lights on. Install security cameras. But unless Robin Hood mistakenly assumes the Sheriff of Nottingham works in my precinct, nobody is going to touch Erin's purse. "Yes."

A couple of other women adjust their purses on the table as if preparing to leave them behind, and I instinctively give them a once-over to see if either of them might be trying to hide something other than food. I'm thinking of drugs, or, as Larry would say, dope. Myrna, a younger woman with short hair and a nose piercing, simply seems to be putting away her nail file. The small older woman with white hair, Barbara, is married to one of the new fire chiefs, so I'm not worried about her. In fact, I like to call her by her nickname, "Boots," simply to irk Larry.

I'll remind them all of the agreements they made last week in case there are any issues. "When we took your fingerprints, you also signed a participation waiver, allowing us to search your person should the need arise. If one of our detection K-9s alerts on you, you'll get to experience a pat-down firsthand."

Larry outright laughs while the rest of the class only murmurs in response.

I glance the lawyer's way, daring him to bring up arguments of what's admissible in court.

He settles in his seat, but the huge grin on his face tells me he's entertained by what I consider a very serious subject.

I ignore him—for both our benefits. "If everyone will simply follow the rules, you'll be saving us time and keep yourself from the close scrutiny of a protective search."

Charlie elbows Kai. "I don't know. Gemma might enjoy getting frisked."

I assume he thinks he's speaking in a quiet tone. Only he doesn't do quiet, so he's just announced Gemma's infatuation with me to the whole class.

They all seem to chuckle in unison. Then they watch for my reaction. The woman isn't even here, and she's causing issues.

"I'm here." Right on cue, she sails in, long ponytail flying from the top of her head.

Now everyone focuses on her, and it's clear by the warm smiles they offer that they adore her.

I'm annoyed nobody else is annoyed.

Gemma squeezes behind chairs down the row to sit with her movie crew. "I'm so sorry I'm late. I came from a different direction and didn't realize how long it would take."

Charlie rolls out her chair.

She plunks down, flips open her journal, and clicks her pen, preparing to write. She looks up, wide blue eyes expectant. "What'd I miss?"

I take a deep breath, thankful I can't smell her tanning oil from here. Unfortunately, that doesn't stop me from imagining all the summer fun that must have kept her from being punctual. Whitewater rafting the Deschutes, windsurfing in the Gorge, waterskiing the

Willamette River. With all the options a beer commercial might feature, why is she even here?

Erin spins sideways in her chair, faces Gemma, and pats the ginormous purse by her side. "Karson was just saying that if you have any food in your purse, you'll want to leave it in the classroom during K-9 demonstrations."

". . . unless you want to get frisked," Aaron finishes with a smirk.

A few snickers don't even faze Gemma. Completely unaware of the insinuation, her shoulders sag in relief. "I'm glad I made it in time for the demonstrations. Where do you get your dogs?"

And just like that, she puts us back on track. I clear my throat to give the lesson I'd prepared. "Some of our dogs are bred and trained internationally, but we also find dogs at the pound. The ones with such high energy that make them horrible pets are perfect for us. They always want to play and please people, and they put that same energy into their work. They actually never stop working. When Officer Harris takes his German shepherd home at night, Blaze will search the whole house before settling down."

Gemma scribbles everything I say into her journal. When she looks up, her lips seem to be parted in wonder. "Do you have a dog? Have you ever been a K-9 cop?"

"No." I'd always felt like I could make a bigger difference in the management track. I don't only want to arrest criminals one at a time, but I want to make sure that they are all getting arrested. Thus, I focused on moving up to sergeant and lieutenant as quickly as possible. "I've never been in the K-9 unit, but I have helped Harris, and I do have the scars to prove it." I hold up my right forearm and point to two thick pink spots of skin where the padded sleeve had slipped and Blaze's teeth punctured my flesh. That was fun.

Gemma lets go of her pen to cover her mouth in horror. Others murmur their own concern.

I quickly explain away my pain. "It was an accident, but I wouldn't want to be the suspect Blaze is ordered to apprehend."

Chuckles.

"There are four different divisions of dogs. German shepherds, like Blaze, and other herding dogs are great at catching suspects and holding them hostage. Then we have our detection dogs. Labs, beagles, basset hounds, and other soft-mouth breeds are used for drug or bomb sniffing. Third, we have our tracking dogs, which perform search and rescues. Bloodhounds and retrievers are good at this. Last, we have our cadaver dogs, which can hunt down dead bodies, even underwater. Among the other dogs I've mentioned for tracking, collies are also common."

Gemma isn't looking at me anymore. She's biting the end of her pen and staring into space, and I have the impression she's going to write some new K-9 character that will give Lassie a run for her money. I try to think of tidbits of information that can help her. Not because I care about her career success, but because I want the next K-9 film to be more believable than *Turner and Hooch*.

"Our K-9 units include SUVs designed to keep our dogs cool when they are left in the vehicles. Even their water bowls are chilled. And they have to be trained to remain calm when a suspect is acting crazy." I think back to helping Blaze with that as well. A small smile stretches my lips. "When Harris was training Blaze, he'd have me scream and thrash about to test him. It was actually one of the most cathartic things I've ever done. Sometimes, when I've had a bad day, I ask if any of the officers in the K-9 division need to give their dogs a little extra training."

Gemma's eyes zip back to me as if my emotional baggage just sprang open in front of TSA.

Perhaps I've overshared. Change of subject. "Any questions?"

Charlie's hand. "Do you ever get compared to Mel Gibson in *Lethal Weapon*?"

"No." I'm usually much more controlled.

Gemma lifts her pen. "Have any of your dogs been killed in the line of duty?"

"No." Thankfully. Watching *Old Yeller* as a kid was painful enough.

"Do you ever answer with anything other than a *no*?" Kai, of course.

"No."

The class's laughter sounds a little nervous at this point. We all just want to go outside where Harris can make them laugh for real.

I march toward the door. "If that's everything, let's head out to watch the demonstrations." I lead the class out the back door of the offices and across the rear parking lot to a dog run next to the kennel. It's full of different sized wooden boxes with numbered doors in which the dog trainers will try to hide. I motion for the class to face the fence line. "Anyone want to guess which box Harris is hiding in?"

"Not one of the front ones," Gemma guesses from halfway down the fence. "That would be too easy."

She's made a good guess, and I'm about to commend her, but then right in front of me, she pulls her phone out of her pocket and points it through the fence like a camera.

Right. She wasn't here for my speech on not recording the demonstration. "Gemma?"

She turns her face my way, expectant grin telling me she thinks she's moving to the head of the class.

"No filming."

The shine in her sapphire eyes turns matte. "Oh." She ducks her chin and fumbles to shove the device inside a purse hanging against her hip. "Sorry."

"Be on time next week so you know the rules," I scold while sending her roommates a warning look. They are partly to blame for not keeping an eye on her.

"Okay," she squeaks.

Kai shoves his hands in his pockets, also penitent.

Charlie . . . not so much. "My guess is box number six. What do I get if I'm right?"

I truly hope Drew is not hiding in box number six. Charlie is too competitive for his own good.

"I'll take you out for a drink," Myrna offers.

Charlie glances at her, then does a double take as if noticing her for the first time. Poor girl. "Oh, I can't date you. I'm taken. Or I will be when I win back my former fiancée."

And I thought I'd shared too much info earlier. I press my lips together to keep from commenting on that one.

Gemma's eyes flash bright again, and she flicks her gaze my way as if to share the joke. She seems to have no clue her interest in me is as ill-fated as her roommate's relationship plans.

A trainer leads Blaze from the kennel on a leash. He looks regal, with pointy ears and thick fawn coat decorated by black markings on his back and muzzle. His muscles coil, ready for action.

I cross my arms. "Well. I'm not encouraging betting, but if you were going to make a legal wager of sorts, now is the time to lock it in."

"Box six for bragging rights," Charlie calls.

Nobody argues.

Blaze is unleashed, though he stands still, a soldier awaiting orders. Then the trainer's secret command ignites his engine like a starter pistol. The dog charges directly toward box number six. Dang.

Harris opens the tiny door and comes out in a padded bite suit. If he didn't look like the Hulk before, he does now. He runs his dog through a few more drills before giving him a reward and ushering him to his kennel.

"All right, crew. We're going to bring out Snoops now."

"Snoops." Larry laughs. Perhaps he's a Charlie Brown fan or perhaps he knows another biker named Snoops. I don't find either too funny myself.

"He's our detection dog. Just like Blaze hunted down Officer Harris, Snoops is going to track a certain scent. I've covertly given one of you a handkerchief to hide on your person." I gave it to Boots because she got here first today, not because it gives me pleasure to watch a firefighter's wife get implicated as a criminal. Even though it might. "Please line up along the fence to see how quickly Snoops can track it down."

I glance at Boots out of the corner of my eye to see where she decides to stand. Far end. That will drag out the demonstration. Make everyone wonder if Snoops is really doing his job or not.

I nod toward the same trainer, waiting by the kennel. She leads out a basset hound with big floppy ears and a long belly that rocks ridiculously close to the ground. Snoops doesn't move with Blaze's energy or precision, though he will perform just as well by waddling right down to the end of the row and alerting on Boots.

He doesn't. He never makes it past Gemma, but rather, he sits in front of her and stares up.

Gemma looks at me, her baby blues asking for help.

Blood pulses through my ears. I close my eyes. If she has so much as a leftover peanut from airline travel in her purse, I am kicking her out of the class. We specifically told her the food rule when she arrived late.

"Hey," Charlie calls. "Is that why you were late, Gem? You were stashing the handkerchief in your purse?"

If only.

Harris jogs out from the kennel, wearing his standard movie star smile. "Snoops is definitely alerting us that he's found what he's looking for. Good boy, Snoops." My classroom assistant has removed his bite suit, but he still has some catching up to do.

The trainer looks at me. She knows this was not the plan.

Boots steps out from her spot as the last in line, waving the handkerchief I gave her. "I thought Snoops was supposed to alert on me."

A line of faces swivel toward Boots then back my way. Kai and Charlie continue their head-swivel all the way to Gemma.

Kai groans. "I was only joking about you wanting to be frisked, Gem."

"You said that?" Gemma's hands rise to press against pink cheeks. "I don't wanna be frisked."

And I don't want to have to frisk her. I roll my eyes toward heaven, questioning God's sense of humor.

"Whoa, boy," Harris hoots. Thankfully he's now caught onto what's happening and can take over the class while I have another little chat with my nemesis. "Follow me, folks." He leads them away on what I assume will become a tour of the kennels.

The line of students straggles past, shooting Gemma and me curious looks.

Larry slows to hand her a business card. "I'm a defense attorney. I can get you out of whatever trouble you're in."

Gemma stares at him, too shocked to reach for the card. "What?"

"Move along, Wolfman." His moniker fits this situation. He's a wolf in sheep's clothing.

He tucks the business card back in his shirt pocket. "You can find me online. Larry Murphey at Murphey's Law." He smirks once more before jogging to catch up with the group.

Kai and Charlie stay behind, flanking a rather pale Gemma. Either she's scared or her coconut-scented sunblock has proven very effective.

"I swear Gemma doesn't do drugs," Charlie vouches. "Though she might have some vitamins in her purse or something. She's super healthy, and you didn't say anything about vitamins."

I swipe my flashlight off my belt and stride toward her. "Open your purse, please."

That's a safer place to start than having her face the fence and "spread 'em."

She lifts the purse's long strap off her shoulder and over her head without a word, then flips the top flap open. It's still pretty bright outside, but there are shadows inside her bag that could hide a forgotten ketchup packet or protein shake mix. I should have made all the women leave their purses behind.

My beam of light instantly reflects against something silver and shiny. Something T-bone shaped. My stomach drops.

Gemma gasps with dismay at being caught. I know she's guilty, because there's no way this was an accident.

I reach inside and pull out the foil packet. Who puts a steak in their purse and forgets about it? Or rather, who even puts a steak in their purse?

"Nefarious," Kai says.

CHAPTER SEVEN

GEMMA

Being a hero means ignoring how silly you feel.
—DIANA WYNNE JONES

All three men stare at me as if I'd wanted to distract the dog. As if I'd wanted to cause more problems. I guess I should have double-checked my purse, but I only ever eat fresh food, so I never carry any with me. I had no idea Jewel stashed leftovers in my purse when she was cleaning up. Honestly, she might have told me, but I was distracted by the story the kids and I were creating.

Karson unfolds a crinkly corner of foil to reveal the illicit slab of meat and verify his suspicions.

"I didn't put that there," I blurt. If only I'd choked down more than the required seven bites.

Karson presses the foil back into place and raises angry eyes in accusation. "I suppose your evil twin did this too?"

"Yes!" If he gets it, why's he so angry? Jewel said it's because he's either hurt, scared, or frustrated. Okay, so he's frustrated. I can respect that. I messed up his dog demonstration. Or rather, my evil twin did.

Karson waves the steak, cornflower irises dull with disbelief. "You're telling me that, without your knowledge, your sister wrapped up a steak and planted it in your purse right before you were to attend a K-9 demonstration?"

"Well . . ." I shrug. He makes it sound completely ridiculous.

My roommates take small steps in retreat, as if my story is too much for even them to support. While they know I'm a sincere person, they hadn't known my sister was a twin until last week's fingerprint debacle. I've gone beyond their jurisdiction.

Karson spares them a glance and tilts his head toward the kennels. "Go on. I'll see you two next week. Though Gemma won't be invited back."

"What?" I cry, and I'm not sure whether it's a sea of shame or injustice that floods my core, rising high enough to clog my throat.

I'm the reason Kai and Charlie are even here. I wanted this class more than anyone. Yes, I think Karson is cute, or I did anyway—back before he started accusing me of criminal mischief, but I came to learn about law enforcement to make my screenplays more authentic. This is my summer break. My only time to write. And now my research is being taken away by the one man I thought could save it. I tried so hard, yet my sister robbed me again.

"No . . ." I plead. I reach out and grip his forearm, but the anger radiating from his body separates us like an electric fence, and my stunned hand drops. "I went to her house tonight to tell her about the child support. I was there to do what you asked me to, even though I didn't want to."

He huffs and his eyes squint. Is he relenting, or is he reinforcing this wall between us?

I forge ahead, determined to make him understand. "She claims that when she started her private practice, the state wasn't able to deduct child support from her wages anymore, and she's been paying her ex directly. He simply hasn't reported it yet."

"I've heard that before." His tone drips with condescension, but at least he's listening.

I clutch my purse to my chest, to my heart, daring to hope. "I don't know whether she's telling the truth or not, but I said if that's the case, then she should talk to him and make sure he updates Child Support Services."

Karson's frown softens into a straight line between the shadows of goatee stubble. "And that's when she decided to cram a steak in your purse in hopes a dog would attack you?"

I open my mouth but my thoughts freeze before forming words. Is he joking? I know if Kai said the same thing, it would be in jest, and we could laugh. But Karson still sounds so serious. "No. She must have put it in my purse when she went inside to clean up the dishes from dinner. She didn't know about the dogs but apparently wanted me to have my leftovers."

One corner of his lips twitch, though he doesn't say anything.

I keep going. "I don't put food in my purse, but I should have confirmed I didn't have any before we left the room. I'm so sorry. Please let me come back."

His eyes read mine.

I stand perfectly still, as though I'm in the full-body scanner at the airport. I did once get selected for a pat-down when going through security, and that's definitely not what I'm here for.

He lifts his flashlight and clicks it back on. I hear the click but can't really see the beam. Summer evenings in Oregon are still too bright for that.

"Let me look in your purse again."

Does he think I'm lying about food, and he's going to find a hot dog and hamburger? Of course he won't, so the more important question is whether he'll let me return to class if he sees that I'm honest. I grip the sides of my bag and hold it open, arms extended.

He inspects the contents of my purse, and I inspect his full crown of short, thick hair. It's shiny, maybe from some kind of hair product. Is that what gives him the cinnamon scent?

In the background, I see Kai and Charlie hovering outside the kennel. My belly warms with the knowledge that they are still looking out for me. I may never win over this cop, but I'll be thankful for the men I do have in my life. Jewel can't scare *them* away.

My purse jostles. Karson continues poking around, and I try to imagine what he's seeing. My wallet. Lip gloss. Tampons.

He pulls out a baggie of crushed white powder. "What's this?"

I drop heavy arms to my sides. "That's chalk. You can't kick me out of class for chalk."

He blinks slowly, and when his eyes meet mine again, they aren't angry. They actually lack their usual spark, looking a little bored. As if he realizes he's wasting his time on me when he could be out putting real criminals behind bars. After tonight, he might need one of those dog-training sessions he mentioned earlier. I picture him clawing his hair out and screaming, "Gemma is driving me insane," while Blaze glances over with mild concern that the boss has lost it.

"Do you always carry chalk? Or is it just to get alone time with me like this?" His suggestion heats my cheeks with awareness in spite of how he probably meant it to mock.

I'm reminded of my sister's assertion that I'm only interested in this man because he's not interested in me. But I'm not trying to trick him into spending time together. I really do admire his passion for his job. Even if his intensity can be misplaced. "I don't want to be alone with you *like this*."

He gives a little shake of his head. "Explain the chalk, please."

I hook my purse back over my shoulder. "I took the chalk to my sister's house to entertain my niece and nephew. I had a giant tub of colors, but it didn't include a white piece of chalk, so I grabbed a stick out of my classroom supplies and put it in a baggie in case we needed white for something. I can show you pictures." I reach inside my bag and pull out my phone.

"I saw pictures last week."

I scrunch my eyebrows together. He did? Oh, that's right. "I showed you a picture of Daisy and Forrest. But I didn't show you our chalk art." I tap on my phone and open my favorite photo, turning the screen his way. "See? I made them look like they are superheroes flying over skyscrapers."

His cheek twitches again as he studies my picture. His chest rises and falls with the sound of defeat. Finally his lids lift, allowing him to read my eyes and contemplate my plea with all the power of a judge and jury. "You were drawing pictures when your sister stuffed the steak in your purse?"

"Yes." I bite my lip to keep from saying anything else incriminating. My heart swells, as if the blood inside is being dammed until it knows what verdict to disperse throughout my being.

He extends the aluminum foil package. "Take your dinner and go home."

I reach for my steak, its cool wrapping a contrast from the warmth of my face. Am I being punished or paroled?

"I'm keeping the baggie. If it's chalk as you say, you'll be allowed back next week."

My arms shoot overhead in victory.

"With the condition that you arrive on time and follow rules. You'll be on probation."

I'm twirling before I can stop myself. I'll come early. I'll bring my laptop and write. The police department ambiance might be just what I need to . . .

"On the other hand. If this baggie is not chalk, you'll be arrested for lying to an officer of the law and obstructing justice, along with the drug charge."

"Thank you so much." I shove the steak inside my purse so I'm free to clasp my hands together. "Would it be totally inappropriate to kiss you on the cheek right now?"

He crosses his arms. "It would earn you a demonstration of my Taser."

I've never been threatened with a Taser before. Hopefully Karson is only teasing, but I bounce a safe distance away.

"Go." He unfolds his arms to point toward the parking lot. "Before I change my mind."

I bounce once more, then jog backward. "I'll go celebrate with a steak dinner."

"Too soon," he says, but one corner of his lips curves up.

Behind him, Kai gives me the shaka sign as Charlie shakes his head. I assume they can see I've avoided another jail sentence, but I wave goodbye anyway to make it clear I'm leaving.

However, I don't leave right away. I sink into the two-toned leather of my copper Toyota Corolla and just breathe. It's one of my favorite things to do. After a crazy day of teaching demanding high school students or pitching to even more demanding movie producers, I take time to decompress. I exhale the insanity and inhale the wonder of life.

My window is down to let the gentle breeze brush over my skin like the lapping of cool water. The setting sun washes the modern police station in a golden hue. It makes the building look clean and bright and not at all like a place where I just had my life threatened with dogs, Tasers, and prison. Such scenarios make the normal madness of teaching and writing seem mundane, and it's no wonder I need time to breathe.

I bite my lip at the realization that all those things only happened to me. Nobody else in my class has been mistaken for a wanted criminal or carried anything in their purse resembling illegal drugs.

I can't help it. My head falls back and laughter bubbles out. I'm both relieved and entertained. Maybe Charlie is right that I should switch genres from police procedural to romantic comedy.

The roof of my car turns into a movie screen as my brain projects onto it the scenes I imagine. I hear the great line Karson spoke earlier. *Do you always carry chalk? Or is it just to get alone time with me?*

The reel continues to play my ideas, and I slide my hand down the strap of my purse to unzip the jagged teeth that hold it closed. I dig past my leftovers in aluminum foil and smooth lip gloss tube to retrieve a long, smooth pen. The plastic cap is between my teeth before I even realized I needed to chew this idea over. Who wants a steak when I have a story this juicy?

The world around me disappears as I dive into the deep end of plot development. The scenes start to line up, and I'm digging into my purse again. I hit pause on a really exciting car chase scene to focus on what I'm looking for in real life.

Paper. I need paper to write down these thoughts before they disappear.

I grab my pink leather journal and flip open to where I'd been praying for God to grant me success so that I can become known as more than just "the pretty twin." With a huff, I turn the page. Every moment I spend praying over my relationship with Jewel is a moment I could be working on my own achievements.

I rough out thirty or so scenes, but it's hard to see in the dimming light. When did it get so dark?

Jabbing the button overhead, I'm rewarded with a yellow spotlight on my words. Let the show begin! I scribble wildly, making myself alternately crack up and swoon with my creative genius. I just hope I can read my own handwriting later.

The plot isn't complete, but it's beautiful. In the same way the marble statue of Aphrodite is admired even without her arms. All I need is my heroine's career to fill in the blanks.

"Write what you know," they say, but if I did that, all my characters would be teachers, which according to Jewel is basically the same thing as being a failure. So I like to think of an alternative to that phrase. For me it's, "Know what you write." This is why I take classes to research. I just need to research a career that would play off my hero's career of detective. But what?

I picture Karson in my head, and it's almost as though he's standing next to my car.

"You're breaking the law again, Gemma."

I jump at the sound of his stern voice. My pen bounces off the dashboard and falls to the floor, freeing my hand to press against my heart.

Karson really is standing next to my car. In a dark and deserted parking lot.

Talk about alone time.

My clenched muscles tingle in relief that it's only him and not a local drug lord who heard about the supposed drug stash in my purse and suspects I'm a threat to his turf. "Oh, you scared me."

He crosses his arms, looking down from his position above. "You *should* be scared. You're loitering."

He sounds so serious. Batman serious. I picture him as a vigilante against loitering, rescuing our city from random people who hang out in parking lots.

I grin. "Should I call Murphey's Law to defend me?"

He snorts and looks away as if trying to hide his half smile. He should have looked the other way, because I can still see this side curve up. The left side. Unfortunately, he's wrangled his mirth back into place before lassoing my gaze again. "Loitering is the act of remaining in a public location for a prolonged amount of time without any apparent purpose. Tell me your purpose, and I'll let you go."

I have the feeling that wanting to see his half grin is not an acceptable purpose, though it's definitely what my heroine would say in such a situation. I hold up my journal. "I'm plotting a new screenplay."

He blinks slowly, as though he's hoping I'll be gone when he opens his eyes.

I'm still here though. And I'm going to win this staring contest.

He finally gives me the win by looking to the stars starting to peek out overhead. "Is there a reason you're plotting a screenplay in the parking lot of my police station after hours?"

I give a small shrug, wondering how honest to be. Since I want him to know I have nothing to hide, I guess I should tell the complete truth. "You inspired a new idea, and I had to jot it down."

No reaction.

Huh. Most people would be flattered, though I expected him to err on the side of anger, since that's where he seems to be most comfortable. Anger is his default. I'm not sure whether his silence should encourage or discourage me.

I take a chance and continue. "I'm writing about the dangers of dating a detective." I pause at the sound of alliteration. As if I've been momentarily blinded by a light bulb popping on over my head. "That sounds like a cute title, doesn't it?"

"No." Saying no is another of his defaults.

"It's got intrigue, romance, and humor—all rolled into one." I lift my hand to write it down, then remember I dropped my pen. I lean forward and pad my fingers along the fuzzy carpet by my feet.

"I hate it."

I sit upright at his extreme response. Usually I laugh off his gruffness, but this time his words carry an edge. As though he's not simply trying to get a rise from me.

"What don't you like about it?"

"This is a dangerous job, Gemma." He clears his throat. "Do you watch the news, or do you just read Nancy Drew?"

My heart stills. I haven't read Nancy Drew in a long time, but I turned on *Miss Congeniality* the other night. "I watch the news, and I turn it off when it gets too sad."

"Of course you do." His tone is still harsh, but I peer through the shadows to better read his expression. Rather than judging me in anger, his eyes are downcast. Maybe from watching too much news. Though with his job, this response more likely comes from real life.

I want to reach out and comfort him, but the last time we spoke, he threatened to tase me. "We find what we look for, Karson. And I prefer to look for the beauty and joy in life. It's out there."

"Yeah?" he asks, but rather than turn his face toward me, he turns it toward the precinct.

"Yeah." I study his profile. Underneath the forehead lines that draw his eyebrows together with constant worry and the stubble around the firm set of his lips, I can see the young boy he used to be. I'll bet if he shaved and got Botox injections, the smooth skin would make him appear years younger. Perhaps he doesn't shave for that very reason. "It's why I look for your smile."

His eyes flash toward me at that. But they aren't angry or smiling. They question me in the same way Mom did when I accused Jewel of rigging homecoming court. Like whether I'm telling the truth or not, he can't win.

"When strangers look at you, they might simply see someone who is tough and mean, but I know anybody who protects others as fiercely as you do must care a whole lot."

His gaze doesn't waver, but his Adam's apple bobs.

Maybe I'm reaching him. Maybe this is exactly what he needs to hear. I can't touch him with my hand because of—you know—the Taser, but words of affirmation might be his love language. And I've been saving up these words for this very moment.

"When you busted into my apartment to rescue me, you were only doing your job. I now know how inconvenienced you were by that phone call, but in the moment, you made me feel cared for. Protected." My throat clogs as if I need this connection as much as he does. As if I've been neglected. And if I think about it, I have been.

Jewel started it all. She'd been my other half, then she turned on me. I've felt alone ever since. That's when I started getting attention from men, but because of that, women avoided getting close to me. I thought my image might help me in Hollywood, but it typecast me as the dumb blond. By the time I came home, my parents had moved away. So now I'm left with nothing but two roommates and my hopes and dreams.

I stare up at my hero. This is the man who would have risked his life to save me had I actually been kidnapped.

He hadn't burst into the apartment looking for anything for himself. He'd been there to give.

The experience made me yearn for someone to care that much. It made me believe it could be him.

"In case nobody tells you this often enough . . ." My breath hitches as if I'm about to say something much more profound than two little words. But is there anything more profound than gratitude? "Thank you," I whisper.

Though I can't see his expression well, I feel it warm. The outline of his shoulders melts.

Do I invite him to meet me down the street for coffee where there would be enough light to read his facial expressions? Or do I keep sharing my feelings from the darkness like a witness in hiding? Because I do think I'm about to capture his heart in the same way he captures wanted criminals.

The shadow of his chin lifts. "Gemma?"

Just the way he says my name makes my pulse throb in the creases of my elbows and behind my knees. It's full of too much familiarity for him not to care.

"Yes?"

A siren blares in the distance. It grows louder, preceding a cruiser into the parking lot. Blue and red flashers strobe over Karson, spotlighting the way his hand automatically reaches for his gun.

"You need to go," he says.

I crane my neck to see if anyone is in the back of the police car. Probably, since Karson's being all defensive again. "Am I in danger?"

"The only danger you're in is needing to call Murphey's Law

with your one phone call if you don't leave right now." The outline of his features has hardened. The recesses of his eyes are masked by the strobing of shadows and light. He's returning to his professional demeanor, though his warning tone is not as dismissive as I assume he means it to be.

I look for the positive, and so I've found it. He may not even realize it himself, but he's protecting me again.

CHAPTER EIGHT

KARSON

*The hero is commonly the simplest
and obscurest of men.*
—Henry David Thoreau

The bingo caller holds up a ball with a letter and number on it. "B-4."

Before. Teaching the citizen's police academy was so much easier *before* Gemma. Keeping my emotions in check was so much easier *before* Gemma. Convincing myself I didn't care was so much easier *before* Gemma.

I told myself I did my job in spite of humanity, but Gemma's one little thank-you changed that. She made me feel appreciated. That maybe I do make a difference.

Except I actually didn't do anything for her. I responded to a false alarm. She still has no idea what kind of crime I deal with on a daily basis. She turns off the news when it makes her sad, which isn't an option for me.

I'm not sure whether to be relieved or not that the tox report on her baggie o' white stuff came back verifying her claim of being chalk. On one hand, the woman is too innocent to go to jail. On the other, she's being allowed back to class to torment me with her Pollyanna perspective.

I sigh, thinking about the syllabus for next week's class. We're letting the citizens drive our cars through a racecourse of cones. Of course, I shouldn't have anything to worry about if she's as slow at driving my cruiser as she was at driving out of the precinct parking lot on Tuesday.

"Karson." Grams's wrinkly hand pats the spot next to my bingo sheet of nine cards on the top of our long table in the dreary, beige VFW hall. "You didn't dab B-4."

I glance up at the television monitor to see if I've missed any other numbers while brooding over troubles at work. It looks like I missed O-62 as well.

"O-62," the voice booms into a microphone.

"Dab," Granddad orders from Grams's other side, though instead of dotting his card, he's playfully striking the dab pose he learned from my nephew. His arms point toward a corner of the ceiling and his balding crown ducks into the crook of one elbow. Phillip would be proud.

My grandparents are normally very religious and consider bingo gambling, but we're not at one of those "heathen" bingo halls looking to get rich. We're at an annual fundraiser the VFW holds for military vets on National Bingo Day, and I've been coming with them since I turned eighteen. That apparently makes it both legal and not a sin.

With as much as my grandparents seem to be enjoying this event, I can see bingo becoming their vice were they not so disciplined. Personally, I find it monotonous and stressful. I'd almost rather be in a police cruiser with Gemma behind the wheel. Almost.

I search the rows of boxes for B-4 and O-62 and dot my finds with the blue, flat-tipped marker called a dabber. On my last card, O-62 completes a diagonal line.

"Bingo," I shout. It's nice to win for a change. I think this round comes with a $250 pot. That will buy me five hundred bullets for my 9mm, which could really come in handy with budget cuts.

"No." Grams looks at my card, then waves at the caller. "It's not a bingo."

I frown. "Why?"

What's the point of dabbing if I can't win? I wait for Grams to quote the verse about the love of money being the root of all evil. I plan to counter with the Scripture of Jesus telling the disciples to buy a sword.

Granddad leans around her and peers at me over the top of his wire-rimmed glasses. "The free space doesn't count this round."

I groan. "Of course it doesn't."

"Sorry," Grams apologizes to the caller. "Keep going."

The crowd murmurs in relief. They have no idea I was going to use my winnings for the bullets, thus helping to protect people just like them.

Granddad holds up the list with the rules for each round. Some rounds require an L-shape for a bingo. Some require two lines in a row. And some, like this one, don't allow the free space in the center. "You, of all people, should know how to follow the rules," he admonishes.

"You got me." I hold my palms up as if I'm under arrest. Unfortunately, that means I set down my dabber and miss the race to dab N-44.

"Bingo!" shouts a fake blond in the front. I know the color is fake because when she turns to smile at me in victory, she looks to be about the age of my grandmother. Only from behind does her long, shiny hair resemble Gemma's.

I nod congratulations as she hobbles up to collect her prize. Perhaps she's a cancer patient wearing a wig, and the winnings will help pay hospital bills. Not all blonds are fake. I've just known enough of them to become wary.

Grams pauses in passing me a new bingo sheet. She points out a spot on the last card that I should have marked. It would have given me the bingo I thought I'd earned earlier.

I hang my head in proper penitence. I wish there was someone else to blame, but the woman who distracted me isn't even here. I robbed myself.

A soft hand pats my forearm. "You may be quick at drawing a weapon, but you'd lose at a dabbing duel."

"Brutal, Grams."

"I love you anyway."

I know she does. She's raised me since I was two. "And I love you even though you're a bingo shark."

"I'm vicious," she says in a warbly voice. She's trying to sound tough, but she's too angelic. Her short silver bob could easily get mistaken for a halo.

"Yes, you're very intimidating, Patricia." Granddad stands and stretches. He does this in between every round as though he's afraid his joints will rust in place if he sits for too long. "Come with me, Karson. There's someone I want you to meet."

I reach for the bowl of popcorn on the table and toss a few buttery kernels into my mouth, perfectly content to watch everyone in the room from a distance. I'm also instantly suspicious of anybody my grandparents want me to meet. While I'm trying to make up for my mom, they are trying to make up for my ex. Their choices of church girls are probably a safe bet, but they are also too sheltered to handle the world I deal with every day. "Is this person a female between the ages of twenty-five and thirty-five?"

"We're at the VFW," Granddad counters.

I don't move. Because we both know being at the VFW didn't stop him from introducing me to the cook last year.

"No," he finally concedes. "Hank Bellingham has an old gun he wants you to restore."

I stand and look around in hopes of seeing a German Luger or M-1 with a folding stock from WWII. "How old?"

I recently restored a 1974 French military rifle, or *gras*, and my fingers have been itching to make the old new again. There's something satisfying about disassembling and cleaning away the grime from the wood stock with lacquer thinner and sandblasting the metal barrel until it's smooth. In a career where my best efforts can be undone by the court system, it's rewarding to visibly see the results of hard labor.

Working with my hands is much better than the luck required to win at bingo, though I feel lucky when Hank shows me a photograph of the Winchester 1873 he found while fishing. It's the gun that won the West. As I return to my seat, I'm mentally listing all the supplies I'll need for when Hank drops the gun off this weekend, and I don't immediately notice the redhead Grams has waiting for me.

I was right to be suspicious. Has my gut ever been wrong?

I consider walking right past, but Grams has a new bingo sheet laid out, so I stop a few feet away and cross my arms to study the younger woman. She's natural-looking. Ponytail and light makeup. Running clothes. I might like her if we met at the gym.

Her lashes flutter up, and her brown eyes take in my uniform before meeting my gaze with an apology. Is she sorry my grandma is putting us in this position or sorry she's going to have to turn down an invitation for a date because she just discovered I'm a cop?

There aren't many places I'd go after work without changing, but the VFW is one of those places. The older generation seems to have more respect for law enforcement officers, especially the war vets. And seeing me dressed this way invites them to tell their battle stories.

No matter why the redhead is sorry, I can put us both out of our misery. I extend a hand to shake. "Hi, I'm Karson Zellner. I hate drama, fireworks, cats, and rap music."

Her expression sparks with the first sign of interest as she slides her tiny palm into mine. "That's unfortunate, because I'm a rapper."

Her response is so unexpected that I don't have time to stop my chuckle. I give her hand one extra pump before pulling mine away to cross safely against my chest again. "Well, as my grandmother is obviously trying to set us up, you're going to have to choose. Me or the rap music?"

"Karson," Grams chides but in a delighted way as only grandmas can do.

I grin devilishly. "Sorry, Grams. I didn't know you liked rap music so much."

"I'm not trying to set you up," she says in a tone that's squeaky with feigned innocence. "I just like showing you off because I'm proud of you. And I thought you might be able to help Bree."

I look at the redhead and arch an eyebrow. Does she think she needs my help too, or is this all Grams's idea?

Bree has good eye contact, but her expression remains unreadable as she lets my grandmother explain.

"Bree's helping her grandpa put on this bingo fundraiser, though normally she works with juvenile delinquents."

My experience with juvies puts me on guard. If Bree is one of those overoptimistic do-gooders who believes she can rehab young hood-lums and thinks "giving them another chance" is an excuse to put criminals back on the street, we will not have much in common.

On the other hand, there's the argument that Bree's profession means she won't be as naive as most of the women Grams introduces me to. Or Gemma. I'll give her a chance. "So," I summarize, "apart from your aspiring rap career, you're a saint."

She lifts a shoulder, playing along. "Nobody's perfect."

"Actually," Grams interjects again, apparently not realizing that this is already as close as I get to flirting. "Bree has been dealing with some unsavory characters from her job, and because she lives alone, she bought a gun for protection."

Now both my eyebrows arch. The woman is a realist. I'm impressed. "What kind of gun?"

"It's purple," Bree says, as if that's an answer.

She just lost some credit but, like she said, nobody's perfect.

Grams fills the silence. "She needs help."

"Obviously."

Bree's eyes narrow, but in a cute way.

Grams motions to me like Vanna White displaying a prize on *Wheel of Fortune*. "I told her we have a shooting range on our property, and you can teach her all she needs to know."

Ahh . . . There it is. I take a deep breath, considering. There's no reason I shouldn't teach her. Everyone with a handgun needs to learn to shoot. Otherwise their weapon can be used against them.

Bree lifts her chin, awaiting my reaction. This is why she looked at me apologetically earlier. She knew my grandma had volunteered me to train her without my knowledge. But no apology needed. This is what I do. This is what I've been doing with my safety academy class.

We don't teach the class how to fire weapons, so I'll never teach Gemma how to shoot. Though, for some reason, I picture my arms around her, placing her hands where they go on a rifle and helping her aim. I growl internally at the unbidden image and refocus. If I don't stop letting myself be distracted, I could lose a lot more than a bingo game.

"Sure, I can teach you." *Bree. I'm teaching Bree.*

There are three types of people in this world. Sheep, wolves, and sheepdogs. If Bree works with juvies, she's a sheepdog like I am.

Whereas Gemma is most definitely a sheep. Or is she Little Bo Peep, and she doesn't even have any sheep because she's lost them while daydreaming? In that sense, she's more dangerous than a wolf.

I give Bree my phone number, which she enters in her contacts list, then take my seat next to Grams again for the blackout round. Every single square on my bingo card has to be dabbed in order to win. I start by dabbing my free space, which is allowed this time.

Grams leans over. "That wasn't so bad, was it?"

"What?" I look at my bingo card, wondering what I did wrong now.

"Making a date with Bree."

Oh . . . "Is it a date?" I know Grams believes it is, but I don't want her to get her hopes up. "I thought I was agreeing to teach her to shoot."

I expect Grams to admonish me. Instead, her wise old eyes turn sly. "It doesn't have to be a date. I wouldn't want Bree's shooting lesson to interfere in your relationship with the girl in your class Phillip told me about."

My nephew ratted me out after all. I'd been thinking I was going to get away clean. Time to throw out evidence in the way defense attorneys so love to do—especially when the defendant is guilty.

"Nah. No relationship there." I smile smugly at Grams and anticipate her coming overreaction as I say, "I threatened to tase the girl in my class when she asked to kiss me."

CHAPTER NINE

GEMMA

*Who knew such a normal beginning would give
the world such a hero?*
—"My Hero," written about Beverly Cleary

I've been rejected before, but never when I was this confident in succeeding. I thought I finally had my foot in the door with a movie producer. I thought I'd finally found a winning concept. I thought this was going to be my big break.

Why do I allow myself to have expectations? Why do I allow myself hope?

"Why, Ramona?" I ask the bronze sculpture of Beverly Cleary's most famous character.

Ramona doesn't respond. She forever romps in the water being squirted from the park splash pad alongside statues of Henry Huggins and Henry's dog, Ribsy. I used to romp with them as a child. Now I'm here for the understanding and inspiration she's always offered.

Jewel and I had actually been close when growing up, but because of my unidentified food allergies, I hadn't been able to keep up with her. Her friends called me a pest, so when I found the book *Ramona the Pest* in the elementary school library, I felt as though it was written just for me. It kept me company whenever Jewel's friends tried to leave me out. And I can still relate to how trouble always followed her.

I want my writing to do that for others, and I'd believed my latest idea could offer a new world for when people felt out of place in theirs. Apparently, I'd thought too highly of it. Now I hate it.

I'm in the Hollywood District of Portland, where author Beverly Cleary grew up. I came down here because director Zach Price is in town for his latest premiere and agreed to meet me at the Hollywood Theater—the historic landmark this neighborhood is named after. Our meeting didn't last long.

"It seemed fortuitous," I confess to Ramona.

A couple of moms side-eye me and motion their children to play closer to Ribsy. I would feel sorry for the women and their lack of imagination if I wasn't too busy feeling sorry for myself.

Imagining how Ramona might respond to my predicament, I sigh. "No, the script isn't finished on paper, but it is in my heart. Zach was only going to be here for a few days, and I honestly expected him to jump at the premise. Rom-com is supposed to be a hot genre right now."

I study the expression on the laughing bronze figure and naturally assume she's laughing at me. However, had Beverly Cleary's debut novel been accepted the way she'd first written it, Ramona never would have existed. She and Beezus were added in later drafts.

I bite my lip at the implication. Perhaps I need to not only finish the screenplay but revise it in order to touch more lives. The way Beverly Cleary touched mine. The way she's still touching people beyond her years on this earth.

"Okay," I finally agree.

Though I can't help wondering if Mrs. Cleary's success required more than her talent and tenacity. I always pray for God to bless the work of my hands, but sometimes it feels as if He plays favorites. Though maybe I only feel that way because I've always been compared to someone else. And found lacking.

It doesn't seem fair that my sister is the one with the house, kids, and career. I've worked just as hard. Maybe harder, with my multiple jobs and location changes. Sure, I have the looks, but they just seem to keep people from seeing anything deeper.

Chilly drops of water flick against my bare calves, reawakening me to my surroundings.

Giggling preschoolers in swimming suits race past, their feet slapping puddles. A gentle breeze follows them as if playing tag, then it lifts to rustle the awning of leaves high overhead. Sunshine dances through the openings created, its teasing warmth luring me away from the shade, and I suppose I should move on.

My desire to prove myself is what keeps me going in the film industry despite overwhelming odds. My wish is to be as successful as my sister. I'd been feeling stupid for having hope, but maybe my hope *is* God's blessing.

Or maybe it's a curse.

I feel the same way about having hope for a relationship with Karson. I'd thought we connected, but I haven't heard anything from him since. Not even about the chalk. Hope for a relationship with him could be nothing more than setting myself up for more rejection.

I head back toward my car, staying on the paved walkway so my heels don't sink into the dirt. After leaving the theater, I should have gone straight to the precinct, but I was in such a funk that I'd debated even going at all. I'd impulsively pulled over at my childhood playground, where Ramona gave me just the pep talk I needed. Now, if I'm going to keep working on my screenplay, I'll have to attend tonight's safety academy class, whether I feel like it or not.

The idea of seeing Karson is not the motivation it usually is. I shared my heart with him, and he's ignored it. Maybe I got him wrong. Maybe he doesn't care.

I'd wanted to return to class today with industry interest in my screenplay. It would validate my career aspirations—aka my presence in class. Then Karson would know I'm not only there to get alone time with him or whatever.

I drive to the precinct in a haze, then sit in the parking lot, blinking to bring myself back to reality. The last time I sat facing the entrance to this tan brick building, Karson had told me to leave before he arrested me.

I do my best to shrug off yet another threat and grab my purse to go inside, but last week's doggy disaster gives me pause. I'll just stuff whatever I need into the pockets of my jumpsuit. Lip gloss, phone, keys, and wallet—in case there are any more ID issues.

Though Karson didn't call me to verify that my sandwich baggie of chalk was actually chalk, I know it was, so I'm not worried. Jewel might have swapped it out for cocaine or some other illegal white substance had she known it would get me into trouble, but she doesn't even know about the trouble her steak got me into. She'd get too much enjoyment from my predicament if I told her.

I stride through the door to our classroom only to find it empty. Did I get the date wrong? I know I'm a little distracted, and I often forget the days of the week during the summer when I'm not teaching, but I'd just met with Zach, and he specifically said he wanted to meet on a Tuesday.

Maybe I got the time wrong. I scan the boring walls to find a boring, round clock. It's seven on the dot.

It looks like class was canceled. Maybe I'll go buy myself an ice-cream cone since my stomach is already churning.

My phone vibrates in my pocket. Zach? Telling me he's reconsidered? Or simply offering me another roll as a floozy? I flinch in anticipation and pull out my cell.

It's not Zach, and I'm not sure whether to feel relieved or rejected all over again. I roll my head from shoulder to shoulder to release tension, then swipe my thumb across the slick screen. At least my roommates believe in me. "Hey, Charlie."

"Did you forget we're meeting in the back lot to race police cars today?"

My heart rear-ends my rib cage. This class hasn't even started, and already it's a wreck. "It's hard to forget something nobody ever told me."

Charlie pauses, which is not his usual MO. "I forgot you left class early last week. But it's on the online syllabus."

I close my eyes. As a teacher, I have no excuse for not having read the syllabus. "I'm just going to go home."

"Are you kidding me? This is the best day of the whole class. Did you not hear me say we're racing police cars?"

I open my eyes again and scan the ceiling as if it holds outlines for all my works-in-progress. "I don't think I have a single police chase scene I need to research for."

"Maybe not yet, but—"

"Zach Price wasn't interested in my pitch."

"Oh." Charlie stage-whispers to someone else—Kai, I assume—"I forgot she was pitching Zach today."

"Gemma." Kai's taken the phone and attempts to soothe my anguish with his deep, lazy voice.

It's actually calming. The dude should teach yoga. I bet he's really good at relaxation poses.

"Why are you trying to work with Zach again?"

I bite my lip. He has a point. Zach fired me once for taking a stand on the kind of scenes I wouldn't appear in. Maybe today's rejection isn't so much based on the quality of my work but on my principles. "Because I want to have a movie produced, and he has the power to make that happen."

"So does Charlie."

"I'm not writing documentaries on South American tribal religions." I sniff. "Though maybe I should. Witch doctors might be more cordial than Lieutenant Zellner."

Kai snickers. "Probably."

"Does she know she's on speaker?" asks a third voice. A no-nonsense voice I would recognize anywhere.

My dumb imagination pictures Karson standing over my phone with arms crossed and the whole class eavesdropping in the background. I want to call Charlie mean names too, for putting me on speaker in the first place. Just because he doesn't understand the meaning of personal business doesn't mean the rest of us want our private lives to be made public.

I clear my throat and consider adding in a fake cough as an excuse to leave. I really can't think of anything else to say. And it's not as though Karson wants me here anyway. My heart can only take so much rejection.

"You should have called me, Karson." The words are out before I can stop them, and they sound so pathetic. But that's how I feel. "You said you'd let me know if I was clear to return. At which point you could have also told me we're driving cop cars today. I'm wearing high heels."

"Of course you are."

He thinks I'm just a stencil of all blonds in Hollywood. Obviously I'm not, or I'd still be there. "Why do you say that? You've never once seen me wear heels."

Charlie answers for him. "It's a stereotype, Gem."

"It's not a—" Karson starts, but Charlie interrupts again.

"That's why the film industry needs you, Gemma. That's why *I* need you. We're going to break stereotypes. Kai and I were just talking about entering the 48 Hour Film Project again this year. Come join us and help us brainstorm a story that can win."

My brain storms ahead of me as usual, leaving everything else behind.

Making movies is why I'm at the police precinct in the first place. Not to get Karson to like me. Not to drive cop cars. But to create. To be a part of something successful.

"Come on . . ." Kai and his velvet hammer of a voice.

I don't really want to go out to the back lot. I don't really want to face the group of people all listening to this conversation. I definitely don't want to have to stand up in heels for a whole evening. I don't even want to look at Karson, or more aptly, I don't want to see how he looks at me. His scowls were funny at first, but now that I'm trying this hard and still failing, it makes me think we'd all be better if I gave up.

"Is she coming?" Karson's voice asks from farther away. From his impatient tone, he isn't joining in the cajoling. He's trying to move on.

I really wish I could give up. It would make life easier. Why can't I ever be satisfied with what I already have?

I grit my teeth, hunch my shoulders, shake my head, and basically have a little fit that nobody else can see. Then I say, "I'm on my way."

CHAPTER TEN

KARSON

Nobody, they say, is a hero to his valet.
—JOHANN WOLFGANG VON GOETHE

I guess I have to wait for Gemma. Again.

I want to be irritated, but I actually feel a little guilty. Even though I *did* leave her a voicemail about class, I'm supposed to be the reliable one here.

I wouldn't mind if a real criminal compared me to a witch doctor, but she's not a real criminal. She's just a menace. Like Dennis. Which, I suppose, makes me Mr. Wilson.

All eyes turn to watch the woman sail out the back door of the precinct. Her long hair ripples in the breeze as if this is a scene from one of her movies. Her summer dress ripples too. Except it's not a dress. She's wearing weird pants that kind of look like a dress. Whatever. It's the footwear that concerns me most.

Of all the days for her to wear fancy shoes. Maybe she *should* have just gone home. Except class wouldn't have been the same without her.

I cross my arms to keep from letting down my guard and remind myself I don't want class to be "the same." I want it to be free from all the drama she causes. Especially the drama inside me.

"Gemma!" Charlie's trademark enthusiasm.

"Hey, Gem." Kai's casual welcome.

The rest of the class calls out things like "glad you made it" and "you wouldn't have wanted to miss this."

She smiles and waves like a real Miss America. Well, she smiles and waves to everyone but me. This is the opposite of past classes, where she followed me around with a lovesick grin. And I thought it was going to take firefighters to dampen her attraction. I'd been able to smother those flames all by myself.

My students seem to be looking back and forth between the two of us, and I know I'm not imagining the smirks and snickers. I know because Harris is both smirking and snickering as he slaps me on the back.

I shoot him a warning glare.

He holds his palms up and backs away, but the apples of his cheeks appear to be straining against a flood of laughter. "Shall I start the motorcycle demonstration?"

I nod toward his white Harley, already aligned to snake its way through a square of cones set up like the dots-and-boxes game I used to play as a kid. "Don't let me keep you from showing off."

He pops a helmet on and calls the class over. I stand back and watch Gemma expertly ignore me. I should be relieved, but I'm more entertained. Maybe even challenged.

Is she ignoring me because I didn't respond to her erroneous adoration last week or because I'm not surprised she wore the wrong shoes on the worst day possible? I'll find out when I refuse to let her drive in those things.

Harris pulls on his riding gloves, then swings a leg over his bike. "Maestro?" he calls to me.

That's right. He needs his theme song. I stroll to the picnic table in the shade and hit *play* on his phone. "Bad Boys" roars through the Bluetooth speaker he'd brought along for this exact moment.

The class breaks out in laughter.

Drew grins proudly. "Every year, I get to escort a huge motorcycle ride to raise money for the families of fallen soldiers. The very first year, the motorcycle dealership played this song as we pulled up. Now I hear it in my mind whenever I ride."

Larry bobs his head. "I was there, man. Great ride."

Harris responds by throttling the engine, and I feel its rumble in my chest.

While the men in the group, especially Larry, marvel at Drew's cornering skills, Gemma looks a little bored. Her gaze bounces around like a pinball. Until it accidentally meets mine, then I might as well have been one of those pinball game flippers, knocking her attention back to Harris. Game on.

I wait until Drew's demonstration is over and he's divided our class into groups of three to drive our vehicles around the old parking lot turned into a makeshift track. Naturally, he puts Gemma with her homeboys and leaves them to me, while he takes off with three other students.

I retrieve a radar gun from my cruiser and show everyone how to point it at Harris when he zips past in his own demonstration. Through it, I watch him weave around cones, then step on the gas, washing us in a wake of warm air.

I hold up the digital screen. "Forty-two miles an hour. Not bad."

Larry's shadow falls over me in his eagerness to hold a radar gun for himself. "My turn."

I hand the device over and catch Gemma watching us from the corner of her eyes. Before I can even lift an eyebrow, she's all enthralled with Harris's group in the distance, trading seats for someone else to drive.

"Gemma." I say her name as if I'm the high school principal calling her into my office, and I'm rewarded with a look of wary defiance.

At the first glimpse of her attention, I tilt my head toward a picnic table and then turn my back on her to lead the way. Also to hide my smug grin.

I should not be enjoying this. I'd spent the past couple of weeks trying to get her to leave me alone, yet now that she wants nothing to do with me, I'm forcing her to talk. I have no excuse.

I face her and assume my police officer stance.

"What's up?" she asks, her jitteriness betraying her attempt at nonchalance. She was obviously telling the truth about not being an actress. Though somehow, she makes even failure look good.

I wait for her to finally give me eye contact. Despite not wearing sunglasses, her expression is unreadable. Which says more than she realizes. Maybe an argument will snap her out of her mood. "I can't let you drive in those shoes."

Her sapphire eyes flutter wide, all sensitivity and innocence. Then they narrow, blaming every one of her life's disappointments and frustration on me. I'll take it over emotionless Gemma. I'll take it over quitter Gemma. I'll take it over beauty queen Gemma any day. This is when things get real.

"I'll drive barefoot," she counters. I think she's trying to sound menacing, but it still comes out all breathy and sweet.

I pinch my lips together to keep from hooting. "I'm sorry. I can't let you do that." It's true that I can't let her. It's not true that I'm sorry.

She knows, and she's not going to back down. She drops her chin and steps closer so I can hear her hushed tone. "Is this because I compared you unfavorably to a witch doctor?"

A corner of my lips twitch. "While that's probably not a good thing to say to a police lieutenant"—understatement—"my decision is nothing personal."

A little voice inside my head reminds me such a statement might not be entirely true either. Gemma triggers me because she reminds me of someone I used to have a very personal relationship with.

But we're talking about safety. And shoes. I tell myself I'm saving lives by preventing a daydreamer from getting behind the wheel in heels.

"I couldn't let"—I motion toward the closest woman to us, who is middle-aged and has too much life experience to wear stilettos to safety academy, though perhaps not as much fashion sense since she's still wearing her funky high tops—"Erin drive in high heels either."

Erin looks at Gemma's feet. "What size do you wear?"

Gemma props one of her sandals on its stiletto and rocks her perfectly painted toes back and forth. "Around a size eight. Why?"

Oh man. I know what's coming. It's not me against Gemma. It's me against the whole class. Everyone loves her. I should have expected them to gang up.

"I wear a size eight too," Erin says. "Would you like to wear my shoes to drive?"

No, Gemma won't want to. For starters, she made it clear earlier that she didn't care to drive. She simply wants to spite me. Plus, Erin's kicks won't match her crazy striped dress/pants outfit.

"Of course I would." Gemma kindly mocks—if that's a possible thing—my earlier statement, then waves Erin to follow her toward the picnic bench. As she passes, her face pivots to taunt me with a triumphant smirk. It's adorable in a pouting puppy kind of way.

I drop my arms. I'm not going to fight her anymore. I'll let her learn her lesson by having her get what she thinks she wants. It'll be like the time in high school shop class when my teacher caught me chewing tobacco and gave me the option of talking to my grandparents or swallowing the wad. I swallowed, then ended up confessing to Granddad later after I went home sick. And I never chewed again.

Maybe Gemma doesn't need an argument so much as she needs to win an argument. I'll give her this small victory. Even if she runs over all the orange cones and goes so slowly she's almost driving backward, she'll still get a thrill. She'll be living herself instead of writing stories about other people living.

Then she'll fail so hard that she can't continue her show of perfection. She'll forget to care about what other people think. And that's what I want for her. It's what I wanted for my ex. And I'm actually kind of proud Gemma is choosing to try.

She slides her feet into the retro Nikes with a yellow swoosh, hot-pink laces, green toe box, and blue trim. I'm not sure if the local company is bringing back an outdated look or if Erin has owned these things for decades.

"Ooh . . . comfy," Gemma coos, as if she'd willingly pick out those monstrosities for their comfort level alone. Perhaps she's never worn a pair of comfortable shoes before.

Erin remains barefoot rather than put on Gemma's heels. I assume it's because she doesn't have a death wish.

Kai slides a hand across his face, clearly covering a chuckle.

Charlie isn't as smooth. "Gemma, you look like you should be driving a clown car, not a police car."

"The key word is *driving*." Gemma looks directly at Erin, who doesn't seem to be offended in the least by Charlie's brash assessment of her style. "Your shoes are a statement piece. It's rare to find clothing both so functional and trendy. Thank you for letting me borrow them."

I lift my eyebrows in admiration of not only her spin on the situation but also how authentic her gratefulness comes across. Unfortunately I'm still making that face when Gemma glances up at me.

"What?" She's daring me to either say something as inconsiderate as Charlie, which I'm sure she would not respond as gracefully to, or come up with a new excuse for not letting her drive.

I don't get a chance to say anything before Harris's group pulls to the curb in a choking cloud of exhaust. He pops open his door and tosses me the keys. I uncross my arms to snatch them out of the air, giving him the opportunity to engage my students before I can.

Gemma rises from her spot at the picnic table, and he does a double take. "Whoa, boy. Starting a new trend, Gemma?"

She bounces on the balls of her feet, mimicking a basketball player warming up. "Karson was threatening to ban me from driving."

"We take safety seriously." Harris shrugs the boulders he calls shoulders. "But it looks like you're up now."

I lift my chin at Harris in thanks for having my back. Then I hold out the keys to Gemma. "Go get 'em, Tiger."

Her gaze jumps to mine again, as if she's forgotten that she's supposed to be avoiding me or glaring at me. Her eyes remain clouded with uncertainty. Either she's actually afraid to drive our racetrack or she wasn't expecting me to cheer her on.

She reaches for the keys, and her smooth nails tickle my palm. That's all. Just her nails brush my skin. But they might as well be a stylus on a touchscreen, pulling up video reel from all our interactions—from when I took her fingerprints to when she offered to kiss me.

Should she ever be able to capture scenes like this in her screenplays, she'll have directors wrapped around her little finger, not to mention the power to toy with the emotions of an audience. Which is exactly what I don't want her to do to me. Neither the emotions nor the wrap-around-the-finger thing.

Without another word, I turn toward the cruiser, breaking off contact. "Kai and Charlie, you're in the back."

Kai pulls out his phone. "Can I film?"

My default is to say no, but I suspect this experience is going to be way too entertaining not to share with the world. I face Gemma over the hood of the cruiser. I can't see her funky getup from this position, but she still seems completely out of place.

Her shiny lips part. From the rapid rise and fall of her chest, I know she's sucking in air. And there's a flash of fear in her eyes.

She has nothing to be afraid of—I'm right here.

"Sure, why not?" I answer Kai. "Go ahead and film."

Gemma's eyes harden into glacier blue. She flips her hair back and pulls it into a ponytail with some fluffy hair band. Then she bites her lips and drops into the car.

I don't realize I'm grinning until Kai points his phone my way and Charlie says, "Smile for the camera."

I scowl and sink into the passenger seat. When I gave permission to film, I didn't mean me.

The car rocks and doors snap shut. Thankfully Kai's phone is now pointed at Gemma. We all watch her look at the console and the computer system she's not used to. Then she lifts her chin and studies the orange cones on the course.

Kai turns the phone as if taking a selfie. "Charlie and I are in the back of a cop car," he tells his imaginary audience.

"We're not in trouble," Charlie explains, as if he's afraid this video could be used against him in a court of law. "Gemma is simply going to take us for a ride."

So far, our driver hasn't even turned on the ignition.

"You okay?" I ask. She's probably wishing she'd used her shoes as an excuse to back out of this situation.

"I'm just getting my bearings." She straps on her seat belt.

I follow suit, though I barely hear the click of safety before the engine roars to life and Gemma steps on the gas hard enough to give me whiplash.

"Whoa!" I'm pressed against my seat as though we've blasted off toward the moon. I stare in horror out the windshield at the chain-link fence zooming toward us and wish I had one of those brake pedals used for training student drivers. I'm torn between offering up one last prayer of repentance before I die or shouting for Gemma to brake so that I might possibly live another day. I open my mouth to shout when she spins the steering wheel, and we're rounding corners like Lightning McQueen.

I grab onto the door handle and rock violently back and forth while Gemma expertly snakes her way through the cones. The hoodlums in the back seat whoop it up. I just try to point and shout warnings, but we're going so fast that anything I might have possibly helped prepare Gemma for is already behind us.

We make it to the final stretch, and Gemma drives it like she stole it.

Larry and his radar gun are nothing but a blur when we race past, though I can imagine him giving Harris a bad time about how Gemma just smoked his mph.

She screeches to a halt, though my heartbeat continues to race. It sounds louder now that the car is quiet. Then it's drowned out by eruptions from the men in back.

"We're roommates with Danica Patrick," Kai deadpans.

"Gemma, where did you learn to drive like that? Is it the shoes? Are they made out of lead?"

I'm still holding onto the door as I turn my head to catch her response.

She gives a little shrug and fixes her hair in the rearview mirror. "They trained me to do my own stunt driving in that last movie I filmed."

"Dude. I don't want to have to follow you."

"Yeah, you're going to make us look bad."

The guys say that, but they get out of the cruiser to trade seats.

I stare at Gemma. She's still wearing her silly outfit, but she's changed. While I'd thought this would be a humbling experience for her, it's been empowering. And I can't help but be impressed.

Her light eyes meet mine with a glimmer of good humor. "Did I scare you?"

"Yes."

She lifts her chin. "Good."

There's an energy between us that I want to write off as endorphins.

I watched a dumb dating show once where a man went on two dates. One was all his choice. He got to pick the girl and their destination based on what he thought he wanted. Then the second date was determined by science. Experts showed him photographs of women, and they picked his date based on how his body physically responded. The scientists sent the couple bungee jumping to get their hearts pumping. This led to a chemical response that created attraction between the two.

In the end, the man chose the woman scientists picked for him over who he'd thought he wanted.

When Gemma asked me if she scared me, that's really what I was talking about. In my head, Gemma's not who I want, but here I am, wanting nothing else more.

CHAPTER ELEVEN

GEMMA

I shouldn't be the superhero's girlfriend.
I should be the superhero.
—KRISTEN STEWART

It's common after a failure to feel as though every aspect of pursuing the goal has failed, but driving a cop car in citizen's police academy reminded me that it's more about the journey than the destination. If I hadn't pursued screenplay writing, I never would have fallen into a few acting roles. And had I never acted, I wouldn't have taken stunt-driving classes. Thus, I wouldn't have gotten to see that look on Karson's face when he said I scared him.

I scared a big, strong, grumpy cop. He fights bad guys as his day job, and he was scared of little ol' me.

After that, I'm invincible. I don't have to try to avoid Karson's eye contact anymore. On the other hand, I don't vie for his attention either. I simply don't care. It's the greatest feeling in the world.

I proved myself here, at least. I belong. Clown shoes or not.

"Can I get my shoes back?" Erin asks when it's almost her turn to drive. "As much as I'd love to wear your beautiful sandals, I have flat soles and need good arch support."

"Oh yeah." I look down at my funky feet. Of all the reasons why Erin still wears these ancient trainers, I never guessed it was for the arch support. "These shoes are so comfortable, I forgot I was wearing them."

"We didn't," Kai quips.

"You're hysterical." I laugh, not so much at my roommate's sense of humor as at my appearance.

I'm not bothered by Kai's joke, as he knew I wouldn't be. I feel good from my victory on the racecourse, and when I feel good about myself, I don't care as much about what others think. I wish I could bottle this feeling and drink it right before my next pitch to Zach Price. Or my next humiliating moment in front of Karson. Or my next dinner with Jewel.

If my sister saw me dressed like this, she'd definitely have something negative to say. The time she rigged homecoming court elections, my mom told me it was out of envy. I'd thought that was dumb. She was class president. She took AP classes and graduated from high school with her associate's degree. I would have gladly traded her my tiara for such a head start on life. If anybody should have been envious, it should have been me.

As for today, Jewel has everything I'm working toward. Why does she still need to mock me? Perhaps for the same reason I feel as though I have to prove myself. Our whole life has been a competition.

I visualize Esau's response when Jacob returned to ask his forgiveness for stealing his birthright and offered gifts to make up for it. He'd said, "I already have plenty, my brother. Keep what you have for yourself." How do I get to that place?

I sink onto the picnic bench and lean over to unlace Erin's bright sneakers. If my life were a film, these kicks would be used for symbolism. They'd represent the envy that probably every woman has to deal with in life. While Erin wishes she could wear my pretty shoes, I wish I was confident enough to wear ugly shoes for comfort.

I pause, looking at the sneakers, and a video montage of iconic footwear in film history dances through my brain to the tune of "Boogie Shoes." Wonder Woman in red boots, Dorothy in ruby-red slippers, then Cinderella's glass ones. Did they deal with envy?

My lips part as I realize these women could relate. Cinderella, anyway. She definitely dealt with the impact of jealousy. Her stepsisters ripped her dress apart to keep her from going to the ball. If not for those magical glass slippers . . .

I sit up straight. What if Cinderella traded her shoes for Dorothy's, and she'd only had to click her heels together to get home rather than race to a coach made out of a pumpkin? Prince Charming never would have found her.

And what if Dorothy had been wearing Wonder Woman's boots? She would have needed an invisible jet to return to Kansas. Such a mash-up could be a fun story to watch, and it could have a powerful message about how we may envy what others have, but we already have exactly what we need.

I want to write it. And I want Charlie to film it in his documentary style. It would be like a reality show, where fictional characters talk to the camera about their issues, then Kai would cut to funny footage of their incidents. I can almost see Dorothy clicking the heels of Marty McFly's Nikes together and saying, "There's no place like 1985."

"Charlie," I call before I'm even aware of where he's at and which direction I should be yelling.

"What?" His voice bellows from right in front of me.

My vision of the Wicked Witch of the West riding her broom to chase after a flying DeLorean fades to be replaced by my roommate's face. His eyebrows dip in concern.

"What's the theme to this year's forty-eight-hour film competition?" My heart thumps in anticipation. Either my shoe idea is going to work, or it's not.

He shrugs as if my part of our production is the easy part. "It has to tie into local culture."

I bite my lip to keep from grinning in triumph before we've agreed on this theme. But anybody who knows Portland culture knows the Nike campus plays a big part. And anybody who knows Nike remembers the Michael Jordan commercial line: *It's gotta be the shoes.*

Kai's gaze slides my way. "Do you have an idea?"

I do, but I wonder if Kai will get it. The only shoes he ever wears are flip-flops, and there aren't many movies where iconic characters wear flip-flops. Julia Roberts did in *Notting Hill*, but I'd always questioned that style choice. Of course, it made her more relatable, which is what Hugh Grant's character needed. Had she been in her *Pretty Woman* boots, I don't think they ever would have gotten together.

Sadly, I doubt Kai or Charlie have ever watched either of those movies. How do I sell them on my idea?

I start with "It's gotta be the shoes."

They both look at my feet, and I remember I'm supposed to be removing Erin's high-tops. I quickly finish unlacing them so I can tug them off and hand them over.

Charlie rubs his chin, probably trying to guess where I'm headed. "That slogan is from that Michael Jordan commercial."

"Oh, yeah." Kai catches up. "That fits into local culture. He played in the NBA finals against our Portland Trailblazers. But while he could fly, we had Clyde Drexler, who could glide."

I clap my hands once at the connection. The basketball players aren't movie characters, but they are iconic. "What if Jordan had wanted to glide like Clyde, so instead of wearing the shoes that were named after him, he wore Gene Kelly's tap shoes?"

Kai tilts his head. "You want me to film Michael Jordan tap-dancing down the court?"

"Exactly. Well, not Jordan himself, we don't have that kind of budget, but an actor playing Michael Jordan."

"That would be memorable." Charlie narrows his eyes. "But why?"

I hold up a strappy sandal before sliding it onto my sole. "To show how we all want something we can't have. And how if we focus on trying to be like someone else, we miss out on how great we really have it." I nod in agreement with myself. This is the fun part of writing—the idea stage, where an original idea gets better and better. "We can take this theme full circle until at the end of our film, we have a character who envies MJ."

Kai snorts, sounding more entertained than convinced. "You mean we start out with Jordan tap-dancing, then we move to Gene Kelly who wants to do some 'Dirty Dancing,' so he puts on Baby's white Keds . . . ?"

Charlie nods. "But the Keds get soaked when he's singing in the rain."

They are starting to see my vision. I script more of the picture for them. "Then Baby wears Mia's Doc Martens from *The Princess Diaries*, but when Johnny tries to lift her above his head, the shoes are so heavy they both fall over."

The guys laugh. A third chuckle joins their chorus.

Karson's still crossing his arms and looking out at the track as if it has all his attention, but he's wearing a small grin. He doesn't make eye contact or give any indication he even notices me, but he says, "You going to put Baby back in the corner?"

"I might." I try to say this with a straight face, but the visual is too ironic to not be funny. Also, I have to appreciate how he's speaking my language.

"Poor Baby." His eyes flick my way, and I feel as though he might be seeing me for the first time. Seeing I'm not only a troublemaker like Ramona the Pest. I can be taken seriously.

The worst part of being considered beautiful is that my appearance is all people see when they look at me. Yet at the same time, I'm afraid to take off my makeup, because what if that's all I am? I have to prove there is more to me, and maybe I've started to prove it to him.

"You know?" Kai's words tear my attention from Karson, though it's going to take some time for my thoughts to catch up and my brain to compute what he's saying.

I stare blindly at my roommate while he speaks, though I'm still wondering about that look Karson gave me. It made me feel as if I was on stage—both vulnerable and powerful. And perhaps there is power in being vulnerable. Dare I look at him again? Dare I let him truly see me?

"You're right, Gemma." This comes from Charlie, though I'm not sure what he thinks I'm right about. I've missed a whole conversation they mistakenly assumed I was part of simply because I was present for it. "Your idea has something to offer everyone."

Oh, that's a good thing to be right about.

Kai nods. "It will be both entertaining and meaningful. Though it's going to be hard to find a cast and costumes to fit all those famous roles."

I blink a few times to refocus. We're talking about the logistics of filming now rather than the strength of story. I have to make this doable for them. "I can limit the number of characters to seven. That shouldn't be too much work."

Charlie nods. "Seven is the number of completion."

He makes writing sound as simple as math. Like one can use a calculator or follow a formula to get to happily ever after. Really it's more of a jigsaw puzzle. There are often missing pieces, and until they connect with each other, the individual parts don't make sense. It's not until the picture comes together in its entirety that it's clear there's no other way it could possibly work.

Which is why we need God's promise that in all things He works for the good of those who love Him. He writes endings I couldn't even imagine.

CHAPTER TWELVE

KARSON

Great heroes need great sorrows and burdens, or
half their greatness goes unnoticed. It is all
part of the fairy tale.
—Peter S. Beagle

Gemma is gone. Okay, in reality she's still here, but with the way she's staring into the distance, her mind is gone. She might as well be a zombie. Everyone else has actually left for the day—body *and* brain.

"Gemma." I snap my fingers in front of her face.

She blinks. Smiles. "Hi."

I once heard that the opposite of love is not hate but indifference. Somehow she's gone past comparing me to a witch doctor to the point where she might not even remember my name. If only I could say the same about her.

I cross my arms. "Class is over." I nod to where Drew stacks orange cones.

"Oh." She glances around, pats herself down as though she's looking for a purse that she didn't bring, then digs into her pockets. She absently pulls out car keys. "Did Kai and Charlie leave already?"

I huff. While I'd expected to have to repeat all the info for next week's class, I didn't expect to have to act as her personal assistant. "They mentioned something about grilling hamburgers and asked you to stop and pick up lemonade on your way home. You told them you would."

"Okay."

It doesn't seem to bother her that she's forgotten a whole conversation she'd participated in, but I'm kind of bothered that she's forgotten me. "You okay?"

She sighs and stares past me again with the kind of contentment that would indicate she was watching a sunset. I know we have plenty of daylight left, so I glance over my shoulder to see what she's looking at. Harris polishes his motorcycle with a yellow rag. Not really a sigh-worthy sight, unless you're a biker named Wolfman.

"I got a great idea for a new script." She says this as if it's a positive answer to the question about being okay.

I rub a hand over my head, not sure where I fit into her new script idea or why I would want to. "Does that mean you won't need to come back to class next week?"

Her face jerks my way, light eyes wide in alarm. "Why wouldn't I?"

I lift a shoulder to shrug off my strange relief. "If you're writing a different script, then you won't need to research for a police procedural."

Her shiny lips part in protest. "I'm still writing that one too. Only it's become a romantic comedy."

She must have not heard a word I told her last week about how there's nothing romantic about my work. "All right then. Did you hear what I said we're doing next week?"

"Um . . ."

Of course she didn't hear. She's been like this the whole second half of class.

"We're teaching self-defense." I glance pointedly at her fancy pants. "Wear exercise clothes."

"Right," she says, and I assume she's agreeing with me, though when her gaze lifts to the bright sky overhead, I wonder if she's thinking about a different kind of *write*.

I dismiss her with a nod toward the front parking lot. "Go home. Your roommates are waiting."

Gemma blinks.

I huff. "Don't forget to pick up lemonade."

"Oh yeah." She waves and takes off. "See you next week."

I'm still watching Gemma trot away when Drew's hulking presence joins me. There's a flash of yellow when he swings his rag over the shoulder that's positioned next to mine, so he must be watching her too.

"She's going to forget the lemonade," I tell him.

"I'm pretty sure that girl has the optimism to make her own," he jokes. When I don't respond, he gives a contemplative murmur. "She's the real deal, Zellner. Not fake like Amber."

I grunt my agreement. Gemma's turning out to be even more dangerous than Amber with the way she romanticizes my job. Which is why I'm going to give Bree a call tonight.

I wouldn't call this a date, but having a woman over to my shooting range is exactly what I would have chosen were I on the dating show *The Science of Love*. I doubt the scientists could have picked anything better. Shooting firearms comes with an adrenaline rush that's known for creating date-like feelings. I can only hope it works.

As for Bree, she's got her long red hair pulled through the back of a ball cap into a ponytail, and I'm instantly reminded of my childhood crush on Scarlett from the *G.I. Joe* movie. Of course, a soldier would never carry a purple Ruger.

"Here." I hand her goggles and shooting earmuffs that resemble headphones.

She makes a face, then slides them on. "And I'd thought I was going to look cool while learning to shoot."

I grin down at the gun case she brought and place it on a makeshift table at one end of the shooting range behind my house. "If you'd wanted to look cool, you wouldn't have bought a purple gun."

She watches me the way a student should. She's actually paying attention to what I'm trying to teach her and not daydreaming about how she would write this scene if we were in a movie or something. "I ordered it online and didn't know it was purple."

I click my tongue, and the gun makes a similar sound as I use my palm to slide it open. "Lame excuse."

A grin stretches her voice tight when she responds with, "I thought I was ordering the pink one."

Pausing, I lift my eyes to hers and shake my head. "If your gun was pink, you'd be on your own."

This time I'm looking at her when she smiles. There's a twinkle in her dark eyes. "Real men shoot pink guns."

"That's not a thing." I remove her clip to load it with the bullets I'd luckily had on hand, since she didn't think to bring any.

"I feel like that should be a saying on T-shirts and bumper stickers. Are you sure it's not?"

"Yes."

She's easy to be with. Why don't I ever choose easy? "Do you have any experience with firearms?"

"Nada."

The sun is behind us, and we're shaded by forest overgrowth. It's light but not bright. My range is lined with trees, and I've hung a target on an old dead stump at the end.

I demonstrate, then talk her through imitating my movements. By the time our lesson is over, she's become a crack shot. I could have her move back a few yards and keep going, but the air has chilled and the sky has turned hazy.

I instruct her on how to make sure the weapon is empty and clean it with gun oil before closing it back in its box.

She snaps the case shut and tilts her chin up at me proudly, lips pressed together in a wide smile. "How do I compare to your other students?"

"Well . . ." I study her but imagine having Gemma ask such a question. While I compare Gemma to my ex, I compare everyone else to Gemma. Even Bree, who is the whole package. I refocus to answer her question. "Considering that my other student is in elementary school and shoots Airsoft guns, I think you might beat him in marksmanship."

Her shoulders bunch and her smile slips. "You have a son?"

I pause as the hitch in her voice indicates she considers the thought of my being a dad a negative thing. I'd never thought of it that way before. "Nephew."

"Oh, that's sweet." Her posture relaxes. "For a moment I thought maybe you'd been married."

Now *that* I definitely understand as a negative thing. But more so for me than her. "I was."

Pause. "Did she die?" How does she make such a question sound hopeful?

Amber's dead to me, but I'm not going to get into that. "No."

"Oh." Her tone is both light and definitive at the same time. Like I'm also dead to her, but she wants to lower me into my grave gently.

In a weird way, I'm relieved. Now I don't have to tell her I'm not interested. And I don't have to try to come up with an excuse to give my grandmother about why I'm not dating Bree. Plus, my choice not to date at all has been confirmed yet again.

"I've . . . uh . . ." She looks down to avoid eye contact. "I've heard it said that in a romantic relationship, people who've never been married before struggle to connect with people who have been. They feel like they have to compete with the former spouse."

I cross my arms. How would Gemma react to the fact that I'm a divorcé? If what Bree says is true, then Gemma's better off without me. Even if I decided to take another chance on love, my ex has ruined that as well.

"I can see how that would be hard," I finally allow.

Though Bree is talking about herself and the things she wants, not what I have to offer Gemma.

I stoop to pick up used shells I can refill later. I don't waste brass. "Good thing we're not on a date."

Bree squats in front of me as if to help, but she's looking at me instead of the ground. "This isn't personal. I really do like you."

"It's fine." How do I tactfully say I'm not upset about her rejection but about what her rejection implies for my chances with someone else? Even though I know better than to take the chance. "You're great, Bree, and I want you to find a spouse who is everything you deserve." I look down at the empty casings in my palm. "Not all of us are that lucky."

We stay like that for another few moments. She's probably trying to figure out what to say about my divorce, while I hope she says nothing.

I finally stand. "Now you have all the basics for handling your weapon."

"Yes. Thank you." Bree stands too. "I feel confident."

That makes one of us. "Do you have a gun safe?"

She picks up her black, plastic case and hugs it to her chest like a teddy bear. Which it's not. "No."

"I'd recommend trigger locks then." Especially if she's got juvies around. She may not be as naive as some of the other women my grandparents have sent my way, but I don't want her ever to have to carry unnecessary guilt from her career choice.

"Good to know. I will." She studies me. "Can I take you out for dinner to repay you for the bullets and everything?"

I suppose we could be friends. She kind of had that sisterly feel until everything got awkward. But not tonight. "You don't owe me anything. This is what I do."

She nods and takes a few steps backward toward my house. "Are you staying out here?"

"Yeah. It's my turn to shoot." I don't need the practice the way she did. I need to take out some frustration.

I wait until her cute little navy Passat rolls away before turning to face the target. My gun is in my holster, but I can't grab it with a handful of brass. A normal person would set the casings down on the table, then grab their gun, but this frustration wells into rage. I'm not the one who messed up, yet I keep paying the price. The good guy is the one who gets abandoned.

With a growl, I wind up and throw my handful of metal downrange as hard and as far as I can. All that comes from my effort is a bunch of hollow pings and a mess I'll have to clean up later.

This isn't about Bree's shooting lesson or even my last class with Gemma. It's about living in a world where I teach people self-defense because I was forced to learn when nobody was around to protect me.

CHAPTER THIRTEEN

GEMMA

*Friends are the real superheroes. They battle
our worst enemies—loneliness, grief, anxiety,
depression, fear, and doubt—every time
they come around.*
—RICHELLE E. GOODRICH

I'm still thinking about shoes a week after Erin loaned me hers. I'm standing in the entryway of our townhome, waiting for the guys to be ready to go to citizen's police academy, and I'm staring down at my classic court shoes with the light pink swoosh. They seem so basic compared to the funky '80s high-tops that inspired the short script I finished writing this morning.

Yeah, I wrote a script in a week. I wish writing was always this easy.

Thankfully, it's summer vacation, so I have lots of time to write. Though it's not a full-length script like *Ferris Bueller's Day Off* or anything. John Hughes wrote that story in a week because there was a writer's strike scheduled, and a director friend told him that if he finished a screenplay by the time the strike started, they'd film it. I wish I had such connections.

I guess knowing Charlie is pretty cool. Just not Ferris Bueller cool.

My gaze wanders up the white wall to Charlie's collection of black-and-white photos from classic movies as I try to remember what kind of shoes Ferris Bueller wore. I've already got the seven characters needed to tell my story, and they seem to fit together pretty nicely, but I'm never *not* looking to improve my work.

Kai joins me in the entryway, hands in pockets, keys jingling. He's wearing Nikes today too, which is something I normally only see him in when we go to boot camp class together at the gym. I assume he used to wear running shoes more often when he was a college athlete, but these days he dresses like a surfer.

"What kind of shoes did Ferris Bueller wear?" I ask.

"Stop it."

I narrow my eyes at his weird response.

"Stop changing the script. You know we have to track down all these shoes before filming, right?"

He has a point. But . . . "There's still time."

Charlie charges past and opens the door while checking his watch. "Actually, there's not much time. We're going to be late if we don't go now."

Kai strolls after him into the blinding sunshine. "We were waiting for you, Charlie."

"I didn't realize you were waiting. It sounded like you were chatting."

"In the entryway?" Kai clicks the key fob, unlocking his girl-friend's green Jeep that he takes care of while she's overseas.

I follow them outside and lock our front door. "We were trying to remember what kind of shoes Ferris Bueller wears."

Charlie opens the passenger door to ride shotgun. Usually we let him drive, but today's weather is too nice not to enjoy by taking the top off Meri's Wrangler. "He wears white dress shoes with black laces."

Kai grimaces. "Ew."

I'm still trying to remember. I remember the sweater vest, which is also *ew*.

Charlie folds his seat forward. "Get in, Gem," he says, and I realize I'm just standing there.

Kai groans. "You shouldn't have told her what shoes Ferris wears. Now she's going to change our script again."

"What?" Charlie turns on me. "Ferris won't work in the script. While someone might want his shoes, he's not going to be jealous of anybody else's. The guy doesn't have an envious bone in his body."

"True." That was more his sister's thing. I bite my lip. "What kind of shoes did Jennifer Grey's character wear?"

They both groan, spurring me to action. I squeeze around Charlie and step one foot into the back seat. But then I remember where we're going, and I pause to make sure I won't be embarrassing myself in front of Karson again. I pat my pockets to check for anything I might be forgetting. Or to be sure I'm not hiding a steak. One just never knows.

Charlie taps his fingers impatiently. "You could have used your time in the entryway to make sure you had everything rather than chatting about the Bueller siblings."

"Sorry." My phone vibrates from within the soft pockets of my gray joggers. I pull it out to see Jewel's name flash, and I'm instantly reminded that I agreed to take over the chalk-art book I'd made for the kids today. I'd forgotten because I'd been working on my script. "Speaking of siblings . . ." I step down to the asphalt and back away.

Charlie splays his hands wide. "Where are you going?"

I hold my phone up. "I have to stop by my sister's after class, so I need to drive. Go ahead. I'll meet you at the precinct."

"Gemma . . ." Kai says in a warning tone. "You aren't making up a story about your sister so you can go inside and change your script, are you?"

"Nope." The sister story is true, but I kinda like the idea of running back inside to look at my writing. Just a peek. To see if Jeanie Bueller's Nikes might be a better fit than Baby's Keds.

I head toward my car, where I already have a copy of *Sidewalk Superheroes* waiting, but as soon as the guys turn out of our parking lot, I sprint inside the house to my computer. I wore good shoes for sprinting. These shoes are going to make me so fast that they won't even realize I'm not right behind them.

It took me longer than I expected to conclude I need to keep Baby's shoes in my screenplay. I would have sworn it only took five minutes, but by the time I pull into the parking lot at the police station, I'm twenty-six minutes late.

If I tell my roommates I got lost on the way, will they just assume I took a wrong turn and not that I got lost in my thoughts? Doubtful. Because I only ever take wrong turns when lost in my thoughts. Which is more often than I'd like to admit.

Maybe nobody will notice. Maybe I can sneak into self-defense training without anyone realizing I haven't been there the whole time.

The receptionist at the front desk points me toward a doorway down the hallway from our classroom. I creep over and peek through a small window in the door to see what looks like a wrestling room inside from the way it's covered in blue mats. Everyone is just standing around, so I should be able to join in without missing a beat.

Turning the handle, I crack the door open. I hear Karson's voice, giving instructions. I can't see him yet. Hopefully his back is to me, and I can just mimic what everyone else does as if I know what's going on.

"Now with your partner, assume the ground fighting stance we just demonstrated."

So far so good. I hold my breath and step into the room on my silent rubber soles. I'm in.

But as I stand there, everyone around drops to the floor. Then they do this weird thing in pairs where one of them lies on their back while the other one straddles their waist in a kneeling position. I'm sure I'm making the most confused/horrified expression as the door thuds shut behind me and everyone's face turns my way.

The only other person standing is Karson. He crosses his arms.

"Oh good," Drew says from where he's kneeling over Wolfman. "Now Karson has a partner too."

And I'd been doing so well avoiding the idea of being partners with Karson. "Uh . . ." *Ferris Bueller, you're* not *my hero.*

Karson's side-eye slides from me to Drew. "How about we switch—?"

Before he can finish his sentence, Wolfman bucks his hips up, knocking the police officer on his side. He rolls Drew over until he's kneeling above, then he pretends to punch. "Hiya!"

I jump at the sound, then giggle in a way that wasn't supposed to come out so nervous-sounding. "Is that what we're doing?"

Karson rubs his jaw. "Yeah. Except for the hiya part. He added that on his own."

Drew's laugh erupts like molten hot fudge from a chocolate lava cake. "Well done, Larry. Now everyone try it."

Karson shrugs and motions for me to take my spot on the mat in front of him.

My heart thumps louder. I am not emotionally prepared for this. So far Karson has held my hand when fingerprinting me and threatened to frisk me when the dog mistook my steak for drugs, but this seems even more intimate.

No, I tell myself. No, it's not. It's simply self-defense training. He could be doing this same thing with Aaron or Erin. It means nothing that I find him attractive or that his touch makes me want to shiver.

"Okay." I take a deep breath, choosing to be completely professional. "I don't know what I'm doing."

"Do you ever?"

Well, there went any mushy feelings I might have had. I turn to face him directly and smack a fist into my own palm. "As you saw with my driving last week, I'm pretty good at figuring things out."

His eyes flinch. He studies me through slits. "Have you had any fight training before? For the roles you've played."

I plop onto my rear and lie back, keeping my knees bent and feet on the floor. The whole time I'm mentally scrolling through my previous acting jobs. Now that I think about it, the characters I play usually end up dying.

Huh. That doesn't bode well for fighting Karson in self-defense.

Instead of confessing my lack of martial arts experience, I say, "You're about to find out."

He grins. The kind of grin that tells me he's up for, and might possibly enjoy, such a challenge. It makes me want to punch him for real.

The mat is cushy and cool underneath my spine, but when Karson steps one leg over me and kneels down to pin my waist against the floor, he is the opposite. Solid muscle and heat. This could be a very scary position were I being attacked by someone I didn't trust. Someone who didn't smell warm and spicy like cinnamon.

He examines me from above, the creases in his forehead deepening as if he's concerned. Maybe he senses my apprehension and figures out I've never done this before. Maybe he's more sensitive than he wants to admit. Maybe he does care after all.

"Bring your hands to guard." He pulls his arms up in demonstration. His blue eyes watch me from over his fists. "You missed this part earlier."

If I'd been on time, I wouldn't have ended up as partners with him. Does he still think I plan stuff like this?

I mimic his guard position to block myself from his attack. "Sorry I'm late."

He nods, either in acceptance of my apology or approval of my form. Or maybe just acknowledgment. "Your roommates said you were right behind them."

"I was. I got . . . lost."

His lips press together, and I realize he's holding back from saying something that would have me comparing him to a witch doctor again. I hear his words in my mind anyway. *Of course you did.*

I got offended when he said that about my heels last week. Only this time I know he's right. This is really why I drive him crazy. What makes me a good writer would make me a really bad cop. A really bad student. And a really bad potential girlfriend.

My guard drops. I deserve that blow.

"Keep your hands up," he advises. Because once again he sees my mistake and knows I can do better. "Now use your forearms to knock away my punches."

In slow motion, his right fist comes toward my face.

I hunch and cover my head with my arms.

His fist connects lightly and then pulls back. He may not like me, but he's a good teacher. "Don't hide. Fight back. Use my momentum against me."

I try to process what he's telling me to do. But rather than absorb the message, I let myself get distracted by it. Mostly by the word *momentum*. Because Momentum would be a good superhero name if it hasn't already been used. I want to call Zach Price and suggest it for his television show.

"Gemma, focus."

Oops. Though I like to think my writer brain is a strength, sometimes it can be a weakness. Kind of like Karson's momentum. I get it now.

He comes at me with a left cross. I need to keep his punch going. Keep it carrying him past me.

I use my forearm, not to block his fist, but to slide by his fist and guide the punch to the ground. With the force of his weight shifting to my left side, I push through my right foot, popping my hips up and knocking Karson sideways the way I'd seen Wolfman do.

Then I'm rolling toward him, pressing my right palm against his chest to throw him all the way onto his back. I don't stop there. I flip upright onto my knees, pretending to punch him the way he had done to me.

To keep him from continuing the flip so that he's over me again, I tuck my toes into the ground and rock backward to shift my weight onto my heels. Then I'm standing. Throwing one last fake punch, I finish with Wolfman's line. "Hiya!"

Karson palms my fist the way I'd palmed it earlier when trying to intimidate him. He's on his back, staring up at me with eyes so piercing they could be considered a weapon. All the while, I'm leaning over him, breathing like I just woke from a nightmare.

Kai slow claps from where Charlie has flipped him onto his back.

"Wow, Gemma." Though Charlie flipped Kai, he's still on his knees rather than having leapt to his feet. It's rare that anyone goes harder than Charlie.

Kai, meanwhile, looks relaxed enough to take a nap. He nods

at my stance. "I should have warned Karson you go to boot camp with me."

"She-wolf." Wolfman shares his moniker.

I step back and shake out my arms. Then I peek over at Karson, who is rolling to his feet with a hand from Drew. He dusts himself off and glances at me long enough to give a small shake of his head that appears to be as disbelieving as it is impressed.

I shrug. "You told me to focus."

The class cracks up.

Drew sends his giant smile my way. "And that's how it's done, folks. Now we're going to move on to choke holds."

Karson pops his knuckles. "Let me at her," he says.

But he's grinning, and my classmates chuckle, so I know it's a joke. It's almost as if we're friends. This feeling is better than being smitten or being rivals. It's only taken four weeks to learn to get along.

And just like that I realize it's my final class on the police academy side. Next week we'll be spraying fire hoses or something. I approach Karson as my partner. For the first time, the only resentment hovering between us is my resentment of having to say goodbye.

"Face off." Drew demonstrates with Wolfman as he instructs us. "One of you wrap your fingers around the other's throat."

I use my scrunchy to gather my hair, revealing the neck Karson's been longing to wring. "Is this the moment you've been waiting for all month?"

"Not yet." His expression softens enough for his lips to turn up. "I'm going to have you try to strangle me first, so I can demonstrate how you escape."

I take a deep breath of his spicy scent. "Okay." Stepping close enough to reach him with both hands, my thumbs meet at the front of Karson's throat. The rest of my fingers circle against the prickles of hair at the base of his skull, though they don't touch. He's not much taller than me, but he's thicker. And by thicker, I mean muscular. I feel his pulse throb under my touch and take another moment to swallow before lifting my gaze to his. "Like that?"

His Adam's apple bobs against my thumbs. "Perfect."

I search his eyes like a dictionary to see if his use of the word "perfect" might have had more than one meaning. But they remain as steely as a safe.

"Now." Officer Harris vies for our attention. "If you're being choked, drop your chin down to make it harder for your attacker to squeeze your neck. Go ahead and give yourself a double chin."

Karson quirks a light eyebrow before dropping his chin. His stubble scrapes the back of my hands, and we remain in this position even though he knows what to do to escape it.

"From here," Officer Harris's voice booms, "you're going to use all your body weight against your attacker's weakest point—their thumbs. Step back with one leg, lean forward to break their grip, and duck under one side of their arm to pivot away."

Before I can even picture the process in my mind, Karson is free, and I'm grasping air. "Hey."

He pivots back. "Think you can do that?"

"I don't know. You told me you were going to demonstrate, but you just disappeared."

"Here." He grabs my wrists to bring my hands back to his neck. His fingers don't slide away immediately, and his eyes meet mine and linger. But before I can get lost in the look or even question the touch, he's all business again. "Squeeze harder."

I adjust the position for a better grip and try not to use my fingernails. He pulls another Houdini.

Then he's back with his hands around my throat. It's not painful. He's not squeezing tight enough to hurt me. Just to hold me.

I should be able to break away as easily as he did. I step and duck. His thumbs don't budge. Well, except to poke my trachea.

"You forgot to stiffen your neck," he coaches.

That's right. I reset and take a deep breath. I pull my chin in, step, and duck. My head bumps his forearm.

"Duck lower." He slides his finger around my neck again and grins as though he's holding a trophy.

"You're enjoying this too much."

"You're right about this being the moment I've been waiting for all month."

I give a few practice neck-stiffenings. "That's actually not what I was talking about."

He tilts his head. "What'd you mean then?"

Maybe I can distract him and break away. "I was talking about how you must be glad this is your last class before we head to the fire department."

His grip slips.

I make my move. I'm free. "Yes." I pump my arms in the air and bounce around until I'm facing him again.

His arms cross but there's still one corner of his lips curving up. "As much as I'd love to be rid of you, I suppose I should tell you about the announcement we made before you got here."

I pause. He's going to willingly tell me of a way to see him again? Maybe this budding friendship has the potential to blossom into something more. "What's that?"

He sighs as if I'm such a burden. But he's playing. And it's fun. "Anybody who makes it through all four of our classes can sign up for a ride-along."

He wants me to go on a ride-along with him? I wish I could play it as cool as he does, but even as I think this, my mouth is opening, my eyes are bulging, and I'm imagining the two of us on a car chase with sirens blaring. Oh, the true crime stories I'm going to write.

"Okay, team," Drew calls. "Let's take it to the wall and practice how you get away from a choke hold against a barrier."

I'm still grinning as I turn to face the wall, and Karson falls into step beside me. This is what it will be like in his cop car. We'll be side by side. Maybe in the dark if it's nighttime. We'll have lots of time to talk and get to know each other better.

There goes my overactive imagination. I don't even know that my ride-along will be with him. "Will my ride-along be with you?" I ask.

He plucks at the front of his T-shirt, and it reminds me of the time in eleventh-grade gym class when Shawn Fox asked if I'd invited anyone to the Sadie Hawkins dance yet. I'd said no and asked who he thought I should take. That's when he'd done the shirt-pluck thing. Except he'd cleared his throat too.

Karson clears his throat. "Only if you request me."

He just told me I could request him. He didn't have to say that. He didn't have to pluck his shirt and clear his throat. He didn't have to tell me about the ride-along at all. "Okay."

"Once you find a spot . . ." Officer Harris uses one hand to slowly press Wolfman to the bricks by his throat. "One partner needs to pin the other against the wall with their hand."

Karson backs up, hands raised as if in surrender. While I had a crush on angry Karson, I am enjoying this side of him so much more. This side is likable.

I step in and pretend I'm going to strangle him, though I feel like he could break from my hold simply by flexing his neck muscles. He is a picture of controlled strength. Our eyes meet, and I wonder what else he's holding back.

Officer Harris continues our lesson. "All you have to do to escape this hold is pivot toward the attacker's fingers, breaking the thumb's hold."

I'm pretty sure the officer also demonstrates the move, but my gaze is locked on Karson. What's changed? Why is he suddenly willing to look me in the eye without his standard scowl?

"If you want to add onto the pivot, you can push your attacker's hand away at the same time. This actually sets you up to wrap *your* arm around *their* neck."

Karson's eyebrows jump.

Now it's my turn to shake my head at him. "You're not going to put me in a headlock."

That one corner of his lip curves higher. "You're going to have to squeeze really hard then."

I lock my arm straight and lean into him with all my weight.

He is the calm before the storm. "Ready?"

Very ready. In fact, I've been waiting for this moment all month. As much as he's been waiting for it to be over.

"Oh man," Drew's voice booms from behind me as he's coming by to personally coach us. "She's really going for it, Karson. Did she find out about your date with the redhead last week?"

My fingers tingle. My grip slips. Then there's a blur, my arm goes flying, and I'm bent over with my head locked in the crook of Karson's elbow.

We're closer than we've ever been, yet it's only because our proximity doesn't matter to him anymore. That's what's changed. He doesn't have to defend himself from me because there's no threat.

He's in a relationship with someone else, and once again I've been too distracted by my daydreams to notice.

CHAPTER FOURTEEN

KARSON

The real hero is always a hero by mistake;
he dreams of being an honest coward
like everybody else.
—UMBERTO ECO

Gemma has never been so quiet as she is the day of our ride-along. I strongly suspect it has something to do with Harris's mentioning my "date" with Bree. While he'd meant his comment as teasing, she seemed to have taken it seriously. Of course, this happened right after I'd resigned myself to enjoying her company, since it was the closest we'd ever get to a relationship. And I'd never enjoyed self-defense day more.

I'm not sure if Gemma decided to respect me as off the market or she's hurt in thinking I'd chosen someone else over her. Either way, I should probably be grateful. Now I'm not going to feel betrayed when she ends up falling for a fireman next week.

But I'm baffled as to why she still signed up for the ride-along and requested me if she's going to make it so awkward. Maybe this is about her writing research as she'd claimed all along. Though she doesn't seem to be doing much research. We're just sitting here on I-205 in the golden glow of a long summer evening, watching traffic slow at the sight of my cruiser.

"Do you have any questions?" I can't believe I actually ask her this. But she doesn't seem like herself when she's not being all curious and intuitive.

Her eyelashes lower as she looks at my dashboard. She studies it as if for the first time. "What's"—she randomly points to a button—"this?"

I adjust my posture as an excuse to hide a smile. She'd pointed at the heater, so obviously she doesn't care too much about what my patrol car does. "That's the Bat-Signal."

Her eyes stay glazed for a moment, but I can tell when my answer registers. Her gaze jumps to mine and her pupils dilate as if to see me better. "Does it work during the day?"

"No." I shrug. "That's the problem with bats. They only come out at night."

She gives me a small but genuine smile. The kind that says she likes being with me even if she doesn't think she can be *with* me. "So you have to do your own superhero stuff during the day then, huh?"

I wish I could say yes to that. I wish I could be her hero. "No. I just do my job."

"Spoken like a true hero."

We stare at each other, and I get this heaviness in the pit of my stomach at the realization she honestly trusts me in a way I've never trusted anyone.

"Gem—"

My radio crackles. "Any units in the area of Clackamas Town Square for robbery in progress?"

I report in, along with everyone else in the area, but none are as close as we are.

"Calling party reports shoplifting in progress at Macy's."

I hit my lights, then grab the radio to give my designator number so she can mark me as responding to a situation. "Show me en route."

My pulse picks up speed like it normally does when heading to a call, but there is nothing normal about this. I'm checking over my shoulder before pulling into traffic, but I'm also keeping an eye on Gemma, who is sitting up straighter and pulling out her pink notebook. My attention is torn.

I don't care about living up to her expectations in this moment. I just want to keep her safe. And I'm kicking myself for suggesting the ride-along. I didn't really want her to go on calls. I just wanted an excuse to have her sitting by my side.

I wait until the dispatcher finishes the description of the suspect before preparing Gemma. "You'll need to stay in the car while I go into the department store."

I don't have the imagination Gemma does, but I *can* imagine worst-case scenarios. And no criminal is going to take kindly to an audience.

Her eyes widen my way and she opens her mouth to argue.

"It's for your safety."

Her mouth closes, though her lips purse in a pout. She can be mad at me if she wants, as long as she's safe.

I take the mall exit, and cars pull over to let me run a red light. As soon as I'm in the town center parking lot, I flick off my flashers and go into what I consider stealth mode. If the suspect is exiting the store, I want to see her before she sees me.

I pull behind a tree into a position where I can watch the exit to the department store. I'm about to shift into park when a large woman with cropped, bleached hair matching the description of the suspect pushes through the glass doors, glancing over her shoulder and walking fast.

Gemma jolts upright and points. "Are you going to let her get away?"

I pinch the button on my radio and give my designator number again. "Suspect exiting the west entrance. I'm watching to see where she goes. Requesting backup."

The woman heads to the passenger side of a beat-up brown pickup. I register a second female as a driver behind the wheel at the same time I tap the license plate number into my computer. The truck belongs to a man currently in jail on drug charges.

Another black-and-white glides into position on the opposite end of the parking lot. With the criminal history these women must have, I'm surprised the two of them aren't more alert. Though it does already require a special kind of arrogance to think they can get away with what they're doing.

Time for me to move in. I flick on my siren along with my lights this time.

Both women jump to attention. The thief stumbles backward a couple of steps before freezing. The driver simply shoots me a dirty look. She's going to be a handful.

I roll behind the truck to block it from backing out. "Wait here." Gemma nods emphatically, eyes the size of camera lenses. What I wouldn't give for an actual Bat-Signal right about now.

I open my door and circle to the front of the cruiser. "Good afternoon, ladies."

"Good afternoon, officer," the driver says. She's skinny and has sagging jowls. Her dark hair is styled like it's the 1980s, and from the lines in her grayish face, I would guess that's the era she attended high school. Though people who live hard lives do tend to age faster. She asks, "Is there something you and your princess of a girlfriend need?"

Did Gemma hear the jab? I think she'd be okay with the insinuation that she's my girlfriend but definitely not the princess part. I, on the other hand, want to arrest the woman simply for putting the idea of dating back in my head.

I keep my emotion in check. I can't handcuff any suspects until I find evidence of a real crime. "I got a call about a theft at Macy's. Do you know anything about that?"

"Nope." Gray-faced lady. "We have a receipt."

Of course they do. That's how their scam works. "May I see it?"

The brunette nods at the blond, who fumbles through her pockets and produces a couple of white slips of paper stapled together. She glances at the driver once more before handing over a stapled pile of multiple receipts.

Just as I suspected. I barely have to glance at the dates and times to know what's going on. "So you returned a bunch of stuff today? For cash?"

Blondie nods, her skittish eyes saying more than her lips as she continues to look between me and the truck driver.

"You didn't like the"—I read the first item on the list—"Bluetooth radio?"

The driver answers for both of them. "There are better brands."
The blond nods in a bobblehead sort of way.

Gemma watches from behind the windshield. If she can hear, I assume she's putting the pieces together. She could very well become a witness when this case goes to trial, so I'll give her another moment to figure it out.

"What about the"—I read from the receipt—"earrings?"

The blond wears large gauges in her ears. I wait for that to trip her up.

The truck driver's laughter holds the tone of mockery. "They were a gift for me, but I didn't like them."

All right. If she wants to talk, we'll talk. She's obviously the mastermind. "So why didn't *you* return them if they were your gift?"

The brunette nods at her friend. "Tina offered."

Uh-huh. And she's giving me Tina's name because she wants the other woman to take the fall for this. "That was nice of you, Tina." I arch my eyebrows pointedly at the woman *not* named Tina before pivoting to fully address her scapegoat. "Are you also going to offer to go to jail for your friend here? Because you're the one caught on camera today. There's footage of you swiping the same items so you can return them and get the money."

"No, I . . . uh . . ."

Gemma covers her mouth as understanding dawns.

Time to make the arrest. "Do you get to keep the entire cash refund, Tina, or do you have to give half to your partner here?"

"Partner?" the brunette bellows. "She was just going to give me the money from the earrings so I could buy some I like. And if you caught her shoplifting today, that had nothing to do with me. You know what? I'm outta here. I don't have to put up with—"

"Actually you do. We're taking you both in for questioning."

Thankfully the other cruiser pulls up in that moment. We can divide and conquer.

I let Officer Wong usher Tina into his back seat. I would rather have taken her, since she's less of a threat to Gemma, but I'm the one who deals with the hardnoses. Plus, I know Tina is more likely to open up to him. He'll play the nice guy and get her to confess with a side of implicating her accomplice. She's already given us a name.

Melanie Foulkrod sits in my back seat while I search the truck. A black plastic film cannister on the faded brown dashboard gets my attention. Who uses real film anymore?

With rubber gloves on, I retrieve the small container warmed by the sun. Popping the top, I find a powdery white substance. Bingo. Whatever drug this is, it's more than the legal limit. If we don't get Ms. Foulkrod for theft, we'll get her for dealing narcotics. And I can get her away from Gemma.

Gemma climbs out of the car as I should have known she would. But it's okay now that the suspects have been apprehended. I wouldn't want to stay in the car with Ms. Foulkrod if I were her either.

"You doing okay?" I ask.

"Yeah." Her eyes take in the scene like an investigator. And she'd probably consider writers to be investigators of sorts. "What'd you find?"

I tip the cannister to show her and swing the vehicle door shut. Case closed.

"Um . . ." She twists her lips. "Are you done searching the truck?"

"I am. Do you need something?" Maybe she's actually bored. Or scared. Or has to pee.

Her gaze flicks to my cruiser before she meets my gaze. "I think you should keep searching."

I tilt my head. She's starting to sound like a conspiracy theorist. Which I suppose could also aid her job as a writer. "Why?"

"When you pulled out the film cannister, Melanie snickered."

I knew the suspect was a mocker, but it doesn't make sense that she would mock me for finding evidence unless she wanted me to find it.

"If she was smart enough to set up Tina as a decoy, that film cannister could very well be a decoy also." Gemma almost whispers, and I have to strain to hear her. "It would be like if I'd really had drugs in my purse, and I put the steak in there with the hopes you'd stop searching once you found the obvious package."

She's right, and it's as though we've switched places. I feel stupid for letting my desire to get Gemma back to safety prevent me from being my normal suspicious self.

"Good call." I give a huge sigh and dig back into the truck to find two large baggies of dope duct-taped to the back of the driver's seat. I'd almost missed them.

I'd bet my Beretta the cannister has nothing but baking powder in it. By the time I'd had it tested, someone would have cleaned out the real stash.

I slammed the truck door shut a second time and look to see Melanie's reaction now. There's no trace of snicker in her scowl. It's a good thing she's locked up already. Otherwise she might very well go after Gemma for encouraging me to keep searching.

But what's to stop her from getting revenge once she meets bail?

I turn my back so she doesn't see me close my eyes and suck in a deep breath. I can't show weakness. I can't let the enemy know how they can hurt me. That's how Spider-Man's enemies know to go after Mary Jane.

Unfortunately, I'm not Spider-Man. I'm not even Gemma's boyfriend. She has to be able to defend herself, and she's going to need more than an escape plan from being choked.

My mind rewinds to the shooting lesson with Bree. I'm going to have to teach Gemma how to shoot.

I tamp down emotion the same way I do gunpowder when reloading. After I'm sure my expression is as impenetrable as a metal casing, I turn to face Gemma. "We have to head to the precinct now. But if you're free this weekend, I'd like to give you a shooting lesson."

Gemma's gaze searches mine, and I realize she's more perceptive than I'd ever given her credit for. How can her eyes be both soft and armor-piercing?

The flicker of light in her irises is like a satellite in the sky. It tells me she can see the reason behind my invitation. She can see I'm concerned about her safety. She can see I really do care. Though hasn't she known that all along?

"I'd like that," she says.

This makes me feel a little better about her safety, but now I need to be worried about mine. I'm in deep trouble.

CHAPTER FIFTEEN

GEMMA

The best heroes always have scars. If they didn't,
the heroine would have nothing to do. It's her job
to help the hero let all that stuff go in order that her
man can be strong enough to fight on but when
he's with her he's free to just breathe.
—KRISTEN ASHLEY

In my mind, I've written a million backstories for Karson. A million motivations for why he invited me over to learn to shoot guns today. Being that he's dating someone else, none of them make sense. But they say that's the difference between fiction and real life. Only fiction has to make sense.

As a writer, I'm still trying to figure it out anyway. I've narrowed possible motives down to three options.

1. *Karson is nothing more than worried about my safety.* He's still annoyed by my writing but realizes I tend to be unobservant to the world around. He won't always be here to protect me, and neither will Kai and Charlie. So he's going to teach me to take care of myself. That's his job. Personally, I think I'd be more comfortable with a Taser than a gun. I could never actually shoot anybody.

2. *Karson and I are friends now.* His gorgeous redhead girlfriend (whom I shall visualize as Scarlett Johansson from *Black Widow* since, you know, Karson is basically Hawkeye) has no reason to be threatened by me. Maybe she'll even be at his house today, and we'll

become besties. I'll play her sidekick, because she's certainly tough enough to shoot supervillains. She'll set me up with Captain America, and we'll go on double dates, be in each other's weddings, and laugh about all this someday.

3. *Karson likes me.* This is my favorite scenario. And in my mind, he's not cheating or anything, because there is no redhead. Either Drew made her up as a joke or Karson ended things with her. He may not be ready for a relationship or want to admit his feelings, but our connection during self-defense class and on my ride-along was more than one-sided.

My fingers itch at the idea of scenario three. I get that same feeling when I'm writing romantic scenes, but sadly I don't have the control of a playwright over my own life. I need to stop trying to script my future. I need a blank page.

"Blank page," I say aloud.

Siri's automated voice responds over my car's speaker, "In one hundred feet, turn right."

I refocus on the winding forest road that has turned the sun into a strobe light. Gorgeous roads like this make it seem as if I've driven hours away from Portland, though really, I'm just outside city limits.

A black mailbox marks a long gravel driveway with the address I'm looking for. I slow to turn, and my eyes scan the shade for any sign of a residence. Nothing yet. My tires crunch through the thick trees for a good minute before a home appears. It's a simple one story—kind of a ranch house, but with a dramatic roof that makes it seem more modern. It's painted a natural brown color that effortlessly blends into the surrounding woods.

I pull onto a cement driveway, cut my engine, and just take in the place. "Blank page."

Karson's home is the exact opposite of my sister's home—fresh, peaceful, and simple. Somehow, it's both unexpected and fitting for the man I know who lives here.

I'd pictured an angry cop to reside in a city apartment with horns honking and neighbors' music blaring, but again, I've watched too many movies. It makes sense that Karson would want to get away from all that. Here, it's quiet except for birds chirping over the faint murmur of tires in the distance.

I open my car door and breathe in the musty scent of underbrush that never fully dries. The dewy air is cool and dim, even though the temperature is supposed to reach the 90s. Perhaps that's why the contemporary lights on the house are lit up with a golden glow in the middle of the day.

A mechanical grinding sound startles me, but it's only the garage door opening. Light shines out from underneath as the door rolls up. I'm about to be let into Karson's world.

"Blank page."

While the man was born to wear a police uniform, the raising of the garage door reveals a different look. First, I see scuffed, camel-colored work boots. Next jeans. Not the soft kind that easily gets holes, but the rugged kind that have to be worn a lot to soften. Then a black T-shirt, which I appreciate for being neither too baggy nor too tight.

He's holding a rifle and wearing a baseball cap, and of the two, it's that hat that makes my pulse pick up speed. I didn't realize I liked baseball caps so much. Maybe I just like them on him. Because it means we're hanging out, and he's not getting paid to be here right now.

By the time my eyes reach Karson's face, he's already looking at me. "I thought I heard you out there. What'd you say?"

"Uh . . ." I don't remember saying anything. Do I really talk to myself, like a heroine in a Hallmark movie? "Nice place?"

"Thanks." He sets the gun down on a long workbench full of other gun-looking things and points to the driveway. "If you keep going, you'll run into my grandparents' home. They bought this property in the '60s."

I blink the direction he's pointing. That's another shocker. But super sweet. Now that I think about it, a policeman probably couldn't afford to live in this area at today's prices. "They still live here?"

"Yep." He picks up a bright-yellow rag and polishes the rifle.

"Granddad taught me to shoot, and we have a gun range behind our houses."

I'd thought we were going to head to an indoor range or something. But this feels so much different. It's not just a way for Karson to show off. It's personal. "Your land is beautiful."

"I know." He sighs and looks out at the trees. "I left for a while, but this is home."

I can see that. And I like it. "Where'd you go?"

"College. You know." He shrugs off the specifics. "I majored in criminal justice and minored in gunsmithing." He peeks over at me as if waiting for my reaction.

I don't disappoint. "That's a thing?" I'll have to give a character a gunsmithing degree now.

"Look." He waves me toward his table. Some of the guns appear to belong in a museum. Others don't look fit for any place but the dump. The latter are rusty and the wooden handles are splintered. "I'm restoring these."

I lift my eyebrows. That's a big if not futile job. "Will they be able to fire again?"

I once heard about someone who stole an old gun to use as a weapon, but when he fired it, he only injured himself. I should use that in a story too.

"Oh, yeah. Check out this one." Karson leads me across the garage. There are no cars in here, only tools. "Would you believe this rifle is from the Civil War? My granddad's friend found it in the lake while fishing."

The weapon definitely looks like an antique, but it's shiny and beautiful. Made new. "Can I hold it?"

"Well." He studies the gun, then frowns at me. "It was designed without a trigger guard. I want to add one before letting anyone hold it. Sorry."

I'm used to him saying "no" but not "sorry," so I'm more intrigued than offended.

I glance down at the trigger in question. It sticks out without anything blocking it from getting bumped. I know not to put a finger on the trigger unless ready to fire, but I'd never thought about the importance of the little piece of metal that encloses it. I always just took it for granted.

"That could be symbolic," I murmur.

"Symbolic?"

Do I normally talk to myself this often, and has nobody ever noticed before? "Oh." My gaze jolts to his. We are so close. It was different when we were both looking down, but now that we're facing each other, all that care and attention Karson lavishes on his firearms is washing over me. Like the icy lapping waves of the ocean on the Oregon Coast, it's going to remain uncomfortable unless I back up or dive in.

As if afraid to drown in his eyes, I turn away and nod toward his guns. "The term 'trigger' is used when someone gets angry. A person who is easily angered might just need to add a trigger guard to their life. A missing trigger guard could be symbolic for an angry person."

He stills. Maybe he's not listening. Maybe he's already been swept away by the tide tugging me his way.

I hold my breath and turn to face him again. But he's not even looking at me. He's studying the trigger on his gun.

Oh man. He thought I was referring to him, didn't he? And perhaps I was.

I could use the trigger analogy in my romantic comedy screenplay. Because the best romantic comedies have depth and meaning that make the humor poignant.

But right now I don't want to deal with angry Karson. I don't want to upset him.

I lighten my tone. "How do you add a trigger guard?"

One of his eyebrows arches to give him a better view of my face without lifting his head to look directly at me. Perhaps he's checking to see if I'm still talking about symbolism or his gun collection.

I smile encouragingly.

It must have satisfied, because he launches into an answer that probably could have been taken directly from his senior thesis. It comes with all the demonstration needed for a TikTok video.

He shows me the piece of metal he's already cut out for the trigger guard. He just has to shape and polish it before attaching it to the weapon.

I'm walked through the steps for sandblasting away rust and cutting new gunstocks from wood. It's quite a process, but I can see the catharsis in it. The poetry of restoration. What might once have been considered worthless by whoever threw it in the lake has now become a priceless collector's edition.

I'm pondering all of this in my heart when Karson pulls out a can of gun oil. As soon as he unscrews the lid, the sweet and spicy scent sweeps over me. It's warm but cooling at the same time.

"So that's why you smell like cinnamon."

He pauses the same way he did before. But this time his eyes are on me. I think they are anyway. They're kind of shaded underneath the brim of his cap.

"I smell like cinnamon?" He speaks with hesitation.

"Yeah." I nod so he knows it's good. "I thought maybe you chewed Big Red."

A corner of his lip curves. "You smell like coconut."

My heart trips, thrilled that he's noticed me the way I've noticed him. "Oh, that's my shampoo." It's my favorite scent. Well, it was before I smelled Karson. But what if he isn't a fan? "Do you like coconut?"

He grimaces. Not a good response. Note to self: buy new shampoo.

He ducks his head and gives a shrug. "I mistook the scent for sunblock and assumed you spent your days at pool parties, among other things."

Oh . . . I duck my head to better see under the brim of his hat. "Sounds like the scent is a trigger."

He exhales in a thoughtful huff. "How can you be both so innocent and insightful?"

I'm not sure if this is a rhetorical question or if he really wants to know. "My sister is a psychologist, remember?"

His eyes crinkle in the corners. "The evil twin?"

"Yes." I'm glad we can joke about this now. I enjoy joking about things that hurt me. If laughter is the best medicine, then jokes are the Band-Aids.

The brim of his hat lifts high enough for him to really look at me. And for me to really look at him. I take a deep breath of spicy gun oil.

"You ready?" he asks.

My heart flutters. "I'm so ready." I've been ready since he busted through my front door to rescue me last summer. But I'm not sure we are preparing for the same thing.

CHAPTER SIXTEEN

KARSON

A hero is no braver than an ordinary man,
but he is brave five minutes longer.
—RALPH WALDO EMERSON

Gemma may not have fired a gun yet, but she's already pierced my heart.

I know I have an itchy trigger finger, but I never figured I could add a trigger guard to my temper. I've never thought of myself as dangerous. More like a gunslinger from the Wild West. I'm a quick draw, so I can get them before they get me.

Gemma's now past my judgment of her coconut scent, but I still have the fake-girlfriend defense. Of course, with the way I'm staring into her eyes, and the way I'm soon going to put my arms around her to help her aim a gun, she's smart enough to figure out my first "date" with Bree had also been my last.

Yeah. This is going to be nothing like teaching Bree to shoot.

I sling a bag of ammo over my shoulder and grab both a shotgun and handgun before leading Gemma through the back door of my garage. She's looking all around, and I'm torn between watching her wonderous expressions and viewing my surroundings through fresh eyes. What does she see?

The giant pine trees. The ivy that snakes its way up tree trunks. The ferns and moss that replace the grass of normal back yards.

I do have a little stone patio with an iron scrollwork table and

Traeger grill. It also holds an old porch swing Granddad made of logs, now shiny from overuse. Grams hung the flower baskets on the lone post I used for stringing white lights to the eves of my house like an awning. The scene has me wanting to invite Gemma for dinner sometime. From what she just said, I think she's ready for that.

However, she's currently focused on what lies beyond the stepping stones and wooden arbor. Granddad built the U-shaped gun table and shelter when I was in fourth grade, so it's pretty dilapidated. Nothing when compared to what they have at other gun ranges.

"How cool," she gushes.

"I like it." I set my firearms on the creaky table and pull out the ammo.

She turns from facing the paper target I already set up a hundred feet downrange to look at the guns I brought with us. "I get to shoot a rifle?"

If I'd known she wanted to shoot a rifle, I would have brought one. "This is a shotgun. It fires a bunch of steel pellets called shot." I pick up the shotgun and pump it to make its trademark cracking sound. "You hear that? That's the best home defense unit sold on the market. It will scare away any intruder. They know that even if you have bad aim, one of those pellets is bound to hit them."

She studies the weapon, slim eyebrows arching.

So I place the firearm on the table and load a round. "I recommend getting a pink one. That way if you ever shoot someone, and they take you to court, your defense attorney can hold up the pink shotgun, and the jury will laugh at the weapon and find you not guilty."

She chuckles. "Like you've ever shot a pink gun before."

I snort. "Only purple."

She bites her lip. Probably to hold back laughter. "This I gotta hear."

I pause, focusing on the gun and buying time to decide how I should respond. I hadn't meant to bring up Bree. Too late now. "The last lesson I gave was to a woman with a purple gun." I slowly lift my eyes to meet Gemma's gaze. It's as calm as the sea before a storm.

"Your date?" she asks sweetly, as if my answer to this question won't change everything between us.

The storm is inside my chest. "I never called it that."

"Is *this* a date?"

As much as I hate lying, the truth is that she's more honest than I am. She's more real. More transparent. Forcing me to be truthful with myself. "Yes." Even though I'm taking the risk of calling this a date, I'm careful not to touch her as I hand her goggles and earplugs.

She puts on the goggles and lifts her chin in triumph, not caring if she looks goofy. Though the twinkle in her eye tells me she might even be enjoying this goofiness as much as she did with Erin's sneakers. "Good."

What have I gotten myself into?

She smiles and holds out her hands for the shotgun. She's so confident, I picture her in a SWAT uniform, leading her team into battle. It scares me a little. For her and also for me.

I choose to trust her and hold the weapon out for her, barrel pointing downrange. "It's heavy."

The weight doesn't make her arms droop. She's stronger than I've given her credit for, as always.

"Keep your finger off the trigger until you're ready to fire." I put on my own protective equipment.

"I know."

Oh yeah, we've had the trigger guard talk. "Okay. Tuck the stock against the inside of your shoulder."

She follows my directions like a pro. I advise on how to aim while I move behind her to help her position the shotgun. I angle my feet so I can step in and—

A gun report rocks me back on my heels. My heart hammers in my chest. I look at the spray of holes in the target. Bull's-eye. She's done this before.

Gemma lowers the gun's barrel and spins to flash a triumphant grin. At my close proximity, she jolts away and holds a hand to her heart. "Oh no. You wanted to help me."

My mouth hangs open. It wasn't that I wanted to help her . . . Okay, I wanted to help her. "I thought you'd need help."

"Oh, I'm so sorry. I ruined our romantic moment."

I wouldn't say ruined, though her talking about it definitely diminishes the spontaneity.

She reaches for my forearm as if to soothe my hurt feelings. The sizzle of her touch is anything but soothing.

"It's like on *Swiss Family Robinson* when Roberta pretended not to know how to shoot so Fritz would put his arms around her. Then when Ernst showed up, she fired the weapon expertly to keep him from holding her. I didn't mean to treat you like Ernst when you're a Fritz."

I didn't follow any of that. All I remember from watching *Swiss Family Robinson* in elementary school was the pirates and the tiger. They made the movie cool. As for Gemma's claim that she ruined our romantic moment? "It's okay. You're a good shot. I'll have to figure out another way to put my arms around you."

Her shoulders relax and her smile turns wistful. "That's a great line."

A line is about trying to reel someone in. I've been trying all this time to set Gemma free. "It wasn't a line."

Her steady gaze tells me she knows. "That's what makes it great."

"Yeah, well . . ." I can handle gunfire from a suspect, but I am totally out of my element here. "Did you learn to shoot for a movie you were in?"

"Writing research."

"Of course." What brought us together just kept us apart. "You'll do the scene justice. If the writing thing doesn't work out for you, I'll offer you a job."

Her laughter tinkles like wind chimes. "I may have the gun part down, but I need help writing another scene."

Back to business. My relief feels strangely hollow, like disappointment. I hold my hands wide to offer her my services. "How can I help?"

She turns her back to me and lifts the shotgun to her shoulder. "I need to write a scene where the hero teaches the heroine to shoot. I need to know how the heroine feels to be in his arms. You know, so I can better write it."

My pulse trips. She just made that up. And while I'd been about to circle my arms around her a moment ago, her invitation has given our coming embrace a whole different feel.

She looks over her shoulder at me, waiting.

With a deep breath, I step behind her, positioning my feet wide so I can lean in closer. I press my chest into her spine. Do I feel her heartbeat or mine? I gently brace the sides of her ribs to stabilize us together. Her head turns, so that our cheeks can align, and we might as well be on a deserted island with the way her coconut scent surrounds us.

Either the weapon is getting heavy in her arms, or my nearness has made her weak, because the barrel of the gun droops.

"Careful," I say, sliding my hands up to cover hers.

I've held her hands before when fingerprinting her. I knew her skin was this soft. But I didn't know it could completely distract me from our target. This position would definitely not be allowed in hunter-safety classes.

I turn my head slightly so my lips are by her ear. "Is this what you need for writing your scene?"

Her head nods, but nothing else moves. She stays in my arms. For once, she's speechless.

We breathe together, taking our time. Because the moment the gun is fired, I won't have a reason to keep her in my arms, unless I'm brave enough to give her the real reason I want her there.

"Are you ready?" she asks.

I don't know if she's talking about guns this time or the more dangerous topic of relationships.

"Yes," I say to both. In spite of the way she reminds me of my ex. In spite of the way my marriage crashed and burned.

She fires. The report echoes through the trees. Pungent gunpowder overpowers Gemma's tropical scent. The kickback presses her closer.

I don't even check the target to see how she did. I swing the weapon from her arms, set it on the table along with my goggles and ear protection, and walk her backward, until she's pressed against a tree.

She rips off her own goggles and earmuffs. Her hands slide behind my back and pull me closer.

I cup her satin cheeks and press my lips hard to hers. Again and again. Enough to knock my hat to the ground.

Now that I'm letting myself get close, I can't get close enough. I hate this neediness at the same time it feels so good to take what I want.

I don't mean to crush her, but her response is so gentle and sweet, and this is what has been missing in my life. As if afraid she's not real, I hang on, refusing to let go.

"Hey." Her whisper slows me down.

I nip her silky lips.

Her palms on my chest barely stop me from nipping again. I thought this was what she'd been asking for. She'd said she was ready. She reacted like she was ready. Now she's ending it?

I pull back to search her eyes. I don't know what I'm going to see, but I have the feeling it will make me want to shoot machine guns like Rambo.

Her gaze meets mine, just as caring as before. Just as adoring.

Relief hiccups through my veins. But I'm confused. "Are you okay?" My hands slide down to her shoulders, and I look her over. Maybe I hurt her. She is tall and strong, but she's tiny at the same time. While that tree trunk behind her is as rough as me. "I thought you wanted me to kiss you."

"I did." She grips the front of my shirt in her hands and groans. "I do."

My chest puffs up at that. Did she just stop me from kissing her to tell me how much she liked my kisses? Pfft, writers.

I grab her hips and lean in again. Because if she liked that, then—

"Wait."

I freeze with my mouth inches from hers. The way our bodies fit together, it takes the strength of a crowbar to keep us apart. I give a little growl, debating whether I need to walk away for this conversation or not. "You're killing me, woman."

She grips my wrists to hold me still. "Are you frustrated? Is that why your kisses are angry?"

That stops me. I hadn't thought of myself as angry. Though maybe

I was angry at my ex. Angry at the fear Gemma and I could end up the same way. "I was going for passionate."

"They were definitely passionate kisses." Her fingers slide from my wrists to pull my hands between us. She laces our fingers together and gazes up at me, and though she's literally had me in a choke hold before, this is the position that makes me feel vulnerable. "But they didn't seem happy."

Happy? Wasn't happiness for schoolgirls who linked arms and skipped through meadows? I'm pretty sure those schoolgirls don't kiss like Gemma. "What's a happy kiss?"

Her slow smile takes my breath away. Happy looks good on her. "I'm going to show you a happy kiss," she says. "But first, I need to tell you something."

She's only inches away, and our noses dance around each other's as if finding the perfect position for when we get to mold our lips back together. "Tell me." There's nothing more important in the world than whatever it is Gemma is going to say before kissing me again.

Her eyes implore mine, revving this engine in my chest. She'd better hurry.

"My sister said anger comes from fear, pain, or frustration."

Her sister, again? Anger, again?

Though in a way, what she's saying makes sense. I roll the words around in my mind. *Fear. Pain. Frustration.* They are the opposite of what I want between us. No wonder she refused to angry kiss.

"So, in case the anger in your kisses comes from anything other than frustration, in case it comes from pain or fear, I just wanted to tell you I'm not going to hurt you."

In this moment, I believe her. And I'm stunned. Even more so than when our lips met.

She lifts higher to nuzzle her nose against mine, and her warmth stings like a hot spring after a run through the snow. I suspect it's just as healing.

CHAPTER SEVENTEEN

GEMMA

*Romance is at the heart of our lives. The truly
blessed among us find a hero or heroine of our own
to love, then root for our children to do the same.*
—M. A. JEWELL

Karson's blue eyes still hold a little bit of thunderstorm, but the intensity of his touch has died down from hurricane-force wind to gentle breeze. His fingertips lap at my back and his breathing presses his chest close to mine in long, slow waves. He looks me over as if checking for damage.

"Stay for dinner," he says.

"Okay." My arms circle his neck like a life preserver, and I smile up at him, relaxed as if I'm floating along a lazy river. I've worked hard for this vacation, and I don't want it to end.

"Oh." He scrunches his face as though he's in pain. "It's pizza night."

"Oh." I scrunch my face too. The last time I ate pizza, it didn't stay down very long. As much as I love the taste, I don't want to make that mistake again. Especially in front of my new beau. "I can't have pizza."

His eyebrows dip. "Why can't you have pizza?"

There's a lot about me he doesn't know yet. I hope it takes forever to share it all, though I'm not thinking about the ending so much as our beginning. Karson kissed me. That's mind-blowing in itself. "I'm allergic to gluten and dairy."

"Bummer." He sighs. "But when I said it's pizza night, I was talking about how it's the night of the week where Granddad cooks pizza in the brick oven he built, and my family gets together for dinner."

"Oh . . ." I purse my lips, trying not to let them stay in a pout. It's sweet and endearing that Karson is so connected to his family. "Then we'll have dinner another night. I love to cook."

His eyes study mine, shifting left then right, reading me like a book. "You should come."

My lips part in wonder. Not only did he kiss me, but he's also inviting me to meet his family? He's making up for lost time. "Really?"

He shrugs, but his gaze holds steady. "We don't have to go if you're not ready. It *is* fast."

"I told you I'm ready." I've had a year of cyberstalking to prepare for this day. It's not fast. It's surreal. Plus a weekly pizza night is the coziest thing ever, and I'm actually a little envious. "I'm not sure when I'll get to introduce you to my family though. My parents moved to Salt Lake to take care of my grandparents. As for my sister, you threatened to arrest her."

"True . . ." He slips away, puts his hat back on, and opens a gun case to clean up. "You think that will affect how your parents see me?"

"Nah. As grumpy as you are, you're much more likable than Jewel," I tease.

He chuckles and picks up the shotgun to resume his shooting lesson. "This is when you having an evil twin comes in handy. She makes me look good."

By the time we clean up the guns and pick up the shells, it's dinnertime. He gives me a slick liter of root beer to carry down the gravel driveway while he carries the ice cream for floats. I can't have a float, but I don't complain this time. I'm meeting the Zellner clan.

"So what are they like?" I ask.

He glances over. "My grandparents?"

"Yeah. And your parents."

He slows. "My parents won't be here. My grandparents raised me."

"Oh." I hadn't known. Though he did talk about his grandparents a lot for a man with a mom and dad. "Are they . . . ? Did they . . . ?" How is a girl supposed to ask her boyfriend if his folks are dead?

"I never met my dad, and my mom took off when I was little. She had a drug addiction, and she died from an overdose while I was in the police academy." He says this matter-of-factly. But it's not a fact. It's a story. One that should be filled with all the emotions.

"I'm sorry."

"It's life." He brushes off his statement as if it isn't the saddest commentary I've ever heard on life. "So today you'll meet Granddad, who is a strict rule follower except when it comes to the game of cribbage. He cheats if you don't keep your eye on him. And Grams bakes a pie every day. In the summer, she'll get up at four a.m. to bake because they don't have air-conditioning."

I love them already. Especially for being there when Karson's parents weren't. And my heart goes out to them as well. I assume it was their daughter who left Karson with them.

I smell the smoky campfire scent of a pizza oven before the old farmhouse comes into view, and I stop to absorb the details. It's not one of those modern farmhouses that are so trendy right now. It's better. This one is a giant white box with black shutters, a red brick fireplace, and steps leading to a wraparound porch. It feels like a piece of history. As if it holds the stories of generations past. There's even a clothesline strung from the side of the house to a giant tree.

The front screen door slams and an elementary-school-aged boy charges out, ball cap on crooked. He has no shoes on, but that doesn't slow him when he reaches the gravel. "Uncle Karson!"

I'd thought the grandparent thing was sweet, but I'd never imagined a nephew. I love nephews. They think everything is awesome.

The kid charges, and Karson has to lift the ice cream out of the way of his rambunctious hug. "Excited for dessert, huh?" he teases.

"Uh-huh." The boy is all big white teeth, and dark eyes that keep sneaking peeks at me.

"Phillip," Karson addresses his nephew. "This is Gemma. I was just teaching her how to shoot . . . and stuff." His sparkling eyes lift to mine in a gaze more intimate than a kiss.

Oh no. I'm not going to be the only one with flaming cheeks here. "Your uncle is really good at shooting . . . and stuff."

Karson gives the little headshake I've grown used to, only this time I look forward to possible retribution.

Phillip joins us on our stroll to the house. "I didn't know girls liked guns. Wanna have a Nerf war?"

Time to shift years. I guess I could practice my Nerf skills for taking on Forrest and Daisy. "Sure."

"Really?" The boy grins up at me, his front teeth reminding me of Chiclets, and there's no way I could turn him down. Nerf guns are more my speed anyway.

Karson shrugs a shoulder. "Gemma, you don't have—"

"Do you ride skateboards too?" Phillip interrupts.

Okay, I might have to turn down that invitation. I'm kind of fond of having my tailbone in one piece. "I—"

"We'll leave the skateboarding to Mr. Harris." Karson plays my hero once again. "I'm going to introduce Gemma to your mom, Granddad, and Grams right now, then after pizza you and I can race the RC cars your dad sent you."

"Sweet," he yells and takes off into the house. The screen door thuds again, and though I can't see him, I hear him yell, "Uncle Karson brought a girl."

Karson studies me, lips pinched together in apology. "We can turn around right now," he offers.

I actually don't mind having my presence announced by a kid's yelling it through the house. He's like a little Charlie. "Are you kidding? This is the most exciting pizza party I've ever attended, and I'm not even through the front door."

"That's because you don't eat pizza," Karson teases.

The screen door swings open to reveal a gray-haired couple and a woman in her thirties. She's exotic-looking with long, dark hair and big, trendy glasses. If this is Karson's sister, it explains where Phillip got his darker coloring, though I'd mistakenly assumed Karson's sister would look like him and that Phillip's multicultural ethnicity came from his dad's side. We're both learning a lot about each other today.

All three of these strangers smile and wave at me like I'm a long-lost relative.

I smile and wave back.

Karson runs a hand over his face.

"You did bring a girl," his sister gushes. She's as sweet as he is salty.

Also, has he never brought a girl home before? I guess besides prom dates, I've never really introduced a guy to my parents either. But Karson's family lives a lot closer.

His grandma motions me forward. "Come in, come in. I made pie."

I've never wanted to eat pie more.

"Introduce yourself first, Patricia," her husband admonishes. "Otherwise you'll scare her away."

"I think it's too late for that." Karson ushers me forward with a hand to my back, and of all the ways he's been protective, this is my favorite. "Gemma, meet my crazy family. When you play Nerf war with Phillip, you have my blessing to shoot any one of them. Though I must warn you, Grams hides an Atomic Power Popper under her bed."

His grandma makes a fist in mock indignation. "I told you that's for playing fetch with the dog."

"Sure, Grams." He gives her the all-knowing expression he must use in interrogations. "And how long ago did we bury Bingo?"

"That's beside the point."

"The point is . . ." His grandpa steps to the side to hold the door open for us to enter. "You're welcome in our home, Gemma, and we will not be having any Nerf wars tonight."

Phillip appears in the doorway with a blaster in each hand. "What?" he whines.

Granddad nods for him to put his weapons away. "Though we do like our guns, we are also against excessive use of force and police brutality."

"That's right." Karson's grandma grabs my hand with both of hers. "It doesn't bother you that Karson is a police officer, does it? I think it's a very respectable profession."

"Uh . . ." I pause before crossing the threshold onto worn oak floors and look over my shoulder at the cop in question. He must not have mentioned to them how he's been the one avoiding me for the past year. "I agree."

Karson lifts a shoulder as if telling me not to worry about it. Probably shielding me from all the stories that could be told about my adventures in citizen's police academy. "The good news is that Gemma likes police officers. The bad news is that she can't eat pizza. Or pie. She's allergic to gluten."

All movement and sound stops.

I glance around at their horrified expressions. Are they feeling bad for me or, in a family with a homemade pizza oven, is my diet a dealbreaker?

"More pie for me!" Phillip jumps onto the couch in celebration, and the tension dissolves into laughter.

"Get down, Phillip. The last thing you need is more sugar." Karson's sister takes the soda from my arms and heads inside, past an open staircase and through the living room filled with antique furniture. "Come on, Gemma. We'll make a salad out of pizza toppings."

I shoot Karson a hopeful grin. I think this means I'm being accepted. Also, I would gladly swap him sisters.

"You're Karson's sister?" I check to confirm I've got the family dynamics correct.

She heads through a misleadingly small doorway into a giant kitchen with green-and-white checkerboard flooring, white cabinets, and a backsplash of yellow tile. It smells like tangy tomato sauce and zesty Italian spices. The place is so cheerful and happy that I almost feel like I need to double-check this is the home Karson grew up in.

The woman grabs the refrigerator handle and stops to look at me as if wondering how much he's told me. "Half sister. We have different dads."

"Oh, I didn't mean . . ."

"It's okay. I know we don't look alike. I'm part Korean." She opens the door and has to move bowls around to fit the root beer inside. She continues talking with her head inside the fridge. "My birth father died fighting in Iraq when I was in kindergarten. Mom couldn't handle the pain and resorted to drugs. Her life was a train wreck after that. Karson doesn't have the good memories of her that I have."

My heart tugs even more for the man I've only adored from a distance until now. I picture him as a kid Phillip's age but already mourning the loss of his parents. He told me he'd never met his dad, but it sounds like he didn't really know his mom either. I'm not sure which sibling had it harder. Was it worse to lose parents who loved you or parents who didn't have the ability to love? "I'm sorry."

"Can you believe after all that, I'm now married to a man on deployment?" The woman emerges with a container of spring mix and a self-deprecating smile. "I'm so thankful Karson is here for Phillip and me."

I'm reminded of the scene in the original Superman where the superhero catches Lois Lane, and says, "I've got you." She looks down to see they're flying, and responds, "You've got me? Who's got you?" That's how I see Karson. He's been doing it alone, and I don't want him to have to save the world on his own anymore.

"I'm Taylor, by the way."

I refocus on the woman chopping vegetables in front of me. She just shared some pretty intimate details with a complete stranger. Though how cool that she's free to do so. Her family secrets don't hold any power over her. "It's nice to meet you, Taylor."

She squats to tug a bowl from a cupboard. "That's probably a lot to take in at once, but I wanted to make sure I had a chance to tell you before things get too insane tonight."

I wonder what exactly she means by insane. The Nerf war was called off, so what else could there be?

"My brother is a jellyfish in armor. You need to know that if you're going to have a relationship with him." She stands and faces me. "Of course, if you made it to our pizza night, you probably know that already."

I've never thought of Karson like a jellyfish before. Maybe more like Sully from *Monsters, Inc.* He's a softy who scares people for a living. "Yes."

She smiles her approval. "Finally."

Again, I'm a little worried by her wording. I'd like to think "finally" means she's glad Karson finally found a woman who isn't afraid of the way he growls, but I don't get a chance to ask before the insanity she spoke of ensues.

It starts with a tinny siren that grows louder. An RC cop car races into the kitchen. The cute little vehicle with flashing red and blue lights is followed by an RC dune buggy. Then by Grandma Patricia.

"Outside." She swats toward the miniature cars even though their drivers can't see her.

Phillip runs through the kitchen to drive the dune buggy onto the back deck.

Karson follows with his RC controls. He slows to let his thirsty eyes drink me in, and I note the cool flecks of concern.

There's the jellyfish Taylor was talking about. I was right to see Karson's fierce nature as protective, but part of his fierceness is about keeping a distance to protect himself. At his grandparents' house, he's not taking down the scum of the earth. He's dealing with the people he cares about the most and who have the ability to hurt him the most—his family.

I'm honored to be let inside this inner circle. I thank him with a slow, promising smile.

His chest rises and falls with a deep breath, and I feel its satisfaction to my toes.

"The fire's almost hot enough," Karson's grandpa yells from outside the French doors, reawaking me to the world around us.

His grandma leans over the sink to shout out the window. "Make sure it's seven hundred degrees."

"You're not the only one who knows how to cook a pie," his grandpa hollers back.

The little siren grows louder again, and Phillip's RC car zips back in the room, ramming into a cabinet. He appears in the doorway. "You're losing the race, Uncle Karson."

And so the night goes. It's a good thing Taylor took the time to talk to me when she did. There's not another moment's peace until after dinner at the picnic table, a million car races down the driveway, my first cribbage lesson, and multiple attempts to get Phillip into his mom's car.

Karson steps behind me and reaches past to the porch railing, locking me to him and causing goose bumps. We watch Taylor climb behind the wheel of her hybrid SUV. Even then, Phillip's window is rolled down to reveal his big-toothed smile in the fading purple twilight.

"You're not going to kiss her, are you, Uncle Karson?"

I bite my lip, awaiting his response. I want him to kiss me, but our kisses still feel fragile, like dreams, and talking about them might be the same as pinching ourselves to wake up.

"That's none of your business," he responds. And I'm glad his grandparents are still in their recliners recovering from their carb comas so they can't question us further.

Taylor starts the engine and backs up to turn around, bringing Phillip's face directly in line with ours. "Remember you said being romantic is the same thing as being stupid," the kid calls.

I blink. Those are not the words of a hero. Especially not one of my heroes.

"I'm an idiot," Karson yells, either in his own defense or as a fore-shadowing of the wooing he's now willing to do.

Taylor cackles, waves, and rolls up Phillip's window before pulling away.

Karson's warm lips tickle the spot underneath my earlobe. "I might need a little help in the romance department," he murmurs as an apology.

I turn to wrap my arms around his solid torso. "You've come to the right place."

"Speaking of the right place." He has to peer harder through the dimming light to see my eyes, and the growing darkness makes being in his arms that much more sensual. "Are you glad you came tonight? Was it too much too soon?"

"Hmm . . ." I replay the beautiful summer evening in my mind. Karson may have been raised by his grandparents, but they seem to have more energy than my folks. Mom wasn't able to get pregnant until late in life after years of infertility treatments, so they never yelled or chased us around. He's blessed to have the home he does. "I'm actually glad you invited me before I had time to stress about bringing a side dish or wearing the right thing. Your family is all really accepting. As if they've been waiting for you to bring a woman home for years."

He's quiet. Maybe embarrassed that it took him three decades to open himself up to a serious girlfriend. "About that . . ."

"It's okay. Taylor told me."

His spine stiffens. His muscles tense under my fingertips. "She did?"

"Yeah." I rest my head on his shoulder to share my peace. "I'm so sorry you had to go through that."

He exhales, allowing me to sink deeper against him.

"That had to be so hard not growing up with a mom who loved well. I can see how it would affect dating relationships."

He takes another deep breath, which pushes me away again momentarily. "You two talked about my mom?"

"She told me you don't have good memories the way she does. When was the last time you saw her?"

He tilts his head back as though he's looking for the first star of the night. Maybe this isn't the right moment to ask, but coming over here made me feel like we are on the fast track to love. I presumed that meant I could ask hard questions. Though my questions seem to be squeezing between us.

"You don't have to answer."

He hugs me tighter but turns his face to the side. "I'm afraid you won't like my answers."

I reach up to cup his cheek and turn his face toward mine. "We can take our time getting to know each other. I mean, I've been waiting for this night quite a while, so I can wait a little longer."

He leans his forehead against mine before his eyelashes lift and he looks at me, though the connection is more visceral than visual. "She didn't come to my high school graduation."

Pain crackles through my heart, igniting a million more questions.

Was she in prison? Was she too drugged to make it in time? Was she invited? I don't ask any of them, because that's not what matters. What matters is that I'm here for him.

"She sent me a thousand dollars in a card."

Oh, that's more than I expected. A peace offering that could have led to reconciliation.

"I drove across the country to find her in South Carolina and return the money." His tone hardens. Turns rigid. "If you could relate to Jacob and Esau, then I relate to Jacob's son Joseph, who was abandoned in a pit. I'd made something of myself without her, and I told her that if I hadn't needed anything from her before, then I didn't need anything from her then."

The broken pieces of my heart shatter even more for him. This was the last time Karson saw his mom. He'd picked up his weapons and attacked rather than run to her with open arms. "But you did need her."

"No. I didn't."

Is this what Taylor was preparing me for? I knew Karson was angry, and now I know why. He doesn't only need a trigger guard. He needs to drop the old firearm back into the lake.

CHAPTER EIGHTEEN

GEMMA

Every damsel in distress deserves a hero.
—Tracy Anne Warren

Kai pulls into the parking lot of our new class location. It's a brick firehouse with a tall cinder-block tower in the back for training.

I scan the area, searching for my favorite hero. Instead of his black uniform and shiny badge, I see a group of men walking across the parking lot in thick khaki pants held over their navy T-shirts by suspenders. They're young and fit and would probably be considered attractive if not for all their strange mustaches. One man even has the huge sideburns that, along with his handlebar mustache, make him look like an old-timey boxer.

"They're pretty much a scene from a movie montage." Charlie must be watching them too.

"I'd film them in slow motion." Kai parks and shuts off the engine.

"Special effects would add a huge fireball exploding behind them." Charlie pops his door open and holds it for me while still looking at the firefighters. "I've never thought about doing a documentary on firemen before. But if the police thing doesn't pan out . . ."

I climb out and stare with him. I'm still not over the mustaches. "Why do their faces look like that?"

I know facial hair is kind of a trend, but I'm more used to my clean-shaven roommates and my boyfriend's five-o'clock shadow.

Kai clicks his key fob, then shoves the keys in his pocket and walks around the Jeep to join us. "I think it's supposed to make them more manly. I'll admit, I'm a little jealous. I can't grow much facial hair."

"Huh." I try to picture Kai with a mustache, but my brain keeps morphing him into Magnum, P.I., even though the only thing those two have in common is Hawaii.

Charlie rubs his own chin. "Maybe I'll grow some."

Now Charlie I can definitely imagine as an artsy outdoorsman on film location in Ecuador. He already drives the Subaru. "Are you wanting to look manly, or do you just need a new challenge?"

Kai chuckles. "I heard the county fair has a beard competition every summer."

Charlie perks up. "Really?"

This is not going to end well.

"Hey. Over here." Karson's voice draws our attention away from the crew headed into the garage. He's snuck up on us while we were entranced by the firemen.

I give him my full attention, as I always do in class. "I was looking for you."

"Really?" He's joking, though there's an edge. I've heard policemen and firemen often have rivalries, but he's got nothing to worry about.

"Yeah, I was just"—I pull my long braid around to hold under my nose like a moustache—"trying to figure out the weird facial hair."

He smirks. "Firefighters can't grow beards because the hair would prevent their oxygen masks from sealing correctly, so they do the mustache thing."

I nod as if his explanation justifies the look. "Ah . . ."

"That settles it." Charlie plants his hands on his hips. "I'm doing it. I'm growing a beard, because I can."

Kai shakes his head at me. "We created a monster."

My roommates head off, arguing, but I stay put with Karson.

One of the best parts of falling in love is the pockets of alone time where we don't have to worry about anything else but looking into each other's eyes. Today, Karson's eyes remind me of when the sun glitters off the ripples in a lake. I call them "water sparkles," and I take lots of pictures of them.

"How was your pie?" I ask, and I don't mean his grandmother's. I baked an apple pie using almond flour for the crust and dropped it off at his precinct so he would know that a relationship with me didn't mean he'd never have pie again.

"Interesting." He says this in a PC kind of way. Like he wanted to say gross, but one doesn't say that to a new girlfriend. "I'm used to Grams cooking with lard."

That's a kind way to say he thought it tasted like cardboard. Though it can't be that bad. I made one to help Kai's girlfriend find a man, they ate it together, and she wound up with him. "I'll keep working on it. So do you get to hang out with me through today's class?"

His laser eye contact raises my temperature. "And make everyone think you're a teacher's pet?"

"They already know." They knew before we did.

His lips quirk as though he's trying to fight a smile. "The fire chief asked me to give rides in the basket at the end of the truck ladder, but if you time it right, you might be able to get me up there alone."

My gaze jumps to the red engine with a long white ladder. I hadn't realized we'd get basket rides. Best alone time ever. My pulse picks up speed like a fire truck with its sirens blaring. "Oh, I'm going to time it right."

He backs up to lead me toward the group gathering inside the giant garage. "It should be easy, since the rest of your class seems to prefer the men with mustaches."

"They're crazy."

He turns to walk side by side with me. "Yeah, *you're* the normal one."

I grin over at him, remembering the past month of abnormal situations we'd both found ourselves in and how they somehow brought us together. I would have loved to grab Karson's hand, but he's working. Also, by the way his cheeks redden when Aaron and Erin look over, he's embarrassed by the extra attention.

The fireman with mutton chops heads our direction. "Hey, Zellner."

Karson crosses his arms and lifts his chin in greeting.

Mutton Chops passes Karson to hold out a helmet and jacket toward me. "Everyone is putting on gear, so I thought I'd offer you mine."

Ooh, I get to wear gear. "Thanks." I take the helmet and settle it on my head. It's heavy, and the face shield distorts my view of Karson. His eyes don't appear as sparkly as they did earlier.

Mutton Chops holds up the shoulders of the yellow coat for me to try on. "I'm sorry I'm not staying for the whole class," he says. "But I wanted to introduce myself before I head out for my camping trip. The name's Thad."

"Aka Wolverine," Wolfman calls over. "With your chops, you look like Hugh Jackman as Wolverine."

That name fits too. I turn to slip my arms into the heavy material. "Thanks, Thad. I'm Gemma." I'd get my phone out of my pocket for a selfie if I could reach it, but the long sleeves hide my hands. I smile over at Karson. "Do you want to take a selfie?" Our first selfie will be of us dressed as a police officer and firefighter. How cute are we?

"Not right now, Gem." He nods toward a real female firefighter who's apparently already started our tour of the facilities. Oops.

I try to pay attention, but Wolfman seems more interested in Thad. "Are you Thaddeus Barker of the Portland Pickles?"

I've never heard of Thaddeus Barker, but I do know the Pickles are our local baseball team. "You're a baseball player?" I whisper so as not to disturb our tour guide.

Thad shrugs nonchalantly. "I was until I injured my rotator cuff rescuing a little girl from a fire."

I tilt my head in sympathy, imagining a million possible scenarios. "Oh no . . ."

Karson elbows me from the other side, and when I look over, he motions toward our class filing through a doorway into the living quarters of the fire station. I'll have to hurry so I don't get left behind.

"Gotta go." I wave goodbye to Thad and tromp after the group.

I pause to see where Karson is. I have no peripheral vision in this helmet, and it shifts around when I move my head. When I do find him, he's still back with Thad.

He waves me on. "I'll be getting the basket ready. I'll meet up with you later."

By later he means our alone time a hundred feet in the air. I think back to how I'd compared falling for Karson with the free-fall ride at the amusement park. This is so much better.

Thad waves too. "Nice meeting you, Gemma. Hope to see you again next week."

Next week we'll be learning CPR. I nod excitedly. That could come in handy in my writing.

I try to pay attention to our tour and how it can benefit my screenplay, but Karson steals the show. Thoughts of him would make me melt even if this getup didn't have me dripping sweat.

I vaguely notice the living area and bunk rooms as we file through. There's no actual fire pole because there's no upstairs, and I'm a little disappointed since firemen sliding down a fire pole makes a great visual in movies, but my movie is going to be about police officers anyway.

We head over to the tower. It would definitely make a good movie backdrop, with five stories and a roof the firemen practice rappelling off. I watch for a moment before craning my neck to find Karson in the basket high overhead. The long white ladder reaches toward the bright blue sky like a stairway to heaven.

There's a crackle sound, and a hot rush of wind draws my attention down to a controlled flame set in an open area on the bottom floor. The woman leading our class talks about temperature and smoke alarms or something.

I glance back up and wave to the figure in the basket. I don't think he sees me because he doesn't wave in return. How long until we get to go on basket rides?

"Gemma."

At the voice calling my name, I turn to find Charlie motioning me to follow him up the stairs to the second floor of the tower. Our group has been divided, and the other half of class is heading toward the fire engine. I want to go that way, but Karson himself would probably chide me for not following directions. Maybe if I'm last, I'll get more alone time with him.

I take the stairs two at a time to catch up with my roommates. "What are we doing?"

Charlie leaves us behind in order to be first in line, so only Kai remains to answer. "We're taking turns going in pairs into a smoke-filled room to rescue dummies."

"Oh cool." I look around at my classmates lined against the bare cement walls in their yellow protective gear. I'd thought I'd enjoy the police side of our class the most, but this side seems even more immersive.

"Gemma." Charlie calls me again. "I need a partner."

I look to Kai who's going to get left out if I join Charlie. He sweeps an arm to usher me forward anyway. "Ladies first."

I head toward the white smoke pouring through a doorway. It smells like Karson's grandpa's brick pizza oven but looks more like fog than smoke. This is when I'm glad for my face shield.

Charlie leans toward me as if we're football players in a huddle. "They hid two dummies, and they are timing how long it takes for us to get them out. I want to win, so I picked you since you were so fast at driving the cop car."

I blink. I can try to race, but it's not the same without Karson here to impress. "Okay."

"Let's stay together and circle the room to the right. If we haven't found one of the dummies when we get to the door, we'll go into the second room."

"There's a second room?"

His eyes bulge from behind protective plastic. "Didn't you pay attention?"

"Uh . . ." I shrug. "We just drag the dummies out, right?"

He huffs, fogging up his face shield. "I should have picked Kai."

The female firefighter at the door laughs. "You'll both be fine. I'm following you in, and if you get scared or need any help, just yell."

What is there to be scared of? This is all a simulation, right? No real fire. "Thanks."

"Ready?" She holds up a stopwatch.

Before I can even nod, Charlie yells, "Go," and grabs my hand to drag me after him.

I squeeze to hang on when he disappears into the dense haze. I can't see a thing through this white cloud, but true to the man's game plan, we seem to be circling the room to the right.

His hand slips away from mine to feel against the wall, so I reach for the back of his coarse jacket to keep up. I'm afraid to take actual steps in case I trip on the dummy, so I just shuffle my feet forward.

My breath echoes inside the helmet and grows louder. I've never been claustrophobic, but if I was, this would be terrifying.

Charlie's jacket pulls to the left. He must be turning a corner. I blindly follow.

I know this room is safe. I know there's no actual threat. I know that at any time I can be rescued. But firefighters do this all the time without any of those safeguards, which has never blown my mind more.

"I found a door," Charlie's muffled voice shouts. "You go into the next room and look for a dummy while I keep circling the perimeter here."

Tingles of adrenaline surge through my body at the idea of being left alone. But I'm not really alone. There's a firefighter following us.

"Okay," I yell back and let go of him to feel my own way.

My fingers run along the solid wall until I feel open space, and I step into the unknown. As I reach out, my own hands disappear into the smoke. I take baby steps until there's another wall to anchor myself against. Then I start around this room in the same way we had the previous one.

What if there's no dummy in here? Or what if there is, and I don't find it? What if—

My shin bumps something solid and stings like a bruise to the bone. I stop in my tracks and wave my hands, but there's nothing there.

I fold forward to feel for what hit my leg. At knee level, there's something squishy like a mattress. I press against it and hear it bounce like springs. A bed?

This would be a good place for a dummy. Were it a real person, he or she could have been sleeping in bed, not realized there was a fire, and passed out from fumes. I'm so double-checking our fire alarms when I get home.

Still tipping at the hips, I slide my hands all over the mattress and feel a less squishy shape. A bag of sand?

I pat the bag to find it has limbs. My heart leaps. This must be the dummy I have to rescue.

I scoop the dummy toward me and lock an elbow under each of its armpits. I don't have to go far to get back to the doorway. I wish Charlie was still with me to lead the way.

I back up, unsure whether I'm heading the correct direction or not. At least if I bump into something with my rear, it will sting less than my shin does.

Three steps, and I haven't hit anything yet. Maybe I'm through the doorway. I slide my left foot back a step, but my heel snags on something attached to the floor.

Normally I'd be able to set my foot down to catch myself, but I'd already been leaning back to drag the dummy. Its extra weight pushes me toward the ground.

A surprised scream rips from my lungs before I land with a jarring thud. I hadn't meant to yell for help. That only makes my situation more embarrassing. I hear radio static crackle and a voice echo, but I don't make out the words.

At least with all this protective gear, I'm not hurt at all, though I'm surely costing Charlie the fastest time. I need to roll over and push myself up as quickly as possible. Preferably before I have to be rescued.

The dummy pins me to the ground. I rock side to side to knock it off, but the deadweight barely budges. I think back to my self-defense training and the way I'd flipped Karson over. I try to bend my knees to plant my feet, but all this gear restricts my movements. I'm a turtle on its back.

Panic rises in my throat. How long do I wrestle with this thing before calling for help?

And just like that, the dummy sits up. Or it feels like it does anyway. But before I can even figure out what's going on, I'm lifted off the ground as well.

I clutch my arms around someone's thick neck. This couldn't be the female firefighter, could it? I highly doubt it's Charlie. I love him and all, but he would gladly leave me behind if I was moving too slowly.

Could it be Karson? Could he lower the basket that quickly if he heard me scream?

As I'm carried toward the door, I hold my breath and watch for my hero's face to appear. Wafts of smoke clear, and the first thing I notice are huge sideburns. What is Thad doing here? I thought he'd said he was going camping.

We emerge into the hallway. My classmates cheer. Thad carries me past them all, but I catch Kai's eye.

He's rocking in laughter. "If only he'd taken off his shirt."

CHAPTER NINETEEN

KARSON

*If your hero is a firefighter, your heroine
better be an arsonist.*
—LINDA HOWARD

I'm lowering the basket when spontaneous applause breaks out below. Clapping, shouting, and whistling. This never happened at the police station, but I shouldn't be surprised. Firefighters get all the glory.

Larry whoops. "Check out Wolverine."

I think he's talking about himself in third person until I remember he calls Thad "Wolverine" because of the ludicrous facial hair. I'm not a big fan of baseball or of the former pitcher, so I doubt I'll really care what he's up to, but I look over the edge of the bucket in hopes everyone is simply excited to watch him drive away.

When I see him carrying another person in his arms, I know it's Gemma as soon as the possibility punches me in the gut. She apparently caused trouble in the firefighting class the same way she did on the police academy side, but instead of threatening to kick her out the way I had, Thad carried her to safety. I want to pluck out his handlebar mustache with a pair of tweezers.

Larry pats me on the shoulder. "Hey, copper. You think Hawkeye could beat Wolverine in a fight?"

I level my gaze on the hand that's touching me until he removes it. "They're on the same side, Larry."

He strokes his beard. "Like firemen and policemen are on the same side?"

I'm not going to take the bait. "Yes." Thad knows to stay away from me, but does he know I'm dating Gemma?

Myrna gives a dreamy sigh. "Look at those muscles . . ."

We all watch Thad's biceps stretch his T-shirt sleeves as he sets Gemma down. We're still twenty feet off the ground, so we also have a great view of the two together as Gemma removes her helmet and shakes her long hair loose. It's going to smell like coconut, and even if it makes Thad assume she's been sunbathing at the lake, he's not going to mind. He'd love to go with her as an excuse to rip off his shirt.

Gemma throws her head back in laughter. The sound jolts me like an alarm. Earlier, she couldn't take her eyes off me in the basket, but now I'm almost at eye level and she hasn't even noticed.

Finally, she hears us talking and lifts her dancing eyes to tango with mine. "I just told Thad about the speech you gave at the beginning of my training," she calls. "He says had he known, he would have removed his shirt to be funny."

I knew it. "What a joke," I say, though I'm talking about the man, not his comedy.

She laughs again, almost too filled with mirth to continue her story. "Can you believe I tripped and fell when I was trying to rescue the dummy?"

I feel like the dummy.

"A firefighter followed Charlie and me in and didn't realize we'd separated. I guess we weren't supposed to, but you know how competitive Charlie is. When she heard me go down in the other room, she radioed for more help."

Thad chuckles along with her.

I ignore him to scan Gemma's form. She doesn't seem to be hurt unless her stomach is cramping from all the laughter. "I'm glad you weren't injured."

Myrna practically hangs out of the side of the basket to get a better look, but it's not Gemma she's looking at. "I'd be willing to risk an injury to be carried by a firefighter."

I open the basket door to kick Myrna out. She's even less help than Larry.

Gemma beams at Thad once again. "Will you rip off your shirt if Myrna needs you?"

Thad glances warily at me. "No." Smart man.

"Jokes aren't as funny a second time." My tone removes all humor.

My less-than-joyous demeanor dampens Gemma's mood, and her giggles trail off into a long exhale. "Thanks again, Thad."

"My pleasure." He salutes me.

I turn my head to keep them both from seeing my sarcastic eye roll. My best attempt at using a trigger guard.

Myrna exits the bucket and joins the firefighting fan club.

The basket shakes at Larry's exit. "Tough break, brother."

I'm not sure which part of his statement to find more offensive. That he believes he can call me brother or that he assumes my relationship with Gemma is broken. And to think I'd been looking forward to seeing her tonight.

"Sorry your vacation got interrupted, Thad," I call. Hint, hint. Go somewhere you're wanted—like camping with mountain lions, mosquitoes, and rattlesnakes. "Gemma, hop in."

I need my trigger guard right now more than ever. I don't want either of us to get injured here. Friendly fire is the most painful because it should be the most preventable.

She nods at me, then looks down at the coat she's still wearing and the helmet in her hands.

"Here." Thad reaches for his uniform, coming to her rescue yet again.

"Thanks." She hands it over and gives me a measuring glance before stepping into the basket.

I quietly lock the door and press the button to lift us high enough for the breeze to cool me off. We rise above the top of the tower and come to a stop. It's peaceful up here. Or at least it should be.

I fold my arms and lean against the side of the basket. I feel vulnerable, and not because I'm suspended a hundred feet in the air.

She's quiet, staring over the edge toward the ground. I imagine that normally she'd be gushing in awe over the view or taking advantage of our moment alone by melting into my arms. I would much rather she be doing one of those things.

I extend an olive branch. "Sorry about that."

Her gaze slides to mine, though her face doesn't move. "I thought you would get a chuckle over the shirtless thing since you made such a big deal out of it at our first class."

I exhale. Best I can do. "It *is* ironic."

She lifts her chin, now studying my face as if to get a better read. "How so?"

I don't want to tell her, but I need to have told her. I tried Saturday night, but she'd assumed we were talking about my mom, and that was a heavy enough conversation for our first date.

She holds out a hand in a half shrug. "I thought you were scared of relationships because of the way your mother left, but what does that have to do with Thad?"

I shake my head at our situation. Of all the places for us to have this conversation. But I can't let my wound fester between us any longer. "The firefighters didn't use to be part of our safety program. It was only citizen's *police* academy."

Her eyes flick to the tower and back. "Okay . . . ?"

"One of the women in our PR department thought it would be good for our image if we partnered with the fire department."

She nods like I was hoping she wouldn't. "I can understand that," she says.

My stomach twists, forcing out a grunt.

She peeks at my expression, trying to read ahead. "So now you have a rivalry. I think that's pretty common."

I run a hand over my face. There's nothing common about it. "That woman who made the suggestion was my wife."

Her hand drops to her heart, and her eyes widen in horror rather than their normal innocence.

Silence hangs between us. I need her to respond, so I know what direction to go with this. I hate that I'm in this position. I hate that the first woman I loved put me here, and the woman I'm falling in love with might judge me for it.

"You . . . you've been married?" Gemma barely whispers.

This is what I was afraid of. I shake my head and look away, trying to hold back the rage that threatens to turn me into the Hulk. "Yes."

"Yes? Then why did you shake your head? You just shook your head."

Ever the optimist, Gemma hears me say I was married but wants to believe she heard wrong. She's a dreamer, but this situation is a nightmare.

"I shook my head because you're going to break up with me now." I wait for her to end it. I don't want her to end it, but if I expect the worst, then I won't be disappointed. That's what I'd been trying to do from the very beginning.

She doesn't deny it. Instead she says, "Where's your wife now?" She looks over the bucket toward the ground, as if one of the women below is my ex, though I'm pretty sure Myrna is the only single lady in the parking lot. "Did she leave you for a firefighter? Did she leave you for Thad? Is that why you're triggered?"

Why does Gemma have such an overactive imagination? I hate that the idea even enters her mind. Is it because she sensed my animosity or because *she* would leave me for Thad? "No, she didn't leave me for Thad."

Her eyes fly to my ring finger, as though she suspects I ran off and got married in Vegas since the last time we saw each other, and this is how I chose to tell her. "I know you were single when I signed up for your class. I made sure."

I'm lucky she didn't have access to background checks the way I do. "What happened?"

With the way her mind concocts scenarios, I should just let her keep going until the truth is mild in comparison. But maybe she'll *actually* stick with me through the hard stuff the way my wife had vowed to.

I take a deep breath to help rip off the Band-Aid. "She was in PR, like I said. I don't know if she chose that career because she was all about image, or she cared so much about image because of that career. It doesn't matter now." I'm rambling. So I get to the point. "But once she saw how much the community praised firefighters and despised policemen, she begged me to change careers."

Gemma's lips separate. She blinks. "She didn't leave you for a firefighter. She left because she wanted *you* to become a firefighter?"

It sounds ridiculous. But it didn't start that way. "It started with the suggestion of a career change. Then she started giving me statistics on how dangerous it is to be a policeman, which I know. But it got to the point that anytime something bad happened, we'd have a big blowup."

Her eyes bulge wider. Her hands drop to her stomach, and I'm a little afraid she's going to get sick and barf on everyone below. "That's why your grandparents were worried about me not wanting you to be on the police force."

I'd been hoping she wouldn't catch onto that. "Yes."

"Oh . . ." She breathes, which is a good sign. It will keep her knees from buckling and her body from toppling over the edge into Thad's waiting arms. "I thought your family was excited to meet me because I was the first woman you'd taken home. I was way off."

No wonder she's having trouble taking this in. I wish I'd better set up her expectations, but it's not as though I didn't try to scare her away. "Yeah. Sorry about that." At least Gemma knew and approved of my career coming into this. No shock there.

She bites her lip. "Did you consider changing careers?"

I snort at the suggestion and at hearing it from Gemma's lips. "I did. Like an idiot."

Her eyebrows pinch together.

I guess my response sounds a little harsh. She'll want to know that I'm able to make sacrifices, but the issue was never based on my commitment level. "Once the whole defund-the-police thing happened, I realized her problem with my job was never about me or my safety." The thought still makes me want to beat up my punching bag. I was out there, risking my life to defend the city, having friends and coworkers quit for their safety, and all the time being ripped apart in the media for something other people did. While my wife only cared about how it made her look.

Gemma tilts her head away, her eyes skeptical. "How do you know it wasn't about your safety?"

I look past her to the cemetery across the street. I don't want to have to bury a relationship, yet I feel so helpless to save it. Again. "I overheard Amber talking with Thad. She asked him to convince me to apply to work with him." Pent-up fury curls my fingers into fists. I still wish I would have punched him when he'd approached me to try. "She told him that she wanted to quit her job to become an influencer on social media, but she couldn't do that with me still working for the police force."

I lift my gaze to Gemma to measure her empathy. Her eyes are as cloudy as the sky at the Oregon Coast. There's a storm coming, but will the tears rain down for me or for herself?

I'll finish saying what I have to say. Then there might be nothing left to say other than goodbye. "After I confronted Amber about talking to Thad, she gave me an ultimatum. She said if I didn't quit the force, our marriage was over."

Gemma slides her hands over her head and holds back the loose hairs that escaped her braid. "You didn't quit?"

I shrug. "I didn't become a police officer for the image. Or the power. Or even a hero complex. I did it to prevent other moms from following in the footsteps of my mother. I did it to protect kids from the pain I went through."

"I know." She reaches a hand to my forearm, and the gentle touch waters my parched soul. We are still connected. There is still hope.

I can't help it. I close my eyes in relief. "I figured that if our marriage depended on giving up my passion and purpose to make her look good, then it wasn't much of a relationship to begin with. I suggested a separation, not realizing she would move on to someone else rather than work on us."

There's still a line between her eyebrows.

I rest my hand on top of hers to comfort her the way she comforted me.

But her eyes don't meet mine. Rather, they slide past me to the tower and the fire engines below.

"So that's why . . ."

"Why what?"

Her gaze leaps back to mine. The clouds have been swept away, but the lightning of panic flashes. "Why you were triggered by me in the beginning. Why you didn't want anything to do with me. You thought I only cared about my image the way your ex did."

"Guilty." I hold up my hand as if I'm being tried in a court of law. "But now I know that you're not—"

"Do you?" she demands, though I'm not sure what she's demanding because I didn't even finish my sentence. She snatches her hand away. "You were triggered when Thad carried me out of the building because you were comparing me to your ex again."

"Right." We just went over that. I'm trying to connect the dots that took her from consoling to accusing.

"I didn't do anything wrong." Her tone is pleading for some reason.

"I know." I'm not blaming her of anything. I'm explaining why I'm triggered.

She waves her arms wildly. "That's between you and Thad. It has nothing to do with me." Her mouth opens and closes a few times before I hear her say, "I can't . . . I can't . . ."

I inhale sharply. "You can't what?" My chest constricts as though the drawbridge to my heart is being raised. I don't want to have to put my armor back on.

She covers her face with her hands. "I can't believe I've put myself in a relationship where I'm being compared to someone else again."

This isn't happening. Though I should have known. I should have listened to my intuition. It's my fault for letting her enter in the first place. "So you don't want to be in this relationship?"

Her hands drop. Her eyes plead with me to understand, but it's as if she's on the other side of the moat, just standing there as the bridge rises and the gap widens between us. "I didn't say that."

"What *are* you saying?"

She looks down at the imaginary crocodiles that keep her from swimming to me. "It's a lot to take in. I mean the divorce is one thing, and I think I could get past that. My dad was divorced before he married my mom."

I didn't know that about her. There's still a lot I don't know. I long to know more. And she just said she could get passed my divorce, which is more than Bree had said. But her tone isn't hopeful. "Okay . . . ?"

"I'm saying I don't want to be compared."

My chest rises and falls, and I try to get ahold of my breathing. "Are you jealous? Because you have nothing to be jealous of."

"No." She bites her lip. "I honestly wish you would have had a better relationship with your ex. For you. For her."

I throw my hands up. Of all the potential responses to my confession of divorce, I didn't expect this. If she wanted me to have a better relationship with my first wife, then why is she acting jealous? I shake my head. "It would be stupid of me *not* to compare possible future relationships with a relationship that failed."

"Why?" Her chin crumples. "So you can leave me too when I fail? I'm human. It's going to happen."

My drawbridge halts. My heart wants to connect again. "Gemma . . . I'm not going to leave you."

"If I prove myself," she adds. "You're not going to leave me if I prove myself."

How did we get here? I don't want her to feel as though she has to prove anything. I just want to know she's a sure thing.

"I'm tired of trying to prove myself," she whispers, and the words are carried away like bubbles in the wind before I can pop their implied accusation. "I already feel like I failed simply because I tripped and was rescued by the man who also tried to help your wife. You're angry even though I didn't do anything wrong."

I rub a hand over my face. "I'm trying to use my trigger guard."

"Your weapon is still pointed toward me."

I picture myself on the SWAT team, clearing a house. In such instances, I keep my gun pointed ahead of me until I know I'm safe. There may be innocent people inside the house, at which point I would lower my weapon, but not until I remove any potential threat. I'm not sure how this is any different. "So what now?"

Her lips turn down and her eyes apologize. This is the expression of compassion I'd wanted to see earlier. But not in this moment. "I need time to process."

"Of course you do." Because she's such a sweet woman, she's not going to come right out and say the harsh words required for breaking up. I look down and shake my head. I'm angry at myself.

"Karson, I care about you. This is just a lot to take in."

I hit the button to lower us toward the parking lot. "I get it."

She reaches for my arm. The gentle connection is probably meant to soothe, but it's like the thread holding a kindergartner's tooth from naturally falling out. It needs to be yanked away.

"You want me to see where you're coming from, but do you see where I'm coming from?" she begs, as though I'm asking too much of her. "How would you feel if I had an ex-husband I'd left, and I got upset every time you did something that reminded me of him?"

I snort at the unfairness of her comparison. At the unfairness of life. "I'd punch him."

She gives a sad smile. "If punching your ex is all it took to fix us, I'd do it."

I ache for her all over again. "No, you wouldn't."

"Because it's going to take more than that."

"What's it going to take?" I slow our descent. We're almost to the ground, and there's a group of wannabe firefighters waiting for their turn. I'm going to have to let Gemma go.

"I need some time to think about it."

I know my fear of losing her is what's driving her away, but I don't know how to stop it. "Okay."

And she told me she wasn't going to hurt me.

CHAPTER TWENTY

GEMMA

Heroes act in spite of their fear, while the rest of us
act because of our fear.
—Jonathan Lockwood Huie

It's a good thing I'd finished my screenplay in a week because since my ride in the basket with Karson, I've been doing nothing but comparing myself with the woman he left. I don't know much about her, but that makes this even worse. Because I possess the world's biggest imagination.

I told Karson I wasn't jealous of Amber, but I am a little actually. She got to marry the man of my dreams, and she wasted the opportunities I would have savored.

I'm not one to moon over men, so I didn't plan to be all dramatic and depressed. It's just that since I found out about Karson's divorce, I've spent so much time every morning trying to figure out how to fix us that by the time I get myself up, it's bedtime again. Not that I've been sleeping well, but bed is a good escape from my roommates' worried expressions and sad attempts at cheering me up.

Here it is, the following Tuesday, and I have yet to decide if I'm going back to class. I want to see Karson, to see if he's struggling as much as I am. But if he's still not over Amber, then I shouldn't expect him to regret ending our three-day relationship. How naive that I'd been obsessing about the redhead he'd taught how to shoot, when he'd actually promised to love someone else forever.

I'm so focused on comparing myself to Karson's ex that I don't really care anymore about being compared to my sister. In fact, she might have some more psychological insight to offer. So I drop by her monstrosity of a house before heading to the fire station with the excuse of an early birthday gift for Forrest. Also, since I'd gotten him an RC police cruiser, I need to get it out of my bedroom to help me stop thinking about my favorite policeman.

I step into the shaded entryway, knock on Jewel's door, then stand there feeling dumb. I didn't even check to see if the kids were here or at their dad's.

The sound of slapping little feet floods my senses with tingles of relief.

"Hey, kiddos," I yell. "It's me."

Excited screeching reaches my ears. At least someone is happy to see me today. I don't expect their mom to react with such enthusiasm. And maybe not even Karson . . . if I go to class.

Their feet pitter-patter away, and I wait for Jewel to climb the stairs. She wasn't in the back yard below. I already checked.

The door swings open before I get the chance to rehash the entire fire truck basket scene in preparation for telling Jewel about it. I'm good at reading my stories from different people's perspectives, so I'm trying to consider what my story will sound like from hers.

"This is a surprise," she says, but I don't think that will sum up her thoughts about what happened with Karson. I'm kicking myself for how surprised I'd been.

I hold up the fuzzy turquoise gift bag with giant googly eyes. It looks like a Muppet, and though I'm not sure kids these days know about Muppets anymore, they can still appreciate googly eyes on a gift bag. "I couldn't wait to bring Forrest his birthday present."

Jewel tilts her head with suspicion.

Forrest dances in the background. It's a bouncy, butt-wiggle of a dance. I've always wanted my own butt-wiggling children, but I don't see how that will be happening anytime soon. I wanted to give a relationship with Karson a go, but then I think about his ex and I want to run the other way.

"What'd you get me?" Forrest shouts. He must not remember his last birthday and how opening presents works.

"It's a car," I joke, even though that's what it really is. "You're turning sixteen and will be old enough to drive, right?"

Forrest wrestles to hold his thumb down with the opposite hand so only his four fingers remain upright. "I'm gonna be this many."

"Oh, that's right. Silly me."

"Silly Aunt Gemma."

Daisy charges over and tries to peek inside the gift bag. I should have thought to bring her something too. As I always shared my sister's birthday, I never experienced being left out when my sibling opened gifts. Though that didn't stop me from wanting what she got when her toy was bigger or her clothes cooler.

"Daisy, that's not your gift," Jewel admonishes, then pulls the girl back so there's room for me to enter. "Come in, Gemma. If you'd told me you were stopping by tonight, I would have made a cake. Not that you would have eaten any."

Comments like that usually make me as nauseous as gluten, but I already felt sick when I got here so . . . "No cake necessary."

I precede them down two levels to the boxy modern living room with its blue velvet sofas and sparkly chrome chandelier. Taking a seat in front of the slate fireplace, I clasp hands around my knees.

Jewel eyes me as if she thinks I should lie down on the couch like a patient. She doesn't say anything, though that could be because I wouldn't be able to hear her over all the noise my niece and nephew are making.

Both kids are wearing swimming suits, and the house smells meaty, like Hamburger Helper. I interrupted a day in the life of a mom.

"Can I open my present now, Mom? Can I open it?"

Jewel shrugs. "That's why Aunt Gemma's here," she says with more than a tinge of skepticism.

Sometimes I hate our twin ESP. Though it's probably why she got into psychology in the first place. She likes being able to read other people's minds.

I avoid her eyes when handing over the gift.

Forrest turns it upside down, and out falls the box onto a floor that looks like wood but is actually as hard as tile. For the first time in my life, I'm thankful for overpackaging. At least Forrest didn't rip up the bag with the Muppet's face.

"It *is* a car," Daisy squeals.

"Awesome!"

Daisy is older and faster, so she beats him to the box. But as the good big sister that she is, she holds up the picture for him to see. "It's a police car."

There goes my twin's all-knowing eyebrow again.

"Can I drive it, Mom? Can I?"

"Outside."

The siblings pretty much spin out the sliding glass door in a whirlwind reminiscent of the Tasmanian Devil from Looney Tunes. Daisy slides it shut, and suddenly it's quiet.

Jewel gets up from the couch and crosses the room to open the stainless-steel refrigerator behind her white marble island. "Want something to drink?"

I flop back into comfy cushions to stare at the chandelier and contemplate the beverages I know she has in her fridge. If I chose a certain one of them, attending tonight's class wouldn't be an option anymore. Tempting. "I'll take a Coke Zero."

A can pops and soda fizzes. "Did you eat dinner?"

I try to remember the last time I ate. Usually I cook my meals fresh, but I haven't had the energy lately. Oh yeah. Kai microwaved frozen zoodles and meatballs and then smothered them in marinara. He must have been really worried about me. "Yes." I'd forced down a few bites anyway.

A tinny police siren makes me jump. Just the RC car. Jewel's going to hate me for that.

She sets my drink on the glass coffee table with a clink, then drops down across from me with the squoosh of cushions. "Why are you really here?"

I groan and sit up straight to reach for my Coke. "Karson is divorced."

Both her eyebrows shoot up this time. "So that's why he's angry."
I reach for the glass, slick with condensation, and guzzle its cool sweetness as if it's the drink I'd wanted to ask for. "I think it started before that. His mom had a drug addiction and took off. He was raised by his grandparents."

Jewel looks out the window at her children. "That's rough." She may not be the best mom on the planet, but she's here for her kiddos. "He's got abandonment issues then."

With that thought, my heart bleeds for Karson even more. It makes me want to be there for him, but will he be there for me in return? "He asked for a separation from his wife when she gave him the ultimatum of quitting the police force or getting a divorce. If he knew the pain of abandonment, why wouldn't he fight for her? Why would he give up?"

Jewel twists her lips as she studies me. "What reason does he give?"

I sigh. It is a sad story, but it could have had a happy ending. "He said she cared more about her image than him."

"Huh." Jewel nods slowly. "Perhaps he felt abandoned again, so he was going to get her before she got him. Probably thought he was protecting himself."

I slump. That's what I'd been afraid of. "He compared Amber to his mom, and now he's comparing me to Amber. I don't really have a chance, do I?"

Jewel tilts her head and narrows her eyes. "Why is he comparing you to Amber?"

"He assumed I was all about image at first."

She looks me up and down and doesn't disagree.

"And then the thing with Thad triggered him."

Her lips press together before she asks, "Who's Thad?"

I take a deep breath. Jewel is not the first person I run to with my embarrassing stories, but I did come here for help. "Well, I tripped when I was trying to rescue a dummy from a smoke-filled room—"

"I'm not even going to ask." She narrows her eyes as though she'd prefer to judge me as cuckoo than actually listen to an explanation of why this was a perfectly sane thing to do.

I expected as much from her. Whatever. "Thad is the firefighter who carried me to safety."

"Gemma." She covers her face and leans forward with her elbows on her knees. Her shoulders shake in laughter.

I sit up straight and flail my arms. Why did I think she'd be any help? "I hope you don't treat your clients like this."

"I'm sorry." She wipes her eyes. "It's just that every woman in the world would love to have your problems."

"You haven't even heard the problem yet."

"Okay." She clamps one hand over her mouth and motions for me to continue with the other hand.

I wait to see if she's going to bust out laughing again. When she doesn't, I look to heaven and share the story. It's not as if our situation can get any worse. I sigh and finish with, "I want to be with Karson, but I don't want to be compared to his ex."

She removes her hand to say, "Okay," again. It's a serious tone and her expression has sobered to match it. "People with abandonment issues often throw the baby out with the bathwater."

This isn't the answer I wanted. It's not even hopeful. "What can I do to fix him?"

"Nothing."

Why in the world did I pick her as the mentor character of my life story? "I don't believe you."

"Because you don't want to believe me, or because the truth hurts?"

I sit up straight, indignant. "Because I write romance, and I know love always wins." But does it? I'm single. And I haven't sold any of my romantic comedy scripts yet. I'm certainly no expert.

Jewel smiles sadly. "Love is letting other people make decisions for themselves. Even when it's not what we want. Even when they make bad choices out of brokenness. You can invite them into a healthy relationship, but that requires you working on yourself enough to know you'll be okay without them if they won't do the work needed to get themselves healthy. Doing the work for them is not love. It's enabling their unhealthy behavior."

That's not how any of my scripts end. That's not how any of my favorite movies end. There's always some grand gesture. Like when Noah restored the old house for Allie in *The Notebook*. I know that wasn't the healthiest relationship, but they spent the rest of their lives together. Literally. "Don't people like Karson need to be loved in order for their brokenness to be healed?"

Jewel smiles sadly. "They already are."

I open my mouth to argue, but she's got me there. Because I know she's talking about Jesus. My mean, selfish, worldly sister is preaching to me, and I hate that she's right. I want Karson to need me too. But that's my own brokenness.

"Karson's ex-wife made an unhealthy demand of him out of her fears. That hurt him, so he made unhealthy choices out of his own fears. They might not be the wrong choices, but they are unhealthy because they're driven by fear." Jewel dispenses more stupid wisdom.

How is it she can know these things in her head and not live them from her heart? How can I?

"Trying to fix Karson isn't going to fix anything."

I huff and look out the window at Daisy teaching Forrest to drive the police car. It'd been barely over a week since I watched Karson racing a similar car with his nephew.

He'd become my hero when he came to my house to protect me, and it was that very job that separated him from his first wife. Is what brought him to me also going to separate us? Was this really all for nothing?

"Karson has reasons to be hurt and angry, but if he doesn't let go of that pain, it's going to haunt his current relationships. He'll be too busy protecting himself to fulfill his purpose of protecting others."

I close my eyes. There's a reason people don't like preachers. They speak some hard truths.

"All you can do is work on you. For example, if there's any truth to Karson's concerns, you start there."

I stand with a dramatic groan. "I'm so tired of being compared to others."

"Tell me about it," she deadpans.

We make eye contact then. The kind that says no matter how different we are, maybe we can relate to one another.

I also have the deep sense that these truths she's speaking, she's learned from experience. Maybe she regrets her choices that led to divorce. And maybe she loved her husband enough to let him go.

Boy, that messes with my view of the world. I take a deep breath and look at my twin.

Even though it's too late for her marriage, maybe it's not too late for the two of us. We've both definitely got some fears to overcome.

I'll focus on our issues later. Right now I have to decide whether I'm going to safety academy or not.

"Isn't there anything else I can do?"

She smooshes her lips together as if she has an answer she doesn't want to speak. Which means it has to be good.

"What?"

Small smile. "You could date Thad instead."

CHAPTER TWENTY-ONE

KARSON

*They say everyone's born a hero. But if you let
it, life will push you over the line until you're the
villain. Problem is, you don't always know that
you've crossed that line.*

—JESSICA JONES

I don't have to be here tonight. I'm not sure why I'm torturing myself. Maybe because I still have stupid hope.

No, I'd been right to be wary all along. I knew to trust my gut. And my gut said Gemma was trouble. I'm here for the same reason I take hot showers with a sunburn—to get the sting over with.

I don't even have to see Gemma to know she's arrived. It's obvious by the way the company of firefighters goes on alert. They stand straighter and punch each other. Does she even realize what a stir she causes with every single entrance? If I'd been afraid of losing Amber, then I should be terrified with Gemma.

I'm not going to avoid her though. I take a deep breath, cross my arms, and look over.

Her eyes are on me, scratching the itch of my heart.

I wish I'd at least kissed her goodbye. Though it wouldn't have been one of her happy kisses.

Charlie and Kai flank her, and I've got their eyes on me as well. Charlie's are wide and demanding, while Kai's glare. Seriously? This isn't a shower for my sunburn. It's a blast from a fire hose.

"I'm glad to see you moving on," Thad says from behind me. Like he has any right at all to comment on my love life.

I roll my eyes his way. "You looked like you were interested in dating Gemma last week."

"You mean when I carried her out of the smoke-filled building and she couldn't keep from talking about you?"

I study him hard.

He holds his hands up as if he's getting read his rights. "You're the muse for the screenplay she's writing."

Gemma's little posse joins the circle of students gathering around mats and dummies in the parking lot, and I warn Thad with my eyes to end the conversation.

"Hey," she says from my right side, and I know she's talking to me even though I can't see her.

I hate that Thad is here to witness our awkward interaction.

I turn my back on him to face Gemma. "Hey." I can't think of anything else to say except to remark on what a cool and overcast day it is, but I've never been the type of person to make small talk about weather.

"Hey," Thad echoes. Worse than just eavesdropping, he's joining the conversation. "Kinda cloudy today, huh?"

I look away and accidentally make eye contact with Kai's glare. Man, that guy holds a grudge. Or is he mad about something else now? Something Gemma told him? She's the one who needed time to "process." He should be glaring at her for ending our relationship. He should be glaring at her for even starting it. She got the cops called on him in the first place last year. I almost wish we'd never been called.

Almost.

Gemma glances up at the sky in question, as if she hadn't noticed the clouds until now. "Is it?"

I can't help huffing a laugh at the irony of her not noticing the clouds.

She frowns at me, her light eyes searching mine as though she wants to reconnect. "What?"

I want to hide behind my shield of anger, but it's hard to be angry with someone who's so likeable. "It's kind of funny that you didn't notice the clouds when your head is always in them."

Her bottom lip juts into the sweetest of pouts, though I'm not sure why this would hurt her. First of all, she knows it to be true. Second, I used to say stuff like this to her all the time, yet it never deterred her from pursuing me.

I pinch my eyes shut. Because honestly, it was a cruel thing to say, and I'd said it for that very reason. It's what I do.

"Let's get started." Lieutenant Rodriguez calls us to attention. "Barker's going to be demonstrating CPR for us today. Barker?"

Thad jogs to the center of our circle.

I glance at Gemma to see if she's watching him, but her gaze locks with mine. In spite of the joke I'd just shared at her expense, there's no anger reflected in her light eyes. There's no shield up to protect her from me. She's just as open and transparent as ever.

And I don't get it. I tried to teach her self-defense.

My heart rams at the wall I've built around it. Maybe I was wrong about her. She's not like Amber. She's not stuck on image.

When class is over, I'll tell her I'm sorry. She needs me to take my finger off the trigger. It's not about fighting for her. It's about raising my hands in surrender.

"Can I get a volunteer?" Thad's words cut through the heavy silence between us.

Gemma's still looking at me, but her eyes narrow into defiance. I didn't wave my white flag soon enough, and now she's going to destroy me. "I will," she offers.

Thad's gaze flicks my way. He gives a little shrug in place of the apology he owes me for ganging up on me with my ex. "Sure, Gemma."

She tosses her hair and sashays to join Thad.

When she moves, I'm now in Kai's and Charlie's lines of sight. Kai shoves his hands in his pocket and lifts his eyebrows as though he'd seen this coming all along. Charlie shakes his head as if he can sadly relate, though with how competitive the guy is, I doubt it. He has to be simply offering pity.

I don't need their judgments. I turn away, only to be faced with the image of Gemma kneeling on a mat across the creepy plastic dummy from Thad.

He shows her how to interlace her fingers and lock her arms when pressing the heel of her hand into the dummy's sternum. "Now if you're doing CPR on your own, you give rescue breaths after every thirty compressions, but if there are two of you, you can work as a team."

Her gaze lifts to mine. Though the two of us are opposites, that's what made us a good team.

"After every fifteen compressions, I'm going to blow two breaths. Ready, Gemma?"

She's got her arms locked into position, but she's still looking at me. Her chest rises and falls as if someone's doing rescue breathing on her, and this little itch in my palms makes me think she's not going to answer him.

But then she lifts her chin. "I've been ready," she says, and I know she's referring to the conversation we had before kissing.

Message received. She's leaving me behind.

That's it. I turn and walk away.

CHAPTER TWENTY-TWO

GEMMA

She preferred imaginary heroes to real ones,
because when tired of them, the former could
be shut up in the tin kitchen till called for,
and the latter were less manageable.
—LOUISA MAY ALCOTT

I hadn't meant to make Karson feel bad last week. I just wanted him to feel what it was like when he compared me to someone else, but I, of all people, should know better. I was acting like Jacob, flaunting my preference for Joseph with a coat of many colors. It was bound to backfire.

I'd like to be able to blame my evil twin, but she suggested dating Thad, not using him to make Karson jealous. Jewel had actually given some good advice that night. Good, but not welcome. Why is the good advice always so hard?

I should have treated Karson with respect, even if I didn't agree with his choices. That's how Jewel described love. Instead, my actions practically proved him right. I cared more about myself than him.

Though it might be too late for us to work things out, I need to apologize for my part. For hurting him when I said I wouldn't. For not being who he deserved. So I'm back at the fire station for another class.

We're supposed to be driving the fire trucks tonight. I wore my Nikes instead of heels in hopes Karson notices and it reminds him of how I wore Erin's ugly shoes to drive the police car.

"Now, Gemma," Charlie chides. He's still a little bitter from how I lost him the smoke-filled-room race. "You can't drive a fire truck like you do a cop car."

I think I nod, but I'm too busy straining my neck in search of Karson to make eye contact or respond verbally. A man in a black police uniform exits the firehouse, and my pulse surges forth like the men in *Braveheart* heading into battle.

Except the dude is African American. And he's ripped. "Drew?"

The policeman turns my way and smiles as if he doesn't know my day will be ruined if he tells me Karson asked him to come in his place. "Hey, Gemma. You ready to race fire trucks?"

A thread of hope holds my heart together. "Did you come just to see how fast I can weave through cones?"

"I did, I did." He rubs his big hands together. "And Zellner asked me to fill in for him. He couldn't make it tonight."

The pieces of my heart are unthreaded in one quick yank.

"Come here, girl." Drew puts his beefy arm around me. He must have read the expression on my face and figured it has something to do with Karson. "Nobody is a hero all the time. We're just all in training."

I look up at his dancing eyes. He's a cop. He should believe in good guys and bad guys. But instead, he makes it sound as if none of us are anything without redemption.

"Now, you ready to drive a fire truck?" Drew moves on as if the only training he's been talking about is Citizen's Safety Academy, though I know better. He points at Charlie. "Your roommate over there seems to want your group to go first."

"I do." Charlie walks backward toward the red truck, waving for me to follow. "Let's go, Gemma."

I force a smile. These people made the effort to be here with me, so I need to stop focusing on the one who didn't.

Since Charlie is driving first, Kai and I have to climb up some diamond-pattern metal steps to an area in the back of the cab with bench seating. It's small and uncomfortable and smells like the grease in a mechanic shop. I'm not sure how big men in thick gear fit back here, but I take my spot next to some kind of equipment locker and pose for all Kai's pictures. Then I watch through a small window as Thad instructs Charlie on how to turn the giant steering wheel to maneuver this rig around orange cones.

There was a time when I would have looked forward to my turn behind the wheel. Especially if Karson was here, crossing his arms and smirking at me. Oh man, I miss his smirk.

Charlie shifts into park, opens his door, and calls to me. "Okay, Gemma. I only knocked over one cone. See if you can beat that."

"Ignore him." Kai waves Charlie away. "This is your chance to research for the script you're writing. Just imagine yourself as Sandra Bullock in *Speed*."

I press my lips together because there's no arguing with that. "I'll do Sandra proud."

Thad watches Charlie and me trade places. "That's so cool you write movies. Would I know anything you've written?"

"No." I shake my head and stare off into space.

Kai raps on the window between us. "She's a good writer," he says.

Except how would he know? He's all about the visuals.

"She just hasn't found her niche yet," Charlie states before climbing up the steps behind me to join Kai.

I grimace. While my roommates are trying to be encouraging, they're just reminding me of something else I want that I can't have.

Thad nods along, as though it's cool to be an aspiring something when really the word *aspiring* just means you're nothing yet. "Oh," he says.

Yeah. *Oh*. As in zero. What my best efforts have amounted to.

"We believe in you, Gemma," Charlie calls.

"Thanks." I don't feel thankful. But maybe I'm just not focused like Karson used to say. If I were a computer, I'd have too many tabs opened. I need a good night's sleep to reboot.

I shake my hands loose to prepare for the role of firefighter, then turn the key in the red console and feel the engine sputter to life. There are a lot of buttons and gauges and a monitor that looks like a backup camera. I assume it's not a screen to control the radio. Well, not the kind of radio that plays music anyway.

I step on the brake and shift into drive. Looking through the giant windshield, I move toward the obstacle course of cones.

Thad does his best to direct me around the first few, but I cut the corners too tightly and pretty much knock them all down. I should have just plowed straight over them. Would have had the same effect, and I'd be done sooner. With two cones left, I decide to do just that.

The cab is silent when I shift into park.

"Wow, Gem," Kai deadpans. "It's a good thing those were cones and not pedestrians."

"Yeah." Charlie's eyes widen in horror. "Did you even try?"

I look over at Thad to find him scratching his head as if stunned by my lack of driving skills.

"Maybe you'd be better at . . ."

It's very kind how hard he's thinking to come up with something nice to say.

"Driving the back end of the fire engine."

"I'm sure that's the issue." Kai's words agree, but his sarcastic tone does not.

"If you didn't want to drive, you should have just said so." Charlie thinks anything that's not a competition is a waste of time. "Now trade places with Kai to see if he can beat my record of only knocking down one cone."

"Come on, Gemma." Thad opens his door. "I'll have the lieutenant take over with these guys, while I show you the steering wheel on the aft of the fire engine."

I'm happy to step out of the competition. I pull the handle to open my door and find a small group of firefighters watching me.

"It's a good thing you're pretty," teases the woman.

Yeah. That's really helping me out now. Especially when the rest of her crew starts laughing.

"Lieutenant." Thad circles the front of the fire truck. "I'm going to let you take over while I show Gemma how the tiller works."

One whoops. "I bet you are."

I look at Thad.

His gray eyes are clear of ulterior motives. "Come on."

By tiller, Thad means the tractor trailer truck long enough to hold the ladder. Because it's so long, there's a little cab on the back with a second steering wheel, or tiller. He motions for me to climb the steps on the side of the truck ahead of him. When we get to the top, he lets me sit behind the wheel while he pulls down a second seat like a theater seat. I assume it's for training new firefighters or for classes like this.

I wrap my fingers around the wheel, unsure of why he brought me here. "With how much Charlie likes to be a backseat driver, he would love this."

Thad chuckles. "I figured you needed a break from him."

I sigh at how transparent I am. "Yeah. If I'd driven myself to class, I would have just gone home. I'm kind of dealing with some stuff."

He nods knowingly. "Zellner, huh?"

"Zellner," I repeat with the tone Seinfeld used to say *Newman*. No matter how well Thad knows Karson, he must have known Amber better. "Where's his ex-wife now? You were friends with her, right?"

Thad gives a sad shrug. "We worked together for Citizen's Safety Academy. She shared that she thought the police job was getting to Zellner emotionally, and she hoped a career change would do him some good. She asked me to talk to him about becoming a firefighter, but apparently that didn't go over too well. I haven't seen her since, but I see her stuff on social media sometimes."

"Huh." That story sounded a little different from the one I'd heard. Though if she became an influencer, that career definitely has to do with image.

Thad looks down before meeting my gaze. "I didn't mean to upset Zellner when carrying you the other day. I never meant to one-up him or anything."

I shake my head. "It's not about you. It's not even about Amber. It's about him being able to see me for me."

"I appreciate that." He pats the steering wheel. "Relationships take the same teamwork as it does to drive this fire truck. While the pump trucks are shorter and easier to maneuver, this one has the ladder that's going to get you where you need to go, but you can't drive it without trusting another driver back here."

The analogy fits. It's the image of the kind of relationship I want to have. "That's really good. You could be a writer."

"Oh, I am," he says.

Man, maybe I should have fallen for him. He's perfect.

"I'm writing a chili cookbook for firemen."

Okay, there's no perfect man. I shake my head. "Not what I meant."

"I know, but love is like chili." He waggles his eyebrows. "Both are spicy."

I groan. "Painful."

"My joke or spicy chili?"

"Love." I give a little huff and wish it was a genuine laugh.

He winces in empathy. "I don't know if you believe in God, but His love is the only perfect love. It's the kind that redeems when the love we'd hoped to get from other people lets us down."

Even though I don't like it or know what that looks like for me, I have to agree. And perhaps my agreement itself is the beginning of healing. "Thanks for the reminder. Can I pay you to write my screenplay?"

He laughs for real. "Come on. I'll show you a few other trucks that you might be able to use in your movie."

We head into the station, where Thad points out different configurations of trucks. Besides holding water, they have compartments that hold equipment. And people. We climb the steps into the back of one cab similar to the truck I drove with my roommates.

A bell sounds. Thad jumps to attention. "I might have to go. Wait here while I check." He jogs away.

I guess that even though he's teaching a class, he still has to respond to emergencies. I look out the giant garage door to see if there's any smoke in the distance, but as the sky is already gray, it's hard to tell.

I'm ready to go home, but I have to wait for Kai and Charlie. And I don't want to get in the way of the sudden activity in the garage. Sinking back into the far cabinet seat, I wish Karson were here with me.

I wonder how he met Amber. Was it from working in the same office? Did they sit back here together at one of these classes? Did he teach her to shoot?

My stomach constricts at the idea of Karson romancing someone else, and I feel a little dizzy. I press a palm against the cool metal of the side of the interior, and it vibrates under my touch. I sway as the truck rolls forward. I guess they are letting my classmates practice driving this truck now.

A siren jolts me from the stories I'm mentally writing. I blink and peek around the equipment locker to look through the window into the driver's seat. It's not Charlie behind the wheel. It's someone else in full fireman garb.

I don't recognize the classmate driving, so I squint to try to place him. He's got a weird mustache. And he's heading the wrong way. He should be winding through cones, not taking off toward the street.

My pulse lurches as we bump onto the road and my reality sets in. I grip the edge of my seat.

My mind whirls like a tornado. Thad told me to stay put. *But I don't think we're in class anymore, Toto.*

Do I bang on the glass to get the driver to stop, or would that delay them from saving lives in time? How far could they be going? Will everyone be safer if I sit here and keep my mouth shut?

While I'd caused some trouble on the police side of Citizen's Safety Academy, I've never been in this much trouble before. I make Ramona the Pest look good.

CHAPTER TWENTY-THREE

KARSON

It turns out a hero's lot is not glory or reward,
but sacrifice.
—PITTACUS LORE

I took an extra shift to keep myself from giving in and going to Citizen's Safety Academy. I wanted to see Gemma, but I just couldn't see her with Thad again. Last week, my presence seemed to actually push her toward him.

Static crackles over my radio. "Any units in the area of Arlington Heights. Child hit by car."

My muscles react in spite of the way my extremities go numb. This is adrenaline. This is reflex. I'm shifting to pull onto the road before I even reach for the radio. I don't waste a second or a movement. And I don't even have to think about it. This is what I'm trained for. This is why I do this job.

"Copy." I respond with my designator number, beating a chorus of voices slower than mine. "Show me en route."

A map pops up on my GPS screen. I'm only four minutes from the location.

I hit my lights and siren, and step on the gas to weave around the cars that pull to the curb in front of me. My heart surges forward with images of my own nephew getting hit by a vehicle. I pray I'm not too late. I pray that whoever is with this child knows first aid or CPR if needed. I pray it's not needed.

My cruiser climbs into the hills, and I have to slow to make turns and avoid other vehicles parked on the side of the tiny roads. "Come on, come on, come on."

No wonder a child got hit up here. He or she could have run into the road after a ball, and a car rounding the corners wouldn't have seen the kiddo before it was too late.

My stomach churns at the horror of being the person behind the wheel who'd hit a kid. The driver will probably need medical attention as well. For emotional damage if not for physical.

That's it. I'm going to ramp up our campaign for speed bumps. I'm going to see if I can get the state to give away signs that say *Caution: Children Playing.* There's enough hurt from the evil in the world without adding in accidents. By focusing on bringing an end to the hurt of others, I can keep the focus off my own.

The blinking arrow on my screen shows only one more turn to reach my destination. All my senses go on high alert. I hold my breath, preparing for what I'm about to see.

I round the corner and scan the scene. Am I at the right place? There are no cars on the side of this road. There's only an empty driveway with a boxy, black garage hidden behind trees and shrubbery. Maybe an ambulance beat me here and has already left with the kid.

Oh wait. There are a couple of children in the shadow of the entry-way on the right side of the house. And there's a woman with them. A blond woman. Gemma.

My stomach turns over.

Gemma looks up, but there's no recognition in her eyes. She's frowning and waving me over. Could she be the one who actually got hit by a car, and now she has a concussion?

She doesn't seem herself. She's gained weight and cut her hair. Is she intentionally letting herself go to prove she's not about image?

The truth of the situation dawns on me. I'm in Arlington Heights. And if those kids are related to Gemma, then this woman in front of me is the evil twin. Though she doesn't look evil. She looks worried.

I open my door. "Did you call 911?"

"Yes." She scoops up the little girl in her arms. "Daisy got hit in the head by Forrest's RC car when he drove it off the side of the hill."

Hit by a car? I rub my temples and stride her way. I'd thought the twin sister thing was a lot to take in, but this? I'll check out the girl to make sure she's okay.

The woman holds a towel to the child's head. "It knocked her out, and I was afraid to move her when she was unconscious in case it was a spinal injury. She's awake now, but there's a lot of blood."

My pulse throbs louder at the possibility Gemma's niece is injured. "Head wounds do bleed a lot. I can administer first aid until an ambulance arrives."

Gemma's twin brushes her daughter's hair to the side to reveal a gash on her temple. "It's not as bad as I thought it was at first." Her light eyes peek up at me, familiar in their color and shape as well as the flicker of indecision. She's torn as to whether to be worried or embarrassed.

"You did the right thing," I say. And I hope for her sake that we will all be laughing about this later when what we thought was a car accident proves to be a false alarm.

There's a little blood still tricking from the cut, but nothing particularly alarming. The child whimpers, but her pupils aren't dilated or shaking. She seems less dazed than her mom does at the moment. Goodness, she seems less dazed than her aunt on a good day.

The boy hugs his mom's leg. "I'm sorry."

"It's going to be okay, kiddo," I console him before responding to his mom. "We'll have the EMTs take care of her. She might need a couple of stitches."

The blaring siren of a fire engine draws our attention to the road. I lift a hand to wave at Mac. He's going to be very relieved that the only car involved in this injury is too small to even be driven by a Barbie.

Speaking of Barbie, another blond comes bounding down the back steps of the fire truck, hair flying. Maybe I'm the one who hit my head in a car accident and am hallucinating because this couldn't actually be happening. There's no way Mac brought Gemma on the truck with them, even if she was at the firehouse and overheard the address of the emergency.

Mac's face pivots to follow Gemma's race across the lawn. His mouth hangs open in shock. So she stowed away.

I guess I shouldn't be surprised.

"What happened?" she yells before she reaches us. "Is Daisy hurt?"

The woman who is *not* Gemma sits on the step of the entryway with Daisy on her lap. "A car hit her."

"Oh no." Gemma kneels in front of her niece, hands on either side of the girl's cheeks. She shoots me a wild glance. "It's a good thing you're here, Karson. You have to go after the driver of the hit-and-run."

I press my lips together. There is no protocol for situations like this. How do I even respond?

Mac and another fireman in yellow join us, wide eyes probably reflecting my own bewilderment. "We didn't know she was on there," he insists.

I nod in understanding. After all, I've had Gemma in a class before.

Forrest stares in awe at the two men in uniform, fears for his sister forgotten. "You rode the fire truck, Aunt Gemma? That's awesome!"

"Yes." She wipes her niece's tears away and kisses her on the forehead. "And it's a good thing I did. Now I'm here for Daisy after she got hit by a car." She glances up at me. "Karson, why are you just standing here? Aren't you going to go track down whoever hit her?"

It would be really nice if the sister would clear all this up, but she's focused on the girl in her arms. I shrug at Mac and company, then plant a head on the little boy's shaggy head. "Found him."

Gemma does a double take to stare at her nephew in confusion. Her azure eyes finally jump to meet mine.

"It was an RC car," I say.

She stands and steps back, hand to her heart. "He hit her with the RC car I gave him?"

"Well, I didn't know that part, but yeah."

Forrest hangs his head. "Sorry, Aunt Gemma."

Gemma hugs the little boy. She's a good aunt. But seeing her with her twin drives home the point of why she doesn't want to put herself in a position to be compared with anyone else again.

I don't even mean to compare the two of them, but I've already had the thought that though her sister's not unattractive, it's obvious Gemma takes better care of herself. I've also had the thought that if her sister is making the kind of money it takes to still live here while paying child support, then it's no wonder Gemma feels the need to prove herself with her writing.

Her gaze seeks mine for help. I wish I could fix this, and I don't just mean the fact that there's another siren blaring louder.

An ambulance angles its way between my cruiser and the fire truck. Here come a third round of emergency workers needing an explanation. I don't envy them the paperwork this event is going to require, but the story is going to be repeated until it's folklore. If any neighbors are filming for TikTok, this thing could go viral. Kai's probably going to kick himself for not stowing away on the fire truck as well.

The EMTs surround Daisy, pulling out gauze and other medical supplies while she watches them for entertainment more than anything. She's going to be fine.

I kind of saunter around the crowd, making small talk with the firemen, though, honestly, I'm just trying to get to Gemma. I squeeze behind Mac and suddenly realize there's not much room between him and the siding of the garage for two people. I realize this because Gemma's the other person, and now we're wedged into a corner, facing each other.

I have more feelings than I can put into words. I default to "Hey."

"Hey," she says, but I read her eyes for all the things she's not saying. They pool with relief that her niece is not injured, waver with humiliation from arriving on a fire truck she shouldn't have been on, then settle with the sadness of a longing that will never be fulfilled.

It tugs me forward. "Come here." I wrap my arms around her and hug her to my chest. I'm using the trauma as an excuse to comfort her, but the truth is I probably need this more than she does.

Her body folds into mine, a reminder of how she's the perfect fit.

Then there's her silky hair tickling the back of my hands, and her fresh coconut fragrance making me wish we were on a tropical honeymoon. I breathe her in, but rather than kiss the top of her head like I want to, I glance over it to anchor myself in reality.

The EMTs take Daisy's temperature and listen to her heart. Mac speaks into his radio, probably letting the rest of the fire department know they can stand down. No Jaws of Life needed to extrapolate anyone from a totaled vehicle.

"This is almost as crazy as the first time I met you," I tell Gemma.

Her fingers fist the back of my shirt, and she squeezes me tighter. "You were mad at me then."

I nod at the memory. If I could have seen the future and how I'd ended up falling for her in spite of my better judgment, I would have been madder. "I knew you were trouble."

She huffs, and when she says, "Double trouble," she turns her cheek to my chest, which is going to look pretty funny on my body camera footage. I hold her tightly anyway, as she studies her sister. If she weren't a twin, would we be together right now? She wouldn't have been so sensitive about being compared to my ex.

Another siren squeals, though this sound is tinny and coming from the ground. I glance down to find an RC cop car circling our feet. This is the vehicle that caused so much trouble today? In a weird way, I'm touched.

"You bought your nephew a police cruiser like the one I got Phillip?"

She pulls away, cheeks flaming. "Oh. Yeah. You know, it fits the theme of the script I'm writing."

Right. Kissing me was nothing but research.

I release her since I'm working. And also, she wanted time to process. I cross my arms to keep from punching things.

I look away to find Gemma's twin watching me with those same icy eyes. Except she's the psychologist who has been psychoanalyzing my every action. I don't want her looking my way.

"Karson, have you met my sister?" Gemma steps between us before I can decide whether to tell the woman off or pretend to be pleased to make her acquaintance. "Jewel, this is the cop who taught the class I've been taking."

The woman holds out her hand. It's not as soft or strong as Gemma's. Man, I'm even comparing their hands. No wonder this drives Gemma crazy.

"I didn't realize you were Karson," Jewel says. "I've heard about you."

In a normal situation, her statement could be considered a compliment. But as I know she's heard about my anger issues, I feel attacked. Rather than play defense, I choose to put her on the offensive. "And I've heard about you."

She smirks. "Don't worry. I've documented my child support, so you don't have to arrest me."

It's probably not a good idea to get on the bad side of a psychologist, especially when she's your girlfriend's twin, but since Gemma and I aren't even really talking right now, I say, "Bummer."

Mac clears his throat. "Miss Bennett, I need to take your statement about how you ended up on my fire truck."

"Uh . . ." Gemma glances at me, and I'm not sure if the uncertain glimmer in her eyes comes from her upcoming attempt at an explanation or the concerns about leaving me with Jewel. Probably both. "All right," she says before stepping away to explain what has to be a pretty unexplainable story.

I look back at Jewel and jut my chin. She's the one who said my anger comes from fear, pain, or frustration, and with as frustrated as I am with her, she wouldn't like what I have to say.

"Anger is energy," she says. "It fuels you to act quickly and take control. It makes you good at your job."

I'm not sure where she's going with this. "That's what I've been trained to do."

"True. But not everyone who is trained to do the job does it as well as you. That's why you've excelled in your career."

I side-eye her because I don't want her to look straight into my soul. "Thanks?"

"You're welcome." She sets Daisy down so the girl can draw on the sidewalk with chalk. Obviously the girl is going to be okay. "I just want to warn you that every strength has a weakness."

That's more like it. Did she orchestrate the whole car fiasco to get me here for a counseling session? "Yeah?"

"There's a time for anger, but there's also a time for letting it go. And that time is when it gets in the way of relationships."

I cross my arms and look out to where Gemma is talking with Mac. How long is her report going to take? "It's not my anger in the way," I say. "It's Gemma's choice. After growing up being compared to you her whole life, she doesn't want to feel like she's competing against anyone else."

Jewel guffaws. "*She* didn't like being compared? She's the pretty twin."

I scrutinize her. Turnabout's fair play. "Did you really rig homecoming elections?"

"Oh my gosh. She's still talking about that?" Jewel rolls her eyes. "Yes, I did. But only because I didn't want to be left behind. She could coast on her looks, but I had to outwit her for anyone to notice me. I'm the only one who has a reason to be envious."

"Hmm." I arch my eyebrows. "There's a time for letting go. And that time is when it gets in the way of relationships."

CHAPTER TWENTY-FOUR

GEMMA

We do not have to become heroes overnight.
Just a step at a time, meeting each thing that comes
up . . . discovering that we have the strength to
stare it down.

—ELEANOR ROOSEVELT

Of all the places I could have accidentally ridden to on a fire truck, it brought me here. To my sister's house. To Karson. He doesn't seem happy about it, but he did comfort me in his arms. Then he had a conversation with my sister. And now he's striding across her lawn in my direction.

I suck in a deep breath and try to will away this shakiness of my limbs. I'm not sure if I'm trembling from the rush of the ride, the fear for Daisy, or withdrawals from my Karson addiction, but I hope that if my jitters don't settle, they'll at least get him to hold me again.

He stops a few feet away. "Do you need a ride?"

I glance over at Mac, climbing into the fire truck. I hadn't thought about whether I'd be allowed to return the way I came or not. I also hadn't worried about being stuck. I mean, this is my sister's house. But if Karson's offering . . . "Yes."

He nods and leads me to his cruiser. It feels as familiar as Meri's Jeep, and I hate to think this could be my last ride with him. But not every relationship ends in happily ever after, as Karson's ex-wife must know.

He opens the door like a gentleman, and I drop inside. As he walks around to the driver's side, I look out the window at my sister with her kids. She's watching us, and I wonder what she thinks of Karson in person.

Could she be interested in him? She's everything he wants, isn't she? Like me, but not so worried about appearances. Plus, they've both been married before, so they'd be on even ground. Wouldn't that just be a kick in the pants?

If they started dating, we'd be spending holidays together. It would be like she stole my homecoming crown all over again. But worse.

He joins me in the front, then radios into his precinct about taking me back to the fire station. I wasn't paying attention to what he said, but the response he gets from the dispatcher includes a couple of dumbfounded expletives.

He studies me from across the console, the intensity in his steely blue eyes turning them the color of gunmetal. He lifts the radio to his mouth. "My thoughts exactly."

The radio goes silent, leaving us to stare at each other. He's so close, and the car smells sweet and spicy like he does. It wouldn't take much to close the space between us. If we weren't surrounded by emergency workers, I'd like to think he would.

He hooks the radio back in its cradle and starts the engine without a word.

My pulse thunders. "Are you angry?"

"Am. I. Angry?" He says this as if it's a factual question, though his tone is tinged with emotion. He pulls away from the curb. "Do you mean am I scared, hurt, or frustrated? Because the answer to all those questions is yes."

I sigh and lean back in my seat. "I was scared too." My fear just doesn't come out the same way in me that it comes out in him. I'm more likely to cry. "But why are you hurt? Why are you frustrated?"

His jaw shifts as he maneuvers down the hill. "It hurts that my ex didn't only destroy what she and I had, but what I could have with someone else."

His pain knifes through me, and my breath escapes like a popped balloon. "Karson." He's hinted at this pain before but never shared it so vulnerably. Except she's not to blame. And actually blaming her is the very problem keeping us apart. Anything I do that reminds him of her will make him want to blame me.

He stops at a traffic light, and his tone deepens. "And I'm frustrated that your sister did such a number on you that you can't even consider giving me a chance."

I press a hand to my churning stomach in hopes of quelling the nausea. "It's not about my sister. It's not even about a second chance. We're damaged puzzle pieces that don't fit together anymore. I can't—"

"I know," he interrupts with a growl.

The light turns green. We drive in silence.

In what world would we have fit? I felt I'd known him the moment we met. I'd seen things to love about him that others hadn't. But the truth is that someone else loved him first, and that hadn't been enough for him, so how could I ever be?

"If we'd met first . . ." My voice breaks.

"It doesn't matter now." His voice goes hard. The rawness of his heart has been surrounded by a wall of stone. But it's still there. Still raw inside. Still throbbing with the ache of this perceived rejection.

The thing is that I don't want to reject him. I see so much potential in him. So much passion. So much strength and determination and protectiveness. But I just can't live the rest of my life in someone else's shadow. I've been there, done that.

"Karson," I whisper.

He pulls into the fire station as though he didn't hear me. Maybe he didn't. My noisy classmates are in a huddle, laughing and shouting. Charlie and Kai break free, waving and holding their arms out in shrugs as if to ask what happened to me. Such a good question.

"Get out, unless you want me to drive you home." Karson's eyes darken with challenge. If I let him drive me home, it would give us time alone, which would most definitely involve more of his angry kisses.

My lips part at the possibility. The more kisses he gives me, the harder it would be to stop kissing. While I do want to kiss, he knows those aren't the type of kisses I want. One of us would have to compromise, and no matter who it was, both our hearts would be broken. Though could it really be any worse than it is right now? "If I get out now, will I see you again?"

He faces forward. "No, Gemma."

I hate his armor. I hate that it makes him the villain of my story. If he'd just put down his weapons, it would give me some hope that we could call a truce.

Goodbye is inevitable, so I might as well say it now. He's not coming back to class. He's got nothing more to offer me. This is how his wife must have felt when he refused to change careers.

I reach for the door handle. "Goodbye."

My roommates start to give me a bad time about my ride on the fire truck, but when I don't laugh with them, their mirth subsides. I stare out the back window of the Jeep as their conversation turns to the film competition, and I'm filled with this inexplicable need to call my sister.

Jewel might offer some insight into Karson. After all, they'd spoken for a little while when I was giving my statement to the fireman. What did she think of him? Did she notice his anger? Did she see through it to the hero underneath?

"What do you think, Gemma?" Charlie interrupts my thoughts.

I blink and realize we're in our parking lot. "Sure," I say.

"Sure?" Kai's tone drips with condescension, and he twists around to challenge me with a look. "Sure, we can call our film *Lost Soles*, spelled S-O-L-E-S?"

I want to get out, but I'm stuck until Charlie opens the door. They have me captive, so I ponder the title aloud. "*Lost Soles*. Like the shoes got lost, but really, it's the innermost beings of our characters."

Charlie smacks Kai. "She gets it."

Kai studies me closer. "That's a little dark for you."

My soul feels dark, but I force a smile. "The pun lightens it."

Charlie nods emphatically. "The writer has spoken."

"Can the writer get out now?"

He pops his door and tilts the seat forward.

He's letting me go because he got his way, but I feel Kai's eyes follow me, and not because of the dumb movie name. I attempt a happy little wave so he can relax. "I'll see you at boot camp class in the morning."

Kai steps out from the driver's seat. "I'm not going to boot camp. I decided to start running again. It's been a while, so I'm doing the 'Couch to 10K' training program."

This time I pause to study him. He used to be a competitive runner, but after an injury, he gave up and pretty much dented our couch with his backside. Falling in love with Charlie's sister has spurred him into becoming a better person.

This would give me hope that a woman can change a man, except Meri left to pursue her own dreams in Africa. He's not doing it for her. He's doing it for himself.

If a person changes for another person, then is the change real? It wasn't in that Clint Eastwood movie where he played an alcoholic who only quit drinking and killing people until his wife passed away.

Obviously I'm not thinking about Clint or Kai. I'm thinking about Karson. Do I want Karson to let go of his anger just for me? No, I want it to be real. Like Kai's changes.

My voice is tiny when I squeak out, "I'm proud of you, Kai." Then I escape to my room.

I fall onto my bed and stare at the vaulted ceiling. I want to call my sister to hear what she has to say about Karson. I just don't want to hear her say it to me because she's sure to use her mean voice.

I dig my phone out of my purse and click on contacts. I stare at my photo of Jewel with Forrest and Daisy. She's like me, but she's made something of herself.

She has multiple degrees. Her own thriving business. A home. Children. While I'm chasing fantasies. Will my desires ever become more than daydreams?

Jewel is who I want to be, and she loves to remind me of it. But even if I never inspire Karson to overcome his anger, maybe Karson can inspire me to overcome this thing with my sister. I tap the green phone icon before I can change my mind.

The phone rings, and I picture her snuggling her kids on the couch while eating ice cream and reading the picture book I made them. They might be too comfortable and relaxed for her to even bother picking up the phone.

"Hi, Gemma." Her tone sounds more breathless than content.

"Everything, okay?"

"I'm only putting Forrest back to bed for the fifth time. I need to get some work done for a presentation tomorrow, but he keeps getting up to ask questions about firemen. What a day, huh?" She pauses but not long enough for me to answer. "Were you calling to check on Daisy? She's doing fine now. Doesn't even have a headache."

"Oh, good." Yeah, I should have been calling to check on Daisy. What kind of aunt am I?

"I'm tempted to hassle you about arriving on the fire truck, but I'm glad you were here."

I'm too shocked to respond. I don't think those words have ever come out of her mouth before. Finally I say, "I'm glad I was too," and actually mean them. Now there's an uneasy silence on both ends. "What did you think of Karson?"

"Aww . . . That's really why you called, huh?"

"Perhaps."

"Yeah. Well." She groans as if she's settling into her couch for the first time that night. "He's not the most hospitable."

I smile at the memory of those long-suffering expressions he liked to give me. "No, he's not."

"I'll bet that makes him good at his job."

I recall his willingness to deal with the most combative of the two thieves on my ride-along. "He plays bad cop."

"In a relationship with you, that would balance out your toxic positivity."

What's wrong with positivity?

"And you could balance out his cynicism."

Ah . . . I see her point. Maybe that's why we fit together so well. Or why we would, if not for the other woman. Tonight we said goodbye. "I'm not going to see him again."

"Hmm . . ."

I sigh and roll onto my side, feeling lonely even while talking to my sister.

"Because he's been married before?" she asks.

That's part of it. "Yeah."

"And because you are tired of being compared to someone else."

So he'd told her. "Yeah." I hope she doesn't blame herself. Though with the animosity that has been between us lately, she'll probably see it as a badge of honor.

"Gem." Her tone dips like a bucket, dumping out its judgments and scorn. "Until Karson told me, I didn't realize you played the comparison game too."

My heartbeat thumps to a stop. What does she mean by *too*? It makes us sound like we are the same in more ways than our genetics. Like we've both wanted to wear each other's shoes.

But what would my shoes get her? Taken advantage of in Hollywood? Killed off in a bunch of TV roles? The upstairs bedroom of a townhome?

I don't say any of this because I'm not ready to go there. I'm not ready to confess my failures to Portland's Woman of the Year. "Of course I'm envious of you. You can eat dairy and gluten."

She snorts. "You can't really have allergies. We're identical twins."

"What?" Those allergies changed my whole life. "You think I made that up?"

"You needed a good excuse to diet and be skinny."

My eyes bulge at the ceiling. At all my memories flashing on it like a movie screen. "You don't remember when I started throwing up almost every day after lunch?"

"Yeah, weren't you bulimic?"

My mouth falls open. "No way."

"A lack of calories also explained your flightiness."

Flightiness? "You mean my brain fog, a symptom of a gluten allergy?"

"Sis, you gotta admit you're still flighty."

I open my mouth to argue.

"Fire truck."

I close my mouth. She has me there. But I can't believe that all this time she'd thought I had an eating disorder. No wonder she harasses me about food. "I didn't think I could have allergies either, but Mrs. Prescott, our volleyball coach, is the one who recommended I stop eating wheat and dairy."

"Then you lost all that weight, and everybody started telling you how you looked like a model. You seriously have allergies?"

"Yes. I was sick a lot in elementary school too, just not as bad." Her view of my world is blowing my mind. "I didn't know you were jealous."

"Jealous *is* the correct word for it. My favorite definition of the word jealousy is being vigilant in guarding something you already have. I was afraid of losing my relationship with you." Her voice breaks, and I feel it in my own throat.

"I miss it too." For ten years I've missed our friendship. I've missed sharing clothes and jokes and adventures. "I've missed being your biggest cheerleader. Lately, I've been cheering against you. Jealousy is awful."

She's quiet for a moment. I must have said too much too soon. "What damaged our relationship wasn't the jealousy then. It was the envy."

I'm not following. But I sense she's about to get counselor-ish. And I love that I can sense this.

"While jealousy is the fear of losing what you already have, envy is wanting what someone else has. Envy is destructive."

I inhale that truth, and like Vicks VapoRub, it burns a little in the healing process.

"I didn't see it before," she confesses. "I told myself I was saving our relationship by rigging homecoming court. I was trying to keep us together. But my envy is what drove me to steal your title."

It's such a silly thing, being homecoming queen. Even though I would have rather had the relationship with my sister, the crown is what wedged us apart. I've held it against her for years, but she's not the only one who needs to apologize. "That's when *my* envy started. I mean, I was already envious that you could eat whatever you wanted—"

She harrumphs, like that's not something to envy.

"The fact that you had that much power in student council seemed to elevate you above me. Your grades got you into advanced classes, while I was still struggling with brain fog, and you were awarded scholarships to attend fancy out-of-state colleges, while I was stuck here."

"Next to you, that's the only way I could get any attention," she wails.

I shrug at the ceiling, though I'm seeing her walking down the aisle at her wedding. "What do you mean? You're the one who got married."

"I took what I could get." She sobers. "While you were turning away dates right and left, I only had the one boyfriend. I didn't marry him out of love. I married him out of loneliness."

My heart grows heavy. It hurts for her. It hurts for her ex, even though he was the one who left her. "I didn't know this."

"I didn't want you to know." Derisive chuckle. "That's probably why I became a psychologist. To figure out all my issues on my own."

I'd thought the only reason Grant had cheated was because Jewel spent so much time at work. I blamed her for destroying their marriage. But maybe I'm to blame in a small way too.

Karson had past abandonment issues from his mom that affected his marriage, while Jewel had me. No, her envy doesn't justify the choices she made, but also, if I hadn't been so envious of what I deemed as her success, I could have been there for her in the way a sister should.

"I'm sorry," I say. The phrase is a cliché, but I believe someone means it when they don't repeat the same mistakes. And I'm going to show her I mean it.

She blubbers for a moment before she can say it back. "I'm sorry too, sis. Man . . ." She laughs through her tears. "If I'd known you'd really had an allergy, I wouldn't have made so many cakes when you came over."

I laugh with her. Another small thing that felt like a big thing. It wasn't the action of baking the cake so much as her intent that had hurt. And maybe that's why envy is so destructive. Because one's intentions are never in favor of the other person.

Suddenly I don't feel like such a failure. Not because I'm any different but because I don't have to compete. I don't have to prove myself. I'm Esau when Jacob apologized.

Whereas I'd once blamed God for playing favorites, our relationship with Him is not so much about favorites as it is about favor. It's like that story Jesus tells where the landowner hires workers for his vineyard throughout the day. He tells those he hires in the morning how much he'll pay them, then when he pays the workers hired later in the day that same amount, the ones he'd hired earlier expected more than what they'd agreed to. Their envy wanted less for others, whereas God's favor was about giving more.

I don't want less for Jewel anymore. I want her to feel beautiful and loved. I want her to be lavished with abundance beyond what she could earn. And there is much peace in realizing God wants this for all of us.

"A heart at peace gives life to the body, but envy rots the bones." The verse from the first Bible study I did with Charlie and Kai comes back to me the same way Jewel's psychology training comes back to her. It had stuck in my memory, and now I know why. I needed it.

I've had exactly what I needed all along. I have a rewarding job as a high school English teacher that gives me summers off to write scripts, and two roommates who can make those scripts into movies. What a gift.

I think of my script again. And I realize what it's been missing. Rather than have the last character continue the problem by envying the first, she can start to see how envy made a mess of the first character's life and how she would have been better off with her own shoes. She can then reverse the cycle, reverting them all back to the stories we know and love.

They simply have to choose to be happy. Choose gratefulness over envy, as the Bible says. Then they can all have hearts at peace.

CHAPTER TWENTY-FIVE

KARSON

Being a hero doesn't mean you're invincible.
It just means that you're brave enough to
stand up and do what's needed.
—RICK RIORDAN

Now that I've said goodbye to Gemma, I have to cut ties with her roommates as well. Otherwise she and I will run into each other and become one of those on-again, off-again couples who want to be together but can't make it work. I never understood those kinds of relationships in the past, but with Gemma I'm tempted to reconnect in spite of how much disconnecting again will tear me apart.

To keep that from happening, I've written a report against Charlie's request for filming a documentary about the impact of defunding the police in Portland, and I'm going to present it to the chief. I'm sure Charlie would have done a good job with it, but we're already operating with a reduced force, and the distraction would reduce it even more. Especially my ability to focus. Though I can't present that case for consideration.

I'm not sure if it's good or bad that I'm bringing Harris along. But he's always been my backup.

"Lieutenant Zellner. Officer Harris." Chief McGinty is a jolly-looking, middle-aged man whose hairline has retreated far enough that he really needs to put sunscreen on the top of his head if he's not wearing a hat. It's currently a hot-pink color that can't be healthy.

He stands up to shake hands. It's a very formal greeting from the man who trained me back when I thought I was going to be able to decrease crime and basically become a superhero. I'm not sure how he's kept his jolliness with all our city has been through, but the crow's-feet at the corner of his eyes come from smiling, and his lone dimple flashes even now.

"Hey, Chief." Harris is also grinning his big, teddy bear grin. I've never really questioned his grin before, because it's just who he is, but if both he and Chief McGinty can be joyful after working here for so long, maybe I'm doing something wrong.

I nod at both of them, then address our boss. "Chief."

Harris and I take our places in uncomfortable plastic chairs.

McGinty leans back in his ergonomic one. "How's safety academy going? I heard one of the students bummed a ride on a fire truck last night. Glad you guys didn't have as many problems."

Harris erupts in laughter. "I don't know if I'd say that."

I side-eye him to see if he might have already said something to McGinty about a certain student, but he's leaning forward and covering his mouth as if trying to keep my sad attempt at a relationship a secret.

"I know there's a film director in the class who's interested in doing a documentary on the whole defunding movement." The chief continues as if that was our biggest problem, so obviously he doesn't know about Gemma.

"Yes." I toss my report onto the desk in front of his family picture in an outdated gold frame.

He reaches for the report, but glances at me. "Give me your impression, Zellner."

I take a deep breath and send Harris another measuring glance. He waves me to go ahead.

"Charlie Newberg supports the police force, and I believe he would present our side of the situation with the kind of objectivity that would lead viewers to think for themselves. Ideally, they would ask questions about the future of law enforcement that could lead to reform, not only regarding our negative reputation for using excessive force but actually benefiting our effectiveness and creating an impact in the city."

Harris leans forward, resting his forearms on his thighs. He nods along as if he has nothing to add.

"However . . ."

Harris sits upright and turns his head to frown at me.

"With so many men having taken early retirement and our force already being stretched so thin, I don't see how we could give up the man-hours needed to fit this into anyone's schedule."

"What?" Harris demands as if I've gone mad.

I point to the report. I should have brought him a copy too. "Even with the funding they added back into our budget and the officers who agreed to come out of early retirement, we're still setting records for shootings and fatalities. That's got to take priority."

"Exactly." Harris says but not in the agreeable tone such a word would suggest. "If you want to get more funding back, we need to show the police department's side of the story. We need them to see how not only does defunding put us in danger, but it has ultimately harmed them."

"Them" being the innocent masses—the sheep we, as sheepdogs, are supposed to be protecting. Granted, there are some sheepdogs who need better training and some sheepdogs who go rabid, but with less funding, it makes it even harder for us to weed them out.

I shake my head. "I understand they had a reason to be angry, but now they're just angry because they want to be angry."

Harris holds a palm out as if to display something I'm missing. "Look who's talking."

While his words should have stopped me in my tracks, they felt more like a punch to the face, and I want to strike back. Even as the energy courses through my veins, I remember Jewel saying that anger is energy. Though it's not rational, it makes me feel powerful.

Am I also angry because I choose to be angry? Do I have the ability to turn this feeling off? Do I want to turn this feeling off? If I do and I listen to logic instead, the logic might make me feel defeated instead of powerful. Then how would I do my job?

"Gentlemen," the chief intercedes. "I appreciate hearing from both of you, and I'll look over the report. Zellner, we previously discussed your running point on this project. Can I safely assume you don't have the time for it anymore?"

Harris stands. "I'll run point, Chief. And I'll do it outside my normal hours."

"I appreciate your offer, but hopefully that won't be necessary. If the film can benefit our world and the people we serve, then we'll make it a priority."

"Thank you, sir."

I scowl and give Harris a look out of the corner of my eye, but even while I'm scowling, I feel like a jerk for doing it. He just stood up for something he believed in and even offered to sacrifice of himself in the process. His sacrifice will benefit the community, Charlie, and even me. But resentment still wells from being called out.

I'm angry that I have an anger issue. I preferred only seeing my anger as a strength.

"If that's all gentlemen, you're dismissed."

I storm out before I can be tempted to slam doors in people's faces.

"Karson," Harris calls me by my first name.

I stop and turn to face him in the hallway.

"What's your deal, man?"

What *is* my deal? That I can't just wallow in keeping the enemy the enemy? That I'm supposed to open up about my side and listen to theirs? Because how else do I get over this anger at injustice? This anger at Amber?

In the same way the public cried to defund the police out of rightful outrage, did I settle and concede my divorce too soon? Rather than work toward a solution that would prevent more pain, did I continue the vicious cycle?

I shake my head and look away. "I'm angry."

"Ya think?"

I narrow my eyes at him. I'm not ready to let it go. So I quote Jewel from yesterday. But just the part I liked. "It makes me good at what I do."

"An anger that stands up for others, yes." He plants his hands on his hips. "When it's about protecting yourself, like it was just now, no. It makes you a coward."

His words knock the breath from my lungs. I've never been called a coward before. I'd prided myself on doing the right thing. On fighting for truth.

But when anger takes over, I can't see truth anymore. I only see my side. My feelings become the truth I'm fighting for. They justify my actions even when my actions are wrong.

That's how anger destroys relationships. Like it did with my mom when I drove across country to return the thousand dollars she sent me on my eighteenth birthday. Like it did with my wife when she gave me the ultimatum of career or marriage. Like it did with Gemma.

I meet Harris's eyes without using rage to shield him from seeing my fear. He knows I'm a coward, so what more do I have to hide?

As for Harris, he has every reason to be angry too. Maybe more. He's been discriminated against as both a Black man and a cop. He watched friends die in the military at the hands of terrorists. His dad passed recently, and now he's taking care of his mom. Yet he keeps on laughing and joking like the happiest man alive. "How do you keep from hating the world?"

He takes a few steps forward and grips my shoulder. "I put myself in other people's shoes. And when I do, I see that all they want is to be loved. So I love them."

He makes it sound so simple. "They may *want* to be loved, but sometimes what they *need* is prison time."

His teeth flash in one of his brilliant smiles. "And that's where you come in, bro."

Harris is good at his job because of his great love. We can learn from each other, and today I need to learn to let my anger go.

I blow out my breath. "I've got to go make a phone call."

"All right." He backs away and claps his hands. "Tell Gemma I said hi."

Except it's not Gemma I'm calling.

The wooden sign welcoming visitors to The Grotto is painted with evergreen trees and what I think is supposed to be a cross, though to me it looks more like crosshairs. Of course they aren't crosshairs since the sign reads: A Place of Solitude, Peace, and Prayer.

This was always Amber's favorite retreat. It's an outdoor Catholic shrine built on over sixty acres in the 1920s. I'm personally not big on shrines, but the gardens, ponds, and caves are definitely a sanctuary. And I decided if I was going to invite my ex-wife to meet with me, I should make her feel as safe as possible.

Me, on the other hand? In spite of the birds chirping overhead and the golden sun streaming between giant trees, my guts are a jittery mess. I scan the asphalt walkway in search of a Hispanic woman so tiny she could disappear underneath her mass of fake blond curls. Though she might have changed in the past three years, I know I'd recognize her stance of one leg turned out and her hip popped to the other side.

The walkway opens to an outdoor seating area where I suppose they hold Mass. Wooden benches face the cliff with a cave in it. Steps lead up to the cave, so I head that way. It's cool and damp and smells fresh like earth. Inside the cave is a stone table covered in flowers. Behind it, there are mossy piles of rocks that hold candelabras and statues. The biggest marble statue in the middle looks as though it could be Mary holding a dying Jesus.

I wonder if my mother ever looked at me with such love. Such sorrow. Could she be looking down on me from heaven like that right now?

She wasn't much of a mother, but the fact that she sent me a gift on my eighteenth birthday meant she'd wanted to try. Maybe she'd wanted to ask for forgiveness. God would have given it to her even though I didn't.

"Karson?" The warm voice holds a remnant of accent.

My stomach clenches at the sound of her rolling the *r* in my name. I take a calming breath, then turn to face her.

Her hair is surprisingly dark. The way it was when we were kids, before she started bleaching it. The jolt of seeing it that way unlocks the good memories I'd stuffed away.

I saw her in court during the divorce, but I'd avoided all eye contact. Now I force myself to look into her chestnut eyes. They are free of the huge, spidery eyelashes she used to wear. She looks natural. It's a good look for her.

I blink and look her up and down. She's gained some weight, but in a healthy way. And she has a ring on her finger. Maybe it's from the man she replaced me with. Maybe not. I'm surprisingly unaffected.

"You . . ." I swallow the lump of sorrow in my throat. "You look good."

Her full lips turn up even as her thick lashes lower. "Thank you." Her gaze lifts again to meet mine. "I used to dream of seeing you again. Sometimes it was with the hope of getting back together, and sometimes it was with the idea of flaunting my success in your face."

I start to cross my arms, then choose to lower my defenses. I stuff my hands in my pockets instead. Just this change feels different. But I'm confused by one thing. "If you wanted to get back together, why did you start dating someone else?"

"I wanted someone to make me feel good about myself. I would have preferred it to be you, but . . ." She shrugs. "I was selfish and didn't wait."

I'm surprised she admits this. It's okay if she has malice for me. What matters is that I don't have to have it for her anymore. I can let my anger go.

"I want you to be happy." Surprisingly, the words are true.

"Thank you." She tucks a strand of dark hair behind an ear. "It's been a hard journey. It got worse before it got better."

I narrow my eyes. I'd figured she simply replaced me and went on with her life. "How so?"

"After our divorce, I felt like I had to fake it even more. I wanted everyone to think I was better off without you."

Is she admitting that she's not? I never would have expected that. I thought I'd held her back. Here she is, being real with me. So she's more honest than she ever was in our marriage.

"I put on a show," she continues. "I laughed louder, smiled wider, took more selfies. My social media sites skyrocketed, and I was getting paid to promote all the stuff I used to pay for."

I thought she'd said it got worse. It sounds like we both got our dream jobs. "That's not so bad."

"Well. The problem with putting yourself up on a pedestal is that eventually you fall off." She scrunches her nose. "I said something careless and got canceled. At which point Elliot replaced me the way I'd replaced you."

So she's not with Elliot anymore. The realization gives me a strange kind of peace. Strange, not because it makes me want to say, "I told you so," but because it offers hope that she started off her current relationship from a healthy place. If Elliot left her for getting canceled, then he's no better than a stranger on Twitter.

I only know what that means because she used to tease me that I was going to get her canceled. It sounds like a really dumb thing, but I guess for her career it could be similar to the kind of angry mobs I've dealt with. The crazy thing is we both chose the ungrateful masses over each other.

Just last week I might have felt vindication over her leaving me and still getting canceled. Today I don't want that for anyone. Not even my ex. "I'm sorry."

She huffs. "Best thing that ever happened to me. See, I didn't just get canceled for what I said. They attacked every fake thing about me. All the insecurities I thought I'd hid, every flaw, had been on display without me knowing."

So that's why she looks different now. It's not only about being real on the outside, she's real on the inside.

"Everything I did in our marriage was to get people to like me."

I nod. That's what I'd thought of Gemma at first. "I know."

"But here's what you don't know." She steps a foot wide and pops her hip. But she also drops her head to one side and looks deep into my eyes, which gives the whole sassy hip pop a new softness. "I also tried to get you to like me. So when you were angry, I just did whatever I could to keep you from being mad at me."

I blink. I knew she tried to comfort me, but I'd never looked at it from this perspective.

"After getting to know the firefighters through the safety academy, I thought that would be a job where you could still be the hero but not come home as angry."

I rub my hands over my face. This changes everything. Or does it? "But I heard you tell Thad you needed me to become a firefighter if you were to become an influencer. You wanted me to have a better image."

Her lips purse. "You heard that?"

"Uh . . . yeah."

"Karson." She shakes her head. "It wasn't that I didn't want you to be a policeman. I didn't want you to be an *angry* policeman. I was afraid I'd be doing a live video and you'd be yelling or slamming doors in the background. I asked for Thad's help because I'd rather you be mad at him than me."

I want to be angry that this is all about my anger. But that would be counterproductive. Especially with all the confessions she's making about her selfishness. "I was mad at both of you."

She closes her eyes and lets out a huge exhale. "So that's why your attitude changed toward me. I thought it was because of the riots."

"Those didn't help my disposition. Which is why I'd thought some time apart would be good for us. I felt like you were kicking me while I was down, and I needed to get back up if I was going to be able to fight for us."

"I had no idea." She presses her lips together. "When your attitude changed, you didn't like me anymore. So I found someone who did. Or, I should say, someone who claimed to. I'm sorry."

Her apology pokes a hole that all my hot air seeps out of. She's deflated me. "No, I'm sorry. I shouldn't have taken out my anger on you. I should have taken care of it out of my love for you." So much pain could have been avoided. "I should have at least talked to you about it rather than just take off."

"I forgive you, Karson." She twists her lips. "We both had a lot to learn, and apparently I had to hit bottom before I could even be honest with myself."

She's not on the bottom anymore. She's content. She's joyful. "Where are you now?" I want to know.

Her sly smile says she's proud of who she's become but in a wholesome way. "I'm the coordinator for Nike's community impact fund. I also married one of their sports researchers."

"Wow." I didn't know sports researching was a career. It's like a degree in gunsmithing, I guess. I'm glad she's been redeemed in the same way as my rusty old guns.

I never used to like her Catholic beliefs. Members of the church could simply confess their sins to some priest, then they didn't have to face the consequences. I wanted there to be consequences. But now, as I'm here, seeking forgiveness from my ex for a wrong I didn't realize I'd committed, I understand we're all just doing the best we know how. Confession means we realize we made a mistake, and we want a second chance to learn how to fix it. It also means we realize we don't deserve the second chance.

"Why are you here, Karson?"

I shrug, not because the answer is simple but because it's so complicated. "I want to do better."

"For a woman?" She doesn't say this with any kind of resentment but in the same way that I'd said I wanted her to be happy. She wants me to find love again. Or maybe for the first time, since I've never been able to love before.

I remember my previous application of the Scripture "one who is full loathes honey." I'd used it to blame Amber for how I felt about women, but the truth was that I played a part in the mess we made. Just like honey was part of the promised land, the Bible says, "He who finds a wife finds what is good and receives favor from the Lord." I'd had a good thing, and I failed to treasure her.

"I think it's too late for that." I should have done better for both Amber and Gemma.

"Miracles can happen." She touches my forearm. "For example, you're here."

I cover her hand and laugh at her meaning. I laugh at our unexpected reconnection. I laugh at the freedom from blaming others for my problems.

I didn't know it could be this way. I wish I'd figured it out sooner.

It's not until I'm headed out of the sanctuary that I see a wooden sign for St. Joseph's Grove leading down a separate trail. This sanctuary is named for Mary, so it would be easy to overlook Joseph, but Mary's husband is not the Joseph who pops into my mind.

While Gemma related to Esau and Jacob, I related to Jacob's son Joseph in the way he was abandoned into a pit. But if I'd been wrong about Amber's reason for leaving me, maybe I was wrong about my mom too. Maybe she was also doing what she thought was best for me. She didn't actually leave me in a pit. She left me with my grandparents, who she'd known would take good care of me.

I pause, then change directions. Perhaps the story of this Joseph might have some wisdom to offer.

The trail leads to an alcove of stone with a statue of Joseph holding baby Jesus. On each side, there are scenes carved into marble panels. Again, I'm not into the praying to saints, and I know some people think that even just a painting of Jesus is breaking commandment number two about graven images. But Jesus made it pretty clear that the commandments were about heart issues, and my heart is drinking it all in. The freshness, the freedom, the reflection.

One of the marble panels contains two scenes labeled as Sorrow and Joy. The sorrow side highlights his concern for Mary and Jesus on their escape to Egypt. The joy side is happy at finding safety. This also fits the safety that Jacob's son Joseph found in Egypt. God provides people to lead others to safety, which applies to my job in police work. Only I've been focusing on the sorrow side rather than the joy.

If anger made me good at my job, it might be time to get a new job.

CHAPTER TWENTY-SIX

GEMMA

Be your own hero, it's cheaper than a movie ticket.
—DOUGLAS HORTON

Take one." Jewel snaps the clapboard together on the first shot of our forty-eight-hour competition. She's volunteered as an assistant to support me, so I feel like a winner already.

I stand with Charlie, facing the screen that shows us what Kai sees through his camera lens. I'm pretty excited about this script. Besides the happy ending Jewel inspired, Kai convinced us to change the title to *Sole Searching*. Like my favorite Nikes, the name is a perfect fit.

Granted, the darker films seem to win all the awards, and my light-hearted twist could take us out of the running to move up into LA's Filmapalooza with the possibility of being shown in Cannes. But we're all okay with that. We want to change lives other than just our own.

Preparing for this contest has kept me almost too busy to think about my personal problems. And by almost, I mean that the misery of saying goodbye to Karson slipped my mind until I see the actor playing Johnny raise Baby overhead in their iconic lift scene. I feel their pain when the giant Dr. Martens she stole from Mia's character in *The Princess Diaries* affects their center of gravity, and they fall onto a mattress off-screen. My romance crashed in a very similar way.

"Let's do it again," Charlie calls, and my heart goes out to the actors who are going to get beaten up before we're done filming. He turns to me. "What do you think?"

I consider the couple who have rolled to opposite sides of the mattress. The real Johnny and Baby would have rolled to the same side. They'd want to be near each other. Sharing the experience would heighten it for them both. If they didn't have the pull-push tension of new love, the lift wouldn't even matter. "They need more chemistry."

Charlie rubs his growing beard. "You sure? It's just a quick shot of them falling over."

"No. It has to be more than that."

Charlie is great at documentaries, but he's not used to romance. I've played a heroine in kissing scenes before. Too many of them. This is my area of expertise.

I study the actors as Kai repositions for the next shot. Their characters aren't simply falling. They are falling in love. There's a lot on the line.

"Hey, Johnny," I call.

The actor looks up. He's got the floppy hair, the triangle of a torso, and the confident swagger. But he's missing the magnetic attraction that makes a couple sizzle on-screen. Notoriously, Patrick Swayze and Jennifer Grey didn't get along on the set of *Dirty Dancing* because they'd had a negative experience in the past, but that shared history equated to the connection viewers needed. It's much deeper than sexual tension.

I trot over and speak quietly enough that only the actors can hear me. "Tell me about the last time you fell in love."

He chuckles dryly. "I don't know if I'd call it love."

Okay, he's not there yet. "Tell me about the last time you had your heart broken."

He crosses his arms. A pose I know all too well.

I turn to the actress. "Or you can start."

"I . . ." She scratches her cheek, then holds her hand out as if she's got nothing.

"Fine. I'll start."

They glance at each other, then look at me. At least they're dropping their guard enough for their eyes to soften with compassion.

"He didn't want to get hurt again the way his ex-wife had hurt him, and I couldn't handle him comparing me to someone else, because I'd grown up in my twin's shadow. We wanted to be together, but our wounds from the past pulled us apart."

"That's rough," Johnny laments.

"Yes, it's rough." My voice sounds a little rough. I clear my throat. "And that's what you and Baby are going through. You have past wounds that can separate you, but if you fight them together, they will make you one."

"Wow." Baby stares off at the lake which we will later film them falling into. "I wish I'd had that with my ex. The only thing we fought over was all the other girls he wanted to date."

Johnny eyes her. "My last girlfriend went back to her ex. Evidently I was the rebound."

Baby looks up at him, and for the first time I see a spark. It's not attraction, but empathy. It will draw the actors together in a way that looks like chemistry to viewers.

This is a trick I learned through writing characters. I've used it when filming with actors I really didn't like at all. For the first time, I wonder if this is what drew me to Karson—besides the hero thing. Could I see him hurting through his anger and think that if I could help soothe his pain, then it would soothe mine, as well?

"Are we ready, kids?" Charlie yells, waking me from my contemplation.

I nod at Charlie, then walk backward toward him but point and talk to our actors. "You are connected by pain. This is your one shot to help heal each other. Your whole future is in this moment."

Baby takes a couple of steps so Johnny can practice grabbing her waist in the right place. The difference I see in them from before to now is the difference between the remake of *Dirty Dancing* and the original.

I call out encouragement. "Act as if in lifting her overhead, your relationship will soar, but if you fall, it's over."

"Even though it's not," Kai corrects me as I pass him. "Once we get this scene, we're going to film Baby taking off her boots in favor of the Keds for the ending of the film."

"Right." The happy ending.

Kai has his camera set up, but he's looking at me. "You know why Charlie wanted to start filming with the boots on, right?"

"Well." I shrug. "Because once she takes the boots off, success will be so much easier."

Kai levels his gaze. "Precisely."

He's right. Johnny and Baby come to life as broken souls, desperate to make the relationship work. They don't succeed at first, but how they grow through their trials gives them the strength they need to overcome.

Isn't it crazy how my own writing can offer more of a message than I intended it to? And sometimes it's the exact message I need to hear?

I don't have time to ponder the message long. We barely even sleep that weekend as we put the same amount of effort into every second of film. It's almost midnight on Sunday when Charlie plays the final cut for us in the living room of our townhome. Yes, the film is well-made, but it's also thought-provoking and joyful. As Johnny lifts Baby into the air for the final montage, I'm overwhelmed with the beauty of their victory.

Kai stands from his spot on the couch and gives a slow clap.

Charlie looks to me for my reaction.

My heart thumps its own approval, but I can barely offer more than a watery smile. Is it envy if I want to be Baby?

"I'll take your tears as two thumbs-up," Charlie translates. "I'm sending it now." He thunders down the stairs to the computer desk in his room and leaves me with Kai.

"Thank you, Kai," I whisper.

He plops back down, arms extended along the back of the sofa. "For what?"

"For making me give the story a happy ending. You know it's what I needed." And I'm pretty sure when he reminded me that Johnny and Baby were going to get a second chance, he was really talking about Karson and me.

"You?" he questions in his deep voice. "I needed it for me." His lazy grin flickers with determination. "When we win this thing, I'm taking my share of the prize money and flying to Africa to propose to Meri."

I hear myself screech. Then I'm throwing my arms in the air and jogging in place. I love the idea of a proposal in Africa. I hope there are wild animals and glamping tents and maybe a hot-air balloon involved. But even more than the romance of it all, I love Kai and Meri together.

"What's going on?" Charlie calls up the stairs.

I'd better quiet down or the neighbors will call the police on me again. Though would that really be such a bad thing if Karson showed up? Oops. This is not about Karson and me anymore.

I wrap my arms around Kai and yell to Charlie. "We have to win so Kai can use his prize money to propose to your sister in Africa."

Charlie bounds up the stairs two at a time, a smile splitting his face. "You're proposing to Meri?"

Kai shrugs like it's no big deal. "If we win."

"Oh, we're winning, brother!" Charlie dares the universe to defy him. Then my roommates are in one of those hugs where they pound each other's backs.

I somehow get pulled in, and my bare pinkie toe gets smashed, but I wouldn't trade this moment for the most expensive shoes in the world. I'm celebrating the kind of love I've only dreamed of.

Kai leans away. "You hit *send* on the film submission, right, Charlie?"

Charlie untangles his limbs to charge back down the stairs.

Kai and I pull apart but stare at each other with huge grins. I give a flap of my arms because where do we go from here? "You need help ring shopping?"

He smirks. "Aren't you going to be busy with a love story of your own?"

So I'd been right to suspect Kai had been giving me relationship advice earlier when we were talking about Johnny and Baby. I deflate like one of those hot-air balloons. Because I don't get the same happy ending he does. "Karson said goodbye."

"I know." He grabs his computer from one of the coffee-table cubes and kicks his feet up to use his lap as a desk. He's probably going to look up prices on airline tickets. "But I also know that, like Cinderella, you have exactly what you need to create your happy ending."

"A fairy godmother?" I wish.

He snorts. "You've never needed a magic wand. You're a screenplay writer. You make magic."

"I can't make magic on my own." I trudge toward the stairs. It's late, and I'm beat in more ways than one. "It took you and Charlie to turn my screenplay into a story people can watch."

"Gemma." Something about his tone stops me. "If we win this competition, you're going to have a whole lot of interest from people who want to turn your screenplays into stories people can watch."

My heart throbs with new meaning. How had I not considered the possibilities? That used to be all I thought about.

Finishing my screenplay isn't about proving myself anymore. It's about being free to be me. And the free me has learned a lot about love that she can share through a story she's been researching to write.

Karson might not have thought he had what it took to be my hero, but I'm going to show him how well the shoe fits.

CHAPTER TWENTY-SEVEN

KARSON

*A hero is someone who understands the
responsibility that comes with his freedom.*
—BOB DYLAN

*A*pparently, fear doesn't make me angry anymore because I am terrified of what I'm about to do, but I'm also at peace. It's a strange combination. I kind of like it.

The chief's door is open, but he's intent on his computer screen and doesn't see me.

I rap on the window.

He glances over, leans back in his chair, and rubs his eyes. "How's it going, Lieutenant?"

I pause to consider. "Good."

He leans forward and frowns as though my response confuses him as much as it confuses me. "Real-ly?" His tone dips in disbelief.

I'm good, but he might not like my news. "Well . . ."

"That's what I thought. Come in."

Does he know why I'm knocking, or does he just always expect negativity from me? I stride in and drop into one of his hard plastic chairs. Coming here has always felt a little bit like the principal's office, but since this might be my last time, I feel nostalgic. I take in the warm scent of coffee, the mess of papers on his desk, and the outdated photo frames. Especially the people in those frames. He does this job for all the right reasons.

Whereas . . . "I'm here to turn in my resignation."

He sits up straighter. "Is this because of my decision on the documentary? I know you didn't like how I was allocating—"

"No." I give a half chuckle, half huff. "You made the right decision about that."

"Okay?" He laces his fingers together on his desk. "Is this over the reduced staff and a heavier workload, because I'm planning to—"

I hold up my hand to stop him as if I was directing traffic. "No, sir. It's been an honor to work for you and for the city." I cross an ankle over one knee. The new me is surprisingly chill. "This is about the realization that I want to work with youth to prevent crime. Schools are starting to bring back resource officers, and I'm taking the job at Lincoln High School."

He lifts his chin with understanding. "That's a change in position. Is it . . . ? Does it . . . ?" He props an elbow on the table and leans his face onto one hand as if needing a better angle for studying me. "How's the pay?"

A laugh bursts out. "It's pretty much a demotion, sir. But it shouldn't be."

"No, it shouldn't be." He shakes his head as if in thought. "With all the school shootings, it's still a risky job."

My heart droops under the heaviness of his reminder. I'd always considered myself a sheepdog. Now I actually get to protect some sheep. "That, and I have a heart for children. I can be there for kids the way my grandparents were there for me."

I hadn't meant to share so much, but it feels good to align my position with my purpose. I'm looking through a scope and am able to pinpoint my target.

It's kind of like being angry, but this energy I feel is a passion to protect our younger generation from continuing the downward spiral of pain started by broken people before them. My goal is healing. My heart is toward them, for them. If the energy from my anger could make me good at my job at the police department, then there's going to be no stopping me at the high school.

McGinty's faded eyes still. "That's very honorable, Zellner. They're lucky to have you." He sighs. "I just don't know what we're going to do without you."

I do. And I'd been waiting for this opening. "I'm on my way to tell Drew Harris to apply for lieutenant."

He hoots, then plants his hands on the desktop to push himself to a standing position before holding out a hand to shake. "Kid, you're all right."

His trite words are not trite at all. And as I shake his hand, I feel as though he's passing the baton. He helped me get to the place where I'm all right, and I'm going to do that for those who follow after me.

A little over a month later, Harris follows me into my new office with a box of my old belongings. "Are you sure this is an office? I think we made a wrong turn into the janitor's closet."

I squeeze by the side of my desk and turn to find the large man filling the rest of the room. "I don't plan on being in here too much."

He sets my box on a chair. "Well, if you have to deal with any students who struggle with claustrophobia, you can just bring them in here and scare them straight."

"I'll keep that in mind." I look around proudly at the clock, the coat hooks by the door, and the bulletin board that already has the bell schedule pinned up. There won't be room for much more decoration. It'll be an adjustment in more ways than one. "Were you a good kid in high school?"

"Huh." Harris chuckles. "I didn't have time to get into trouble. If I wanted to play sports, I had to work with tutors to keep my grades up, and I also had to have a job on weekends to pay for my own fees and equipment. What about you?"

It's been a long time since I'd thought about high school, and the distance has freed me to be more honest about who I was. I'd always felt I didn't fit in because I was raised by my grandparents, but I'd go hunting with Granddad a lot, and both grandparents always attended my wrestling matches. I didn't have to work the way Harris did—neither at a job nor for good grades.

"I didn't look for trouble, but I was troubled," I admit. The best part had been Amber. I blink at the realization and the surprising fondness. "Amber kept me on the straight and narrow."

"Aww . . ." The big guy has a mushy heart. "I didn't realize she'd been your high school sweetheart."

"Yeah." I run a hand over my head and stare at the ceiling panels. "I've been so mad at her that I'd forgotten the good things about our relationship."

He backs up into the hallway as if he needs more room than my office offers. He rests his hands on the doorframe and leans in for our conversation. "That's amazing that you two made amends. Do you think you'll try getting back together?"

There was a time when such a question would ignite fireworks inside me. Not the entertaining kind, but the blow-your-head-off-for-getting-too-close kind. Now I'm as cool as the rain that ruined yet another Independence Day in Portland. "She's remarried."

"No kidding. What about . . . ?" He looks down as if trying to be nonchalant, but I know where he's heading. He's going to ask about—

"Gemma?" I say along with him.

"Yeah. The actress who wanted you to play her hero."

I can't help smiling at the memory. At all the memories. "Now *she* was trouble."

Harris shakes before erupting with his contagious belly laugh. "True. But you never smiled this much before her."

I've been making changes lately, and they all started with her. The smile Harris is talking about, I feel it on the inside as well. If Gemma were here to kiss right now, it would be a happy kiss.

Just the idea makes me want to track her down and kiss her. I run my fingers through my hair at the realization. It's not surprising that I want to kiss her but that I'm not scared of reconnecting without knowing it's a sure thing.

I've spent my life throwing people in jail, and I don't only mean literally. If anyone in my life hurt me at all, I'd lock them up. My mom. My wife. And now Gemma.

She didn't even do anything wrong. She just reminded me of someone who had. So I ended things.

Maybe I don't have to be like that anymore. I explore the recesses of my heart. The areas that are usually behind bars and monitored with security cameras now seem to have open doors.

I wait for my mental alarms to go off. A warning. A siren. A phone call about breach of protocol. But there's nothing.

Is my heart completely unprotected? How is that safe? And why doesn't it bother me?

I frown up at Harris as if he has the answer. And he does.

Seeing him hulking in my door, I can't imagine any students messing with him. He's obviously strong. With that strength comes ease. Confidence. He doesn't have Small Man Syndrome. He doesn't have to bark at everyone like a chihuahua. He can just be.

This is what is happening to me. I've grown stronger. Not physically, but emotionally. I'm confident enough to believe I'm worth loving even if I fail at being Gemma's hero. I'm capable of being there for her even if she doesn't stay here for me.

"Harris."

He lifts his eyebrows as if he's already been listening a while for me to say something. "Yeah?"

"I think I made a mistake in saying goodbye to Gemma."

"Yeah." It isn't a question this time.

My pulse not only races but jumps hurdles in its haste to right another wrong. I scramble to grab my phone from out of one of the boxes. I have to call Gemma right now. I have to let her know that I won't be comparing her to Amber anymore. "When were you going to tell me?"

He shrugs. "After I knew for sure that you weren't getting back together with Amber."

"I told you she's remarried. Keep up, man." I truly hope Amber's new husband loves her the way her first husband should have. Just as I truly hope Gemma chooses to give me a second chance at this love thing. Though I'll start with the hope she answers the phone when she sees my name.

I tap on my contacts list. I tap on the magnifying glass icon. I start to type Gemma's name. I'm typing so fast it doesn't pop up before I finish. I type her full name and then hit *done*. No phone number appears. I must have spelled her name wrong.

I retry and tap *done* again. What is wrong with my phone?

No results found?

Oh yeah. In a fit of rage, I'd removed her from my contacts.

My stomach churns. I drop my arms to my side and stare at Drew. I'm an idiot.

"You okay there, buddy?"

"I . . . uh . . ." I didn't accept her friend request on social media. If I was still at the police station, I could look up her application form on file to find her phone number. I wonder if she has a writing website. "I don't know where to find her."

Drew's teeth flash. He's rocking with laughter again. Rocking so hard he has to lean forward through the doorframe.

The new me has started to appreciate his sense of humor more, but I'm not getting the joke. "Why is this funny?"

"Whoa, boy." He hoots and hollers and takes his sweet time getting ahold of himself. "You really don't know, do you?"

I drop my phone back into the box with a *thud* and hold my hands wide. "Obviously not."

He wipes his eyes and takes a step backward. He taps on the wall just outside my office. "The two of you are coworkers now."

I still so quickly that I can feel my blood rush to my feet. Perhaps that's why my brain isn't able to process the meaning of Drew's words—it's not getting enough oxygen.

Finally I recall the fact that Gemma teaches English. She's a teacher. Here. At my school. If Drew is right, that means I'm going to see her every day.

How is she going to respond to this surprise? Will she think I stalked her? Changed jobs to be near her? The coincidence could come across as completely creepy. Kind of like when she signed up for Citizen's Safety Academy to be near me. Hopefully this works out better.

In a daze, I push my way into the hallway to look at the bulletin board of teachers' pictures for myself. Sure enough. Gemma won Teacher of the Month last May. Her stunning black-and-white image could be the headshot used for her page on IMDb. "I can't believe she works here."

But of course she works here. It's like when Joseph's brothers showed up in Egypt to buy grain from him. Somehow my life has come full circle, but this time I have the knowledge to create a healthy relationship.

CHAPTER TWENTY-EIGHT

GEMMA

Dear Diary, the Heroine never cries.
—AMELIA F. JONES

Our film competition win still hasn't sunk in—even as I drop Kai off at the airport for his flight to Africa. I weave through the traffic jam of vehicles and pull up to the curb.

Kai sits and stares out the windshield. "What if a witch doctor puts a poisonous snake in my window to kill me in my sleep?"

The mention of witch doctors reminds me of the time I compared Karson to one, though I don't think the cop has anything to do with Kai's current worries. "You're proposing to a nurse, so she'll have the medical knowledge to save you if she wants to get married."

He faces me then, dark eyes jittery like coffee. "You think she'll say yes?"

I smile at what love has done to him. My chill, lazy roommate is running marathons, willing to tolerate the threat of poisonous snakes, and taking on what he used to consider the biggest risk of all—marriage. That's really what he's afraid of. I smile with confidence. "You know how Charlie predicted we'd win the film competition?"

Kai gives a half grin. "Yes. Charlie has experience with first place."

"True. And I have experience with romance." Not the relationship kind of experience but the writing kind. I just finished my screenplay. I'm all about the happily ever after. "I predict that it's a good thing you started running again, because Meri's going to race you to the altar."

Kai takes a deep breath instead of laughing as I'd expected him to. I've never seen him so serious. "I would have flown to Africa to propose even if we hadn't won the competition. Isn't it crazy how when we met, I wasn't even willing to get off the sofa to pursue her, and now I'm flying around the world?"

My heart melts, and I reach for his hand. "The challenges you've already overcome make your love that much stronger."

He squeezes my palm as though he'll never let go. Is he going to try to take me with him? I'd love to go watch his reunion, but school starts on Monday. Also, I can't park my car here.

"Thanks, Gemma." He releases me to pull his backpack from the floor up into his lap. The dude travels light. "I wish the same for you and Officer Angry Eyes."

It's a good thing I can laugh. Otherwise I'd cry. "So magnanimous of you."

"If I can grow, anyone can." He gives my hand one more squeeze, then steps to the sidewalk and swings his backpack over a shoulder.

Winning the film competition has changed his life, but I'm not sure if it will change mine. I'd expected winning to make me feel more successful or look shinier. Perhaps the reason it doesn't feel real is because I'm still the same person I was before winning.

I'm not any better of a writer. My work is the same quality. It's just recognized now. And I can't help wondering if I deserve this recognition.

I've heard other writers talk about imposter syndrome before, and I thought it a modest brag. But now I get it. If I didn't feel like a winner before, something like a cash award isn't going to change that.

Art can't be about validating oneself. If you don't feel validated before a standing ovation, you're seriously going to question the honesty and/or sanity of those clapping. Art has to be about expression. Which is why the one woman crying in front of me at the theater while watching *Sole Searching* meant more to me than everyone else standing up afterward. I know her tears were real. Without us having ever met, my words somehow touched her.

So maybe I am changed. Not in the way I feel successful, but in the way I'm inspired to keep writing, whether I feel successful or not.

Our win did give me the encouragement needed to submit my finished romantic comedy to all my producer contacts, though I wrote it to reach Karson. If it doesn't get made, I'm not sure how I'll share it with him.

I ponder this on my drive to Lincoln High. I've got to get my mind in gear for students. They have to be my audience now. I want to teach them the love of literature, but I also want them to find the courage to win the battles in their own life stories. And they've got stories. I mean, the mess I created with Karson started back when I was their age. Back when my sister and I began to envy each other in high school.

I park in the teachers' parking lot and head down the empty halls to my classroom, telling myself to focus. Karson used to tell me the same thing, trying to get me to focus on him, and now that he's not with me, I can't get my focus off of him. I can even almost smell his cinnamon scent.

I stop and close my eyes to inhale deeply. Yep. Spicy gun oil. My imagination is like no other. I shake the sense and continue forward, past the new resource officer's room.

The trick for leaving my worries behind has always been to get lost in someone else's story. I'd started doing this as a child at bedtime. I couldn't sleep unless my mom read us a book. When she quit reading to us, I'd read with a flashlight under my covers. When I got caught and my flashlight taken away, I began making up stories in my head. I'd tell them to Jewel, but when we stopped talking, I had to start writing them down.

All my years of envy had melted away like candle wax when Jewel and I reconnected, but this new gratitude washes clean any remaining remnants in the votive holder of my heart. Kai had wished me love with Officer Angry Eyes, but maybe my happy ending is with my sister. I'll treasure my time with her even more because of the years we spent apart.

Maybe that's enough. Or maybe it's God who has to be enough when others fail us, like Thad said. I can avoid envy by always being grateful for Him in my life. Aware He is working in the bad as well as the good. I can have a heart at peace.

I shrug at the simplicity of it all. I understand life in a new way, yet the more I learn, the more I realize I don't know. So I'll keep reading to understand those around me, and I'll write to better understand myself.

I pull open my classroom door, making a mental list of the books I'm going to teach this year. I've pulled my favorite quotes to hang around the room. I'll quote them so many times that when my students graduate, they may forget everything else, but they won't forget the best lines of heroes and heroines. Those lines from writers in the past will help define their direction. Then they'll have no choice but to become heroes in their own right.

On that note, my phone rings the soundtrack from the latest Wonder Woman movie. My heart skips with delight that my sister might be calling about the new tradition I suggested of taking the kids to Enchanted Forest on the last day of summer before school starts.

I drop the armload of books on the nearest desk and dig my phone out of my purse. I blink at the name on the screen. It's not my sister's name.

I hold my breath before realizing I'm going to have to breathe in order to answer. I exhale in a rush. "Hello?"

As I wait for a response, I try to recall if I've gotten a new phone recently. Did my contacts get messed up? This happened once before when Kai became Kai-Kai and Charlie's last name was swapped with a Charlie I used to date. The technical glitch created confusing moments like when I thought my roommate was telling me he missed the sound of my voice. But I haven't gotten a new phone since then, so the person on the line must be who my contact list says it is.

"Gemma? This is Zach Price."

I bulge my eyes toward the wall. I'd sent him my screenplay because I'm a glutton for punishment, not because I had any inkling he would be interested. "Zach?" Wow, that came out with more enthusiasm than any playwright should ever use for a producer.

"Yeah." Small chuckle. "Is your screenplay still available? If so, I'd love to chat when I'm in town next week."

"Yes." I blindly reach for the desk so I can take a seat before falling on the floor. This is why Charlie told me I need an agent. So they can keep negotiations afloat while my emotions jump overboard. I've never wished I was a better actress more than I do right now. "I'd love to get together."

"All I need from you is a new ending to the script."

My overinflated lungs exhale at the request. I should have been expecting this shoe to drop. "What do you mean?"

"Most of the story seems very authentic. You were even able to make the ridiculous seem believable, even when the writer stows away on a fire truck."

I bite my lip. He's not only critiquing my story, he's critiquing my life. "Thanks?"

"But I don't buy the ending."

I lean my forehead forward into my free hand. I'd just claimed to Kai that I knew happy endings, but this one hadn't actually happened yet. I'd written it so I could profess my love to Karson through the Gemma character. The real happy ending won't actually happen until he watches the movie.

"I don't think Jenna would lead the cop on a high-speed chase just to have him pull her over."

I twist my lips in disappointment. "Why?" I question. "Because she's such a good driver he can't catch her?"

Zach chuckles. "That would be an interesting twist. But no. She wouldn't do that, because she doesn't know if he's grown as a character yet. They were both part of the problem, so he could simply throw her in jail the way he'd been threatening to in the beginning when he fingerprinted her."

That ending holds some dramatic irony for my story, but I wouldn't want to experience it in real life. Also, Zach has a point about Karson's growth. I'd been hoping he'd do what Kai did and be inspired to make positive changes in his life while I'm gone, but I have no evidence of that. For all I know, he's even angrier than before because he's now had his heart broken twice.

I hesitate but finally ask, "What do you think she should do?" Not so much for my script as for myself.

"They're your characters, sweetheart."

I scrunch my nose, and not only at the disingenuous moniker. The other part of his response bothers me more.

"Figure it out and bring me the new ending when we meet at the end of the month."

I fold over to rest my forehead on the cool laminate desktop. This churning in the pit of my stomach will give me more empathy the next time I see one of my students hunched in such a position.

"Okay," I squeak. But now I feel more hopeless about the script—and my life—than ever.

CHAPTER TWENTY-NINE

KARSON

A hero is somebody who voluntarily
walks into the unknown.
—Tom Hanks

Gemma walked past my office, took a deep breath, and disappeared. I thought she was waiting outside for me in the hall, but then when I got up to talk to her, she continued on as if she didn't even know I was there. Was she pretending not to notice me? No, she's too transparent to be that good of an actress. Plus, she's always wandering around like she has no clue what's going on.

I seized the opportunity and followed her. Her classroom was the best place to have a private discussion anyway. Once she finally went in, I was about to knock on her door when her phone rang. It was a guy named Zach, and to my dismay, she was pretty excited to talk to him.

I'm disappointed, but I'm not letting myself get angry. I'm also not letting this dissuade me from saying what I need to say. I'm simply waiting for the opportune time. Whenever that may be. So far it's been over a month.

This morning she's helping students hang homecoming dance posters throughout the commons. I know this because I'm watching from a monitor in my office that shows camera footage from around the school.

The longer I wait to approach her, the creepier it will seem when

I out myself, but I just wish our reconnection would happen naturally. Like the time I was doing a locker search right outside her classroom, and she was heading my way. But then she checked her purse and returned to her classroom as if she'd forgotten something. Or when I was in the parking lot, helping with a fender bender, and she approached. But then she breezed right by, telling a student the story of driving my cop car. Evidently, she wrote a screenplay about it, and it has some interest.

I'm like one of these students with a secret crush. Is this how she felt about me back in the very beginning? It's nerve-racking. Though I have the feeling she'll be nicer to me than I was to her.

"Officer Zellner?" A girl in a black cheerleading uniform stands at my door.

"Hey. What can I do for you?" I love when the kids come to me rather than me have to go to them. I get up to join her at the entry since there's not much room inside.

"I'm on the homecoming committee, and I wanted to make sure you'll be here as a chaperone for our dance this weekend."

"Oh." That's one of my responsibilities I'd forgotten about. Not exactly what I pictured when I got into law enforcement, but a dance is a good way to keep an eye on these kids. "What's the date and time?"

She tells me, and I flick open my calendar app to add it to my schedule. My gaze slides toward the commons, where Gemma is finishing up. Maybe she'll be a chaperone too. That would be a more natural way to connect than stalking her in the hallways.

My pulse skips a beat, like it used to when I was preparing for a drug bust or weapons raid. Because this plan also feels life-threatening. "I'll be there."

She bounces on her toes and then waves before spinning to leave. "Thanks for your help."

"See ya." As much as I want to connect with these kids, I was more comfortable dealing with hardened criminals. Which is probably why I need to be here. I thought it was for them, but it seems to be for me.

CHAPTER THIRTY

GEMMA

A true hero isn't measured by the size of his strength, but by the strength of his heart.
—ZEUS, IN *HERCULES*

A meet-cute is the scene where the hero and heroine meet for the very first time." I sigh dreamily and clutch "The Legend of Sleepy Hollow" to my chest. I know it's considered a Halloween story, which is why my students are reading it this time of year, but at the core, it's about a love triangle.

Sardonic laughter yanks me from American gothic literature back into my classroom's circle of desks. The closest thing my students get to a party like the one Ichabod Crane attended will be this weekend's homecoming dance.

"Meet-cutes are just made up for the movies," Brock the Jock scoffs. I picture him as the headless horseman for all the times he forgets to use his brain. The kid is a natural leader though, and I'm hoping I can help turn him the right direction so others will follow.

"Oh, my young friend, meet-cutes are very real." I straighten my favorite houndstooth scarf. "Let me tell you a tale."

The class groans collectively, and I know it's because they are required to as teenagers.

"It's for the screenplay I'm pitching this weekend. I still have to figure out a new ending, but I've got the meet-cute down."

"Maybe we can help," offers Samantha, the cheerleading captain who's in charge of the homecoming dance.

"Sure," I shrug. I'll take all the help I can get. "Here's how it starts. I was duct-taped to a chair."

The room hushes.

Samantha raises her hand but doesn't wait to speak. "Wait. Is this your screenplay or your life?"

"Uh . . ." Why are kids so smart? "It happened to me when I was researching for a screenplay."

Brock gives a scarecrow's smirk. "Of course it did," he says, and I'm reminded very much of the man who used to say that to me all the time.

Huh. Maybe my students will be able to help after all.

"Anyway." I pull out the seat from behind my desk to use the chair for reenacting the story, then plop down. "I twisted and thrashed and growled . . ."

Long blond strands of hair flip into my face. I blow them away to find Brock filming me from his phone. I'll be on TikTok before the day ends, but I just consider this a compliment.

I pause dramatically. "Little did I know that my neighbors saw me through the window and called the police."

The students' eyes bulge.

"Wait." Brock shakes his head. "You had a meet-cute with a cop?"

"Yes." I sigh and picture Karson. "He had the look of Hawkeye from the Avengers. They both have the same brooding blue eyes and widow's peak."

Taylor and Samantha glance at each other. The girls must know the actor I'm referring to. They also pull out their phones, but I'm too lost in my narrative to care.

"When my roommate opened the front door, the officer charged in to rescue me."

Brock's chin drops. "That's how you met your boyfriend?"

I laugh and wave my hand. "No, we're not dating."

"He didn't ask you out?" Samantha flatters me by sounding shocked.

But the truth is that we never went on an actual date. No dinner and a movie. No holding hands and walking along the river. No driving me home and kissing on the front step until Charlie flicked the lights at us.

"No, he did not." I gaze out the window.

"Why not?" Taylor asks.

I blink and find my students waiting for the explanation as to why I need help with my happily ever after. "He has a backstory that wounded him."

As I speak, the door squeaks open. Hawkeye stands there. "You wounded me, Gemma Bennett," he says gruffly. "You flipped me over during the self-defense lesson of citizen's police academy."

Wow. My imagination has never been so vivid.

"Sorry, Miss Bennett." Samantha giggles. "I texted our new resource officer because I thought you might want to meet him, you know, if you haven't already."

He's real. And he's a resource officer at my school instead of police lieutenant?

Karson crosses his solid forearms. "Then there's no emergency?"

"Actually." Brock raises his hand. "There's a shortage of chaperones for the homecoming dance tomorrow. You should help Miss Bennett."

Ah, I knew this kid could be taught.

Karson's gaze warms me from the inside. "I'm already required to attend all football games and dances. I'll be there."

My stomach churns with unasked questions. Though I did ask my students to help me with my story, and they got my hero to join us. Not only now but for every dance I chaperone as the advisor for the dance committee. I hadn't seen this plot twist coming.

Brock whoops. "So it's a date."

Okay, now the kid is taking it too far.

"Excuse us." I rise and usher my new coworker into the hall, away from our audience. He smells like cinnamon, and I can't help thinking if Ichabod Crane had used the same gun oil, Miss Van Tassel would have chosen him, and his story would have ended differently. As for the conflict in my story, I'm still not sure how it will end. At the moment, it's reminding me very much of how it started, back when this man assumed the worst about me. "Karson, I didn't plan for them to call you. I honestly didn't know you were working here now."

"I believe you."

"You do?" Hope swells in my chest.

"Yes." A sheepish smile colors his cheeks. "I took this job because I want to impact the lives of kids like I was before they become angry grown-ups like I was."

He *is* a hero, as I suspected all along.

"Then I saw your picture on the bulletin board by my office—"

His office . . . ? "So that's why I smelled cinnamon in the hallway when coming back to school for the first time." I cover my mouth to let him continue. I didn't mean to interrupt his tantalizing narrative about what brought us back together. It's the best story I've ever heard, and I can't wait to get to the ending. I pull my hand down to prompt, "Go on."

"I've seen you around and started to feel a little bit like your stalker." He shrugs one shoulder, eyes searching mine. "I realized I judged you too harshly for stalking me after we first met. I was only looking for a way to reconnect. As were you."

As was I.

My lips separate to let me breathe in this moment. He wanted this. He wanted to say hello instead of goodbye. I wish I could keep exploring the new avenue of our relationship, but I've got students waiting for me.

I glance back toward the window to my classroom and get a glimpse of the red hair ribbon from Samantha's ponytail as she ducks out of sight. That girl. "Samantha did the reconnecting for us."

"She did." He arches a teasing eyebrow. "I'm just surprised with as much trouble as you get into that it's taken so long for me to be called to your class."

Karson isn't avoiding me anymore. He's seeking me out. I don't want to leave him, but this time saying goodbye holds excitement for tomorrow.

"I've got to get back to my students before there's more trouble, but it's a good thing you're coming to the homecoming dance to keep an eye on me . . . I mean them."

"You," he clarifies. "I know better than to take my eyes off you." He backs away as if to validate his point, but his gaze holds both longing and promise. And the way it makes me feel is better than any homecoming tiara I could have ever worn.

CHAPTER THIRTY-ONE

KARSON

I'm no hero. I'm just a man in love.
Though there's never been anything more
courageous than loving someone.
—KARINA HALLE

I'm as nervous as a junior at prom. Talking with Gemma again made me feel as though I was in the right place with the right person, even though a year ago I never would have imagined myself dating her, let alone being a resource officer at her school. Unfortunately, I couldn't tell her all that with a classroom of students spying on us. So tonight's the night.

I'm in the commons before the doors open for the dance. Gemma's not here yet, but I can see her touch in the decorations. The homecoming theme this year is "Hollywood or Bust" because they'd been playing Grant High from the Hollywood District. There's a red carpet leading in from the glass doors. Gold stars hang from the ceiling. And there's even a theater curtain backdrop as a photo op. Just the setting I need for making this a night to remember for her.

The DJ in the corner energizes the room with some funky new song. The overhead lights dim to highlight the flashes of color from a disco ball. And Gemma wanders in as only Gemma could. Her face is aglow with wonder as she surveys the room, completely unaware she's the most stunning thing here.

I hold my position by the front door, but I can't take my eyes off her in a gold dress that glitters underneath the strobing lights. The front half of her long blond ringlets are twisted atop her head in a way that would never need a crown. If ever I were to feel unworthy of her attention, it would be right now. While she looks like a movie star, I'm wearing my work uniform. But it doesn't matter because I'm a man in love.

It doesn't matter if she gains weight or cuts her hair. It doesn't matter if she trips on the red carpet in her ridiculous stiletto sandals. It doesn't matter if she continues writing screenplays for the rest of her life and never sells a one. What matters isn't the beauty I see when I look at her, but how she helps me see the beauty in the world around us.

I know when she spots me because her gaze stops roving. She pulls her shoulders back and heads my direction.

My heart jitters, and the scene around us disappears. The throbbing music, the pulsing lights, the hundreds of students smashed against the glass doors, ready to mob us. I really hope they behave tonight so I can just enjoy my time with Gemma.

"You ready for this?" she asks.

"I've been ready," I respond, before realizing she means she's about to unlock the doors.

A few dolled-up teenagers surround her, their phone apps open to scan tickets and their stamps poised to mark hands.

Before pushing in the bar on the first door and using a hex key to keep it unlocked, she sends me a smile that looks as though she fears it might be the last time we see each other before we're separated by a mosh pit of students. But I know better. Not only do her students love her and want her to have her happy ending, but as I told her yesterday, I'm not taking my eyes off her.

She unlocks a second and a third door. Teens trickle in slowly at first, then Brock bounds to the center of the dance floor, lets out a holler, and is rushed by the screaming masses.

I didn't enjoy this scene as a student, and it's absolutely crazy that I chose to be here again. The only reason I attended dances in high school was for Amber. I wanted to be with her. I wanted what she could offer me.

I've finally gotten to the place where it's not about me anymore.

I'm here for others. And Gemma helped me get to this place. It's time I tell her.

With hands in my pockets, I weave my way to the red curtain backdrop, where Gemma is directing the line of students getting their photographs taken. I can barely hear her over the music, but that's okay. Being near her is enough.

Her eyes meet mine and she gives an exaggerated huff as if she's exhausted already. She wipes her forehead and steps back to stand beside me. In unity, we turn our faces toward each other. Maybe no words are needed.

"Miss Bennett," Samantha calls from the temporary stage, where homecoming queen will be crowned. I know it's Samantha because she's still wearing the red bow in her hair, though she's not in her cheer uniform.

"Gotta run," Gemma yells over the bass.

I nod. I'm supposed to make my rounds anyway. "Meet you at the punch table?"

She flashes me a grateful grin. I really like this thing called gratefulness. It not only helps us endure situations we never would have planned for ourselves, but it enables us to turn our sorrows into joy. Like Jacob and Esau, who reunited even after Esau threatened to kill Jacob. Like Joseph, who ultimately ended up saving the brothers who tried to destroy him.

Joseph said it best. *You intended to harm me, but God intended it for good.* God's here not only to restore what I'd lost, but also to use my specific wounds to help others find healing. From the peace I see in Gemma, it looks as if she's discovered the same thing. I'd like to think we've helped each other, and I'm looking forward to our punch table rendezvous to find out for sure.

I circle past the entrance and catch a kid trying to sneak another kid in by licking the stamp on the back of his hand and pressing it to his buddy's hand. Not only can he not produce a ticket, but he doesn't even have a student ID. I shake my head and point the direction of the parking lot. They all glare. But even in this, I'm grateful I caught them before they got inside.

I continue around the dance floor and DJ booth to the quietest corner, where Gemma is sipping punch. I watch her for a moment before approaching. Had she possibly felt this same welling excitement when she looked at me in Citizen's Safety Academy for the first time?

I join her at the table. "Last time I was at a high school dance, I was dating the girl I ended up marrying."

She looks up, hesitantly. I hadn't meant to compare her to Amber. I'd actually wanted to do the opposite.

"Yeah?" So many questions in that one word. "This is the last place I ever expected to see you."

"Yeah." I scoop myself a cup of punch and take a sip. Spiked? Nope. No bite. It's all tropical fruit and sugar. "I like seeing you in your environment. This is where you shine. No tiara needed."

The beat dies down and a slow song changes the mood of the room to make it more intimate.

The apples of her cheeks round into a smile. "Thanks. I know it's cliché to say this at a homecoming dance, but I actually feel like I'm coming home. I used to only see teaching as my day job that I needed to pay bills, but now that I'm about to sell my screenplay, I don't want to leave. I want to keep teaching them to live their own life story." She nods out at the kids pairing off into couples to sway together.

I'd love to put my arms around Gemma, but there's nobody here to chaperone *us*. Also, she just said she was about to sell a screenplay. Her stories will be coming to life on the big screen. She's made it. "That's so great. Congratulations. On both the success and the significance."

"Mmm . . ." she says, and I wonder if I've lost her to her land of make-believe again. "I like that. Significance."

I didn't lose her. She was simply mulling over my words. Which bodes well for me saying more of them. "I met with Amber."

Her eyes zip to mine, hopeful yet cautious.

I take a deep breath. "I never had the chance to forgive my mom for leaving me before, so I thought it might be good if I forgave Amber while I had a chance."

Gemma's eyes widen and her long, slim fingers press against her chest. "You forgave her?"

"That was my plan." Silly thing, plans. Do we ever know what we're doing? I certainly don't in this moment. I have no idea how Gemma will react. I just know I need to tell her she was right all along. "When Amber and I spoke, we both realized how much we'd hurt each other. She ended up apologizing too."

Gemma's lips, stained bright with punch, part. "You aren't mad at her anymore?"

My gaze travels her face. If we were anywhere else, I'd gently take it in my palms and show her how very happy I am. "No. And I need to apologize for comparing you to her in the first place."

Her eyes well with tears, the flashing lights making them glisten. "It's okay if you compare me. I know who I am now."

Somehow, I could tell. She's changed since I said goodbye. And not only because she's about to sell her screenplay. There's something more. "*Who* are you?" I ask. I really want to know how she sees herself.

"I'm trouble." She holds up a finger. "But that's okay because it gives me a lot of ideas to write about. And more importantly, I've come to believe that even the bad things in our lives can work out for good if we use them for God's glory."

In our time apart, we'd come to the same realizations. Which is very, very good. I cross my arms in my old cop stance. "It works out for me because I love trouble."

"No you don't."

"I do now."

She bursts into laughter. Not the reaction most men would want after such a declaration, but since I'd first thought there was nothing good that could come from her kind of trouble, I deserve to be laughed at.

I join in.

Oh yeah. If I was in a place where I could kiss her, they would be very, very happy kisses. This is what falling in love should feel like.

An alarm blares over the music. I go on alert, scanning our surroundings. I see the group of kids I'd kicked out, running for the door carrying a lit flare. Somehow, they'd gotten in with that. Looks like

I've got more safety trainings to plan for. In the meantime, I give chase just as the overhead sprinklers shoot icy water down on our heads.

Students scream, and a mob separates me from the culprits. The music screeches to a halt as the DJ tries to cover all his equipment with the bags it came in. We're surrounded by mad panic that I should have prevented. I can at least give directions over the microphone.

"Get out," I shout to Gemma.

She takes off deeper into the building. "I've got to get my committee out of the culinary arts room where they're preparing refreshments."

Of course she does. "No. Let a fireman do that."

"I've been trained," she yells back. As if failing at rescuing a dummy in a smoky simulation has prepared her for rescuing students from a blazing inferno.

I scan the perimeter to make sure there's no threat other than the flare. The room is thankfully smoke-free. I'll direct traffic, then go after Gemma.

I fight the current of slick bodies to get to the DJ booth, then tap the microphone to see if it's still working. The tap echoes through the commons as a static *thump*. That will do.

"Attention, students." My voice echoes over the PA system. "Please remain calm. Don't run but exit the building as quickly and efficiently as possible. I repeat, don't run."

The screaming lowers a decibel. I see students slowing to look around and assist each other. Most of them are out the door now, so the building will soon be clear.

Dropping the mike, I disregard my own advice and take off for where I last saw Gemma. After getting her out, I'll circle the room once more, checking for anybody left behind and possible injuries. Then I'll let my buddies at the fire department take over. They should be arriving soon.

Gemma emerges from a back hallway, waving a couple of girls in front of her. The girls cover their heads with their arms, though their fancy hairstyles have melted over their faces. Their skirts cling to their legs, impeding their steps, but at least they're all heading the right direction.

I wait for Gemma. She's an even bigger mess. She wipes at strands of hair plastered over her face only to leave a trail of black makeup down from her eyes. When I'd met her, I'd assumed she was all about image. But she looks like this right now because she cared more about her students than herself. And I adore her for it.

"Let's go, gorgeous."

She's laughing again, in spite of it all. Laughing and crying and running. Unfortunately, she didn't listen to me when I warned against running.

CHAPTER THIRTY-TWO

GEMMA

*All my life I thought that the story was over when
the hero and heroine were safely engaged—after all,
what's good enough for Jane Austen ought to be
good enough for anyone. But it's a lie. The story
is about to begin, and every day will
be a new piece of the plot.*
—MARY ANN SHAFFER

I thought I'd already fallen for Karson. It's nothing compared to the way my right heel slips out from underneath me, and when I try to yank it to a stop, I topple to the cement floor, jabbing my opposite shin with the stiletto heel.

Fire burns up my leg, but it could be worse. There could be a real fire. My students could be in it. I'm grateful they're safe, and I'm sharing this moment with my real-life hero who just professed his love. Only a man in love would look at me, a drowned clown, and call me gorgeous.

I kick off the very same sandals that got me in trouble on driving day of safety academy and roll over to my hands and knees to crawl toward the door. I don't trust myself not to slip again, and also my shin stings as if it just got hit with a baseball bat.

Karson drops to the ground beside me. "You're bleeding."

"Of course I am."

His eyes flick up to mine. "Don't say cute things. I don't have time to kiss you right now."

I'm about to ask, *Why not?* Kissing in the rain worked for Noah and Allie in *The Notebook.* Who cares if we're getting drenched by fire sprinklers and our lives are in danger?

But then Karson rips his shirt off, and I fall back onto my rear, speechless.

I've never seen his abs before. Hello, six-pack. Maybe the reason police don't take off their shirts before rescuing a victim is so that the victim doesn't swoon and cause more problems.

He rolls the shirt up, then wraps the material around my leg and ties it. Blood seeps through the material quickly at first, then the trail slows.

I hadn't realized how bad my injury was, but now my shin pulses with pressure. "Thank you."

The door is still pretty far away, but crawling will have to work. Strong arms scoop me up.

I squeal in surprise and wrap my arms around Karson's neck. I am literally being carried to safety by a man without a shirt. The very man who lectured me on ever writing a scene with this kind of rescue.

I study his face up close. Rivers of water drip off points of hair. His chilled skin is pale against the darker stubble along his jaw. But most importantly, his cornflower-blue eyes hold intensity without the steely flecks of fury. They meet my gaze, and I see my contentment reflected.

"You know I'm going to have to write this scene as the ending of my screenplay now. It's going to be your fault the police officer takes off his shirt before rescuing the damsel in distress."

His full lips twitch. "Go ahead and tease me about this. I guarantee you can't possibly tease me as much as those guys will."

I look out the window to where a fire truck is pulling to the curb, red lights flashing in the dimming night. Blue lights follow, announcing a police cruiser joining our party.

Karson pushes through the door, the onslaught of water replaced with an icy breeze that stings more than the gash on my shin. Students cheer from across the street.

I shiver and wave. I may not have been homecoming queen, but once upon a time, I practiced my princess skills. I finally get to use them. Elbow, elbow, wrist, wrist.

This will be a homecoming they never forget. Most importantly, they'll all be going home safe tonight.

"Hey, there."

I recognize the confident tone.

Thad jumps from the fire truck. "Had to show me up, huh, Zellner?"

"Whoa, boy." Another familiar voice hoots in laughter. Drew claps his hands as he circles his cruiser toward us. "Too bad the students don't know about the lecture you gave Gemma on her first day of safety academy."

Karson's gaze holds mine even as he speaks to his old partner. "Let's not tell your old safety academy classmates about this."

Kai pops out of Drew's cruiser with his camera in hand, as if he came back from getting engaged in Africa just for this moment. "Nobody has to tell them. I've got it all on film."

Charlie climbs from the back seat. "Gemma, did you pull the fire alarm to get Karson to rescue you?"

I smile at my hero. "No, I never could have plotted this."

Karson doesn't even seem to care about our audience. He's looking at me. Carrying me to the ambulance. Setting me down for the EMTs to inspect. Wrapping the scratchy blanket they give him around my shoulders.

My students all shout and whistle.

Karson's smile quivers. His eye contact doesn't. "If you want a good ending to your screenplay, I'll give you one right now."

And I thought I'd been swooning before. I'm not cold anymore. My skin burns. My breath hitches. My pulse thunders through my veins.

"Gemma, as you admitted tonight, you are trouble."

He's keeping it real, and I can't keep from laughing. Ramona the Pest would be proud.

He chuckles along, then his grin sobers. "You triggered me. You saw through my shield of self-protection, and you pointed out my mistakes."

Okay, now my heart hurts for him. I didn't mean to cause him pain. I only want the best for him.

"You could have had any man you wanted, but instead you cared enough to make me want to be a better man."

I shake my head. Because I didn't do anything for him that he didn't do for me.

"Yes, you did," he argues. "And I don't care if I'm making a fool of myself in front of everyone tonight. They already seem to know what I'm about to say anyway."

"I know too," I say. "Because I'm also in love with you."

He shakes his head and gives me the smirk I can't get enough of.

I reach for his face to kiss him, letting the blanket fall away. Our lips meet to the cheers of the crowd around. He tastes sweet, like fruit punch and commitment.

I smile against his lips.

He smiles with me. "It's a good thing you're not shallow the way I once assumed you were, because we are a sight."

"It's true." Kai's camera lens is practically in our faces. "Gemma, you look like you belong in an '80s hair band."

How kind of him to record this moment so I can laugh at myself later . . . along with the rest of the world.

I bug my eyes at Karson, probably making myself look worse. His gaze caresses me in return, as if I'm the most radiant woman he's ever seen. This is what it's like to be loved.

"Thank you for rescuing me," I whisper.

He kisses the top of my head. His kiss is so much better than a tiara that tarnishes. "You rescued me," he responds. "Gemma Bennett is my hero."

Read on for a sneak peek of *Fiancé Finale*, the third book in the Love Off Script series!

Chapter One

NICOLE

*It is better to be hated for what you are than to be
loved for what you are not.*
—ANDRÉ GIDE

It's rare for me to be awakened by the sound of an incoming text message because it's rare for anyone to beat me out of bed. So when the phone on my nightstand starts to vibrate, I'm lost in the dark. Then I see a glow of blue light and hear the buzz. A rush of warm fuzzies reminds me what day it is.

It's the day my campaign launches. And by "my campaign," I mean the one that is going to skyrocket my career in advertising. It's what I've sacrificed for.

It took some finagling, but I finally persuaded a well-known Christian golfer to represent the pizza restaurant Slice of Heaven. Naturally, because he's made some memorable slices in his career. All the billboards have been designed, all the radio spots recorded, and all the commercials filmed. Hence the fact that I was finally able to get a good night's sleep. Now I'm just waiting for audience response, and by the sound of my cell buzzing, I don't have to wait any longer.

I reach for my phone with a smile in my heart.

MORGAN: *Dante is trending on social media.*

Already!

I sit up straight, the text more energizing than a shot of espresso. I'd known my campaign was good, but I hadn't expected such instant results.

I fumble for the switch on my reading lamp, and a warm glow spills across my all-white bedroom, reflecting off the black windows that will give me a great view of the Portland skyline once it wakes. I rub the sleep out of my eyes and try to focus on my phone.

If this campaign turns out to be as big as I think, I'm taking myself to Jamaica for vacation. Better yet, Costa Rica. No, wait. Peru.

My pulse stills in a silent moment as I think about the man who left me for a film gig in South America. I could have gone with Charlie, but that would have required giving up my own dreams. Now look at me. I'm going to have both the job and the journey. Who needs the man?

There's another man in my life now, and he's a star in the PGA. I bite my lip and click on the app that might as well be a magic wand, because it's going to make all my wishes come true.

Dante Sullivan. His name pops up first on the list of popular subjects.

I jump to my feet and do a little dance right there on top of my mattress. "Thank you, Jesus."

I pause my celebration long enough to find out exactly what I'm celebrating. I click on Dante's name. But then I bounce again while waiting for the app to load. Because I can't help it.

The first post reads like a political ad ripping on a rival in the opposing party. I should have expected as much. Christianity is considered offensive these days. Religion is a punchline. Believers are the new blonds. But that's okay. Dante has a huge platform, so not everybody who sees him is going to be a fan.

I scroll to the next post and cringe at a sexual comment. Weird. Pizza isn't that kind of hot.

I shake my head. Moving on.

The following post is a link to a news article about . . . I gasp and smash a hand over my mouth.

Either my phone vibrates with another text, or I'm trembling in shock. Probably both.

MORGAN: *Dante apparently sent some inappropriate texts to a single mom of a kid in the junior golf camp he's helping coach. Slice of Heaven is dropping him.*

"No . . ."

My legs give out. I sink into a nest made of sheets and pillows. Not that I feel any of their comfort. I'm numb. I'm horrified. I'm mad.

My college psychology teacher taught us to use the word *angry* rather than *mad*, because *mad* can mean crazy. But I think *mad* fits this scenario.

Tingles shoot through my body, and my breathing comes out in gasps. This is the stuff of mental breakdowns. Or at least panic attacks.

I'm mad at Dante. I'm mad he propositioned that mom. I'm mad that his followers are going to blame his poor choice on God. I'm mad about the company that just spent their whole advertising budget on a "pillar in the community" who is turning out to be more like one of the pillars Samson knocked over. I'm mad about how this is going to affect me.

There's no trip to Machu Picchu in my future. There might not even be a job in my future.

But you know who I'm most mad at? Me.

I should have known this would happen. Everybody falls off their platform eventually. It's just more devastating to a community who prides themselves on being wholesome.

This is my dad's fall from Grace Chapel all over again.

I can practically feel a cold sore forming on the outside of my mouth from the onslaught of stress. I rub my lips together. Yep. There's the tender bump. Because public humiliation wouldn't be complete without an open lesion on my face.

The phone rings, startling me back to the present. It's Morgan, of course. Soon it'll be the owner of Slice of Heaven, my boss, and the press. I don't know whether to laugh or cry.

I'm not one to hide under my covers, but I'm also not sure what I can possibly do about this. I feel the devastation that's coming for all involved. There's no spinning it, and I wouldn't want to.

"Why, God?" I just want to understand.

My phone rings a second time. I take a deep breath of the soothing lavender sachets, though they are not currently cutting it. I must come across as poised. It's my brand.

I look at Morgan's wide brown eyes staring at me from the contact photo on my screen, then I slide my thumb over its slick surface to answer. "I saw the news," I state calmly. "Have you spoken with Dante?"

"I've left messages for him with his agent and his mom." Her voice is pitched higher than usual, and mine would be too if I'd spoken with Mrs. Sullivan. The matriarch wears an apron with all the charm of June Cleaver but brandishes her rolling pin like a weapon. "There's an apology forthcoming."

I can't hold back my huff. Dante's apology is only going to split the justice and mercy arms of the church even wider—not to mention in the eyes of those who don't go to church. What should be used as proof of how badly we all need a Savior will be used as evidence of hypocrisy. Though honestly, I don't feel like anything can save me right now.

> "A masterpiece of comic timing, unbeatable chemistry, and a zany but relatable cast of characters."
>
> —*Midwest Book Review*

978-0-8254-4710-5

Meri Newberg feels like the last young Christian woman on the planet to be single. So when she's handed a strange present at her best friend's wedding—a 1950s magazine article of "ways to get a husband"—she decides there's nothing to lose by trying out its advice. After all, she can't get any *more* single.

> "As hilarious as it is charming!"
>
> —Betsy St. Amant, author of *The Key to Love*

KREGEL
PUBLICATIONS